TITANS

TITANS

VICTORIA SCOTT

SCHOLASTIC INC.

Copyright © 2016 by Victoria Scott

This book was originally published in hardcover by Scholastic Press in 2016.

All rights reserved. Published by Scholastic Inc., *Publishers since 1920*. SCHOLASTIC and associated logos are trademarks and/or registered trademarks of Scholastic Inc.

The publisher does not have any control over and does not assume any responsibility for author or third-party websites or their content.

No part of this publication may be reproduced, stored in a retrieval system, or transmitted in any form or by any means, electronic, mechanical, photocopying, recording, or otherwise, without written permission of the publisher. For information regarding permission, write to Scholastic Inc., Attention: Permissions Department, 557 Broadway, New York, NY 10012.

This book is a work of fiction. Names, characters, places, and incidents are either the product of the author's imagination or are used fictitiously, and any resemblance to actual persons, living or dead, business establishments, events, or locales is entirely coincidental.

ISBN 978-1-338-09555-5

10 9 8 7 6 5 4 3 2 1   17 18 19 20 21

Printed in the U.S.A.   40
First printing 2017

Book design by Nina Goffi

For my daughter—
Whatever you decide to do in this big, blue world,
your mama will bet on you to win.
I love you, I love you.

CYCLONE TRACK PROGRAM, TITAN DERBY

Final Results, Previous Season

COURSE NAME: Earthquake
DISTANCE: 32 Furlongs
BREED TYPE: Titan 3.0
ENGINE OIL: Diesel
SURFACE: Dirt

TITAN NAME	JOCKEY	TRAINER	SPONSOR	TIME RANK
The Man	M. Franklin	O. Richey	Richey Enterprises	10.50 1/4
Fuzzy Constellation	A. Gaston	C. Norman	B&B Oil and Gas	11.03 2/4
Prince of Tides	S. Barrins	B. Lovato	Stanley Stables	13.60 3/4
Sylvester	H. Wells	V. Pletcher	Ned and Carol Wells	---- 4/4

PART I
FRAGILE THINGS

CHAPTER ONE

Tonight, the Titans will run.

I can see their eyes glowing red from my hard-won place outside the fence. Grown men jostle me from both sides, sloshing pints of beer, hollering over one another as they place last-minute bets. The moon dips low in the sky, lured by grumbled curses and bare-knuckle fights and cigarettes pinched between dirtied fingertips.

My parents don't know I'm here. I snuck out my bedroom window with Magnolia an hour before midnight, an hour before the race would begin. Last year, I watched the machines run on a local sports channel—one of the few my family could afford. The Gambini brothers should have been thrilled. The first year and already they had cameramen and a spot in homes across Detroit.

This time, though, I won't watch from under my mother's arm, her fingers working their way through my hair. I breathe in the pungent smell of sweat and urine, and press closer against the fence. Magnolia stands beside me, her sight set on the course. She takes my hand in hers and gives it a good squeeze. I squeeze right back, and narrow my gaze to the Titans.

From inside the starting gate, the steel horses stamp the dry earth and toss their heads. I can make out the jockeys' colored jerseys and anxious hands as they work their Titans' control panels. I know from reading online that they're sending manual instructions to the horses' control centers, setting speeds and calculating lean percentages and determining how close they'll push their horses to the slay zone.

The horses are a mixture of the real things and race cars. That's why I've studied both. There isn't much to do in the suburbs of Detroit, especially when where you live is less suburb and more slum. As working conditions at my father's plant worsened, and my parents began to argue, the horses were transported into the heart of the forest that nuzzled my house. A glittering promise of hope in the form of iron bolts and smooth steel.

The starting light in the center of the track flicks on, throwing red across the dirt. The Titans lose their ever-loving minds when they see that particular shade of cherry. They may not have *real* minds, or *real* thoughts, but like any other computer they have the potential for recognition and reaction. The jockeys toe their stirrups, lean forward in their black leather seats, and grip the handlebars as their horses thrash.

I see all of this through the bars of the starting gate.

And then the light changes colors.

It blinks yellow—on and off, on and off.

Yellow.

The crowd moves in, bodies flush against my back until my nose is pushed through the chain-link fence.

Yellow.

My heart thunders in my chest so that I can feel it in my throat. Magnolia tightens her hold on my hand.

Yellow.

Finally, finally, the onlookers quiet. The absence of sound is jarring. It's the loudest thing I've ever heard—all those men breathing rapidly, eyes widening, hands clenching their bet cards.

Green!

The gates slide away. A gun fires.

And the Titans run.

They run and the world trembles beneath my feet. Steam puffs from their nostrils and their eyes cut a crimson path and their bodies clash against one another, steel on steel. As the Titans rumble past, a smile sweeps across my face. Watching them is like kissing a speeding train. Like dancing with a hurricane. The horses are terrifying and beautiful at once. They are mindless beasts, but under the stadium lights, their bodies moving down the track like ghosts, they are glorious.

I'm thirteen years old the day I first witness the Titans run. It's the same day I watch a grown man die.

CHAPTER TWO

Four years later

It's the first Monday of summer. There's no Ms. Finchella with her chalky fingers and history papers. There are no Styrofoam trays with steak fingers and questionable gravy. And there's definitely no gym class where kids are separated by the volley-ball kneepads they don: florescent white for those who come from money, and murky gray for those who grab from the used pile.

Who needs those things when it's finally summer? When the sky spreads out over our neighborhood with blueness so deep you could slurp it through a straw. I dig my hands into my pockets and tip my head back, open my mouth like maybe some of that blue will float down like snowflakes. Once my eyes are cast upward, I find myself counting those fluffy clouds, sorting them into categories based on size and shape, seeing mathematical calculations dance across their white bellies.

Of course, I see numbers everywhere—in the leaves, in the way the grass grows, even in the lines that cross my palms.

My feet carry me between two clapboard houses while my brain keeps sorting patterns, until a sharp rapping sound steals my attention. It's Magnolia waving from inside her window. She slides the glass pane open and music blasts into the warm air like it's relieved to escape her room.

"Whatcha want, Astrid?" she asks with a smirk.

"Nothing," I reply. "Wrong house, wrong window."

She laughs. "Even so, it's your lucky day, because I'm in the market for a little adventure." She climbs through the window, knobby knees getting stuck in the frame before she yanks them out. My best friend wears black shorts and a black tank. She's even got black sandals on her feet. You'd think she was allergic to color, but that's not it at all.

"You like my new piece?" she asks when she rights herself.

I admire the orange headband in her long blond hair. Attached to it is an orange veil that lies backward, just begging for a breeze so it can flip forward and cover her heart-shaped face. Now the black makes sense. Magnolia claims people should dress to accommodate their accessories, not the other way around. And Magnolia's favorite accessory of choice is one worn on the crown of her head.

"I made it this morning." She nudges the band back. "Still need to sew on a line of sequins to the bottom."

"Nah, no sequins."

"No?"

"No."

She grimaces. "What do you know?"

I smile. "I don't. I just like to get a rise out of you."

Magnolia's white teeth flash behind red lipstick. It clashes with her orange headband, but I won't tell her that. The only thing Magnolia likes better than her custom headpieces is her Revlon red lipstick, No. 22. "What do you want to do?"

I shrug. "Go for a walk?"

"Yeah?" She's already heading toward the street, our footsteps retracing the same path we've cut countless times before. "You think anyone will be out there this soon?"

"Maybe."

We don't have to mention the place by name to have this conversation. It's why we spend so much of our summers in the woods past Candlewick Park—to catch a glimpse of them in the daylight, though most don't ever make an appearance until nightfall. Just thinking about the Titans running at Cyclone Track gets my blood pumping.

"How'd your dad's interview go?" Magnolia asks.

I cringe at this question. Both our fathers lost their jobs at the electrical plant a couple of months ago. "Strategic restructuring," the newspaper called the layoffs, which only made my father angrier. The company replaced the men with machines made in Taiwan, is the truth. I know because Dad went around the house in the weeks following his "restructuring" and searched for anything in our house made in Taiwan. A couple of my younger sister's stuffed animals, our microwave, and one of my mother's favorite hand shovels were among the culprits. He threw them all away, save the microwave. "It's today," I tell her.

"Oh, I thought it was last Friday."

I step over the curb and into crisp leaves. "Rescheduled."

Magnolia nods like this is something she expected. "Dad says he might apply there too if your dad likes the place and the monkey who interviews him."

"No point in doing it before then," I reply. But we both know Magnolia's dad has probably already applied. Between the two old friends, they've marched their way into every plant and factory Detroit has to offer. Magnolia's dad even took a class at the library on creating a resume. You'd think he'd discovered another planet, listening to him gloat over that manila-colored piece of paper.

Little good it did him.

Magnolia must notice the distant look on my face because she rubs my back. I smile with one side of my mouth and return the favor. It's our ritual. Our *we'll get through this* one-two dance. On some twisted level, it's nice to know I'm not alone in this situation. That Magnolia and I are both waiting for things at our houses to implode. But it's also twice as scary, because there's a specific something Detroit factory workers do after they've exhausted their options.

My stomach twists, imagining my family packing their bags for another town, another house. I can't do that again. I won't survive the nights in grimy motels, or worse, the days huddled in our car while my dad hunts for jobs *elsewhere*.

It nearly broke my family the last time we lost our house. But this time would be even worse, because it would mean leaving Magnolia. Of course, she could leave first.

My mind spins as I skip from one potential solution to another. This is what I've done every day since Dad became unemployed: think through the ways I could help my family. Yes, my dad needs another gig. But at this point, we just need money. Enough so that if he lost another job in the future, we wouldn't have to entertain worst-case scenarios. My landing a minimum wager could help, but the last time Mom came home with an application from a craft store, Dad shouted about respect and a man's responsibility to support his family. My sisters and I watched the vein in his neck throb, making ourselves small at the table.

CHAPTER THREE

It must be almost noon when we reach the Gambini brothers' pride and joy. Young girls and women aren't the norm at the midnight races, but during the day, no one shoos us away. So we linger near the woods, a good distance from the chain-link fence, and watch for signs of life. In the middle of the season, jockeys and managers and sponsors bustle back and forth between the stables and track. But there's time still before things are in full swing, and most jockeys elect to train on private tracks, on private property, paid for by family money.

Magnolia sits on the ground and produces a deck of playing cards from her pocket. I sit next to her and she deftly shuffles and splits the cards, five to each of us. Magnolia gazes at the empty track and says, "Let's start with lowball, aces down."

She's suggesting low poker on my account, because I always end up with crap cards. It doesn't matter, though, Magnolia will beat me either way. Her father taught her, though she's since become a much better player than him. Admittedly, that's not saying much. Magnolia's dad has lost and repurchased a family vehicle more times than I can count with his own deck of cards. If you ask the man, he's always up. But tell that to his children, who are living on the dwindling dollars tucked discreetly inside his wife's hatbox.

Although Magnolia despises her father for what he's done to them, the card games stuck.

I suppose gambling runs in the blood. I would know, after all. It was my grandfather's own addiction that cost us a home the first time. That one-story, green-shuttered, ranch-style house was supposed to be left to my father and our family. It was my grandmother's adamant wish. But she went quietly one night when I was very young, and my grandfather was not a quiet man.

He gambled everything he had in his bank account, and then every hard-earned wad of cash we hid between his walls. Finally, he gambled away that house note too, and onto the streets we marched.

My grandfather's affinity for cards was worse than an addiction. It was wild and frenzied.

My father's addiction is of the softer sort. Slow to grow, but steadfast once it bloomed. He likes cards too, and Magnolia's old man because of it. But it was the Titan races that lost us the last safety net we had.

Magnolia and I play for an hour or so, our eyes flicking to the barren track, until finally, after my best friend has made a mockery of me hand after hand, the sound of someone approaching reaches my ears.

The guy is wearing an orange hunting vest over a plaid shirt. Hairy forearms protrude from rolled sleeves, and he's got a perma-grimace thing going on, as if he's never had a real, gut-clenching laugh in his entire life. White hair that's on its last legs, a tall, thin frame, and eyebrows so thick they demand respect—that's this guy. He looks pale. He also seems angry about who knows what, but pale nonetheless. I notice trickles of sweat running down his face, and consider telling him to lose the hunting vest. It's summer, for crying out loud.

The old guy is barely holding himself up, and he's breathing rapidly. Magnolia notices the man and his condition, and whispers that we should go get my mom. But I have a motto I've stood by since I was eleven years old, and it's solid as the sun.

Don't let others do for you what you can do for yourself.

I can help this man as easily as Mom could. So I stand and approach him. "Hey, you okay?"

He grumbles.

"Want to sit with us?" I ask, gently taking his elbow.

The man looks at me, his grimace extra grimace-y. He looks familiar somehow. "I'm fine," he says.

"Uh, you don't look fine," Magnolia adds, coming to stand beside the two of us.

He tugs his arm away and nearly tumbles backward in the process.

"You're already sweating bullets, old man," I tell him. "You want a mouthful of dirt too?"

The man snaps at me with his vicious dentures. Not that I'm certain he wears dentures, but it seems likely. "I don't need your help. Leave me alone."

"When people say they don't need help, you know what they usually need?"

He glares at me.

I keep a firm grip on the man and look at Magnolia. "Get his other side. Let's get him down."

Magnolia juts her chin out. "Uh . . ."

"Just do it, Mag," I clip.

The man releases a string of profanities lovely enough to make my younger sister sing with delight, but still we strong-arm him toward the ground, next to our playing cards. He's not fighting us that hard. Not really. And after he settles himself in the leaves, he resorts to silently scowling.

"Since you're no longer speaking, we're gonna have to stick

around for a while to make sure you don't bite it." I sit a few feet away, and Magnolia flops down across from me, eyeing me like, *Can we just get out of here?*

"Take off that hunting jacket, at least," I tell him.

His jaw tightens.

"Take it off."

He grumbles.

"And here we have it, folks," Magnolia booms. "The two most stubborn individuals ever to grace Warren County." She laughs nervously while the man and I have ourselves a nice staring contest.

Eventually, Magnolia gets comfortable enough, or maybe bored enough, to change the subject. "How'd you finish junior year? Have you gotten your grades yet?"

"Yeah, they posted Sunday."

Magnolia grins. "Well, how did the math genius make out?"

I can't help the smile that lifts the corners of my mouth. "I did okay."

"Pfft. You probably got a hundred on Slander's final."

I don't respond.

"No way." Magnolia's eyes widen. "You got a hundred on that slimeball's test? Doesn't that mean he puts your name in next year's final?"

My laughter gives me away, and Magnolia shakes her head. "Just think of all those future juniors cursing your name as they try and work through . . . through . . ."

"Division postulates?" I offer.

Her nose scrunches. "Gross. Don't speak of such foul things around me. I'm a lady."

For the next few minutes, I trace my newest theories on what track lengths and jams this Titan season will hold for Magnolia in the grass. I wish I had chalk. And a clean sheet of paper. And the parts my dad used to bring home from work. When I realize Magnolia's eyes have glazed over, I stand and shoot a pointed look at Old Man.

"We're going to leave now, unless you need us to stay longer."

"I didn't need you to stay at all," he growls.

"Manners," I joke.

But then Magnolia and I raise our heads to Cyclone Track, holding our breath. Magnolia doesn't speak. Nor do I. We're both afraid if we make a noise, the possibility will dash away. We were hoping to glimpse an aspiring jockey inspecting the grounds, or maybe a Gambini brother.

But this is better than we dared hope.

CHAPTER FOUR

There in the distance is a flash of steel against the sun, and the clatter of hooves as a horse is led toward the track. I clamber to my feet and Magnolia does the same, double aces forgotten, Old Man left to his own devices.

The horse approaches the starting gate and tosses its head. I squint against the shadows thrown by the trees, and make out the rider. It's a guy I don't recognize, but of course that isn't surprising since jockeys can only ever enter the races once. That goes for Titans too. Once a Titan's serial number has been entered in a prelim race, it can't ever be run again after that season. This limits the number, and *kind*, of people who invest in Titans. It also ensures there will always be new customers.

The aspiring jockey is dressed in blue, no number or surname or slogan on his back. He's a free agent then, as many are around this time. Without a sponsor, he may not be able to cover the $50,000 entrance fee. Heck, his Titan may be borrowed for all I know.

Slowly, the Titan's eyes change from black orbs to a red burning solar system—a sure sign that the horse's racing engine is warmed up and ready to operate. The jockey guides his horse into a lane, not bothering to enter the starting gate. He works his fingers across the control panel, turning the two joystick-type devices on either side to straighten the creature out.

"Think he's working on start speed?" Magnolia whispers.

I nod, though he should use the starting gate if that's the case. Raising a hand to my forehead, I inspect the guy more closely. He's built lean, taller than most jocks I've seen here, and is wearing dark shades and a handkerchief over his mouth.

Where is his helmet?

The jockey logs a few more commands and the Titan stiffens, neck rigid, legs bolted to the ground as if roots stretch from his hooves down into the earth.

There's a low churning noise that grows in volume, signaling that the horse is about to be let loose. It sounds like an airplane rumbling down a tarmac, gaining speed. But the horse hasn't moved an inch. Magnolia looks at me, and I look at her. We smile. This is our place. Always has been. No matter how difficult life gets, and despite the money my father lost here—we share this love.

The sound builds.

And builds.

The guy leans backward, but he should know better. You're supposed to lean forward. His shoulders tighten and he breathes out. I can almost see the oxygen leaving his body. And then he slams his hand on that glittering black button, and his Titan roars to life.

It's off, running, momentum building until I feel as if I'll burst from excitement. The jockey leans back even farther and straightens his legs in front of him in black leather stirrups. He holds on to the grip bar with his left hand, and moves his right over the control panel to kick his horse into the next highest gear. It's wrong, though. He should have done it earlier. The first turn is rapidly approaching, and the tight radius means he'll need to slow soon. Two seconds earlier would have been best. Two and a half, even. His dash has a stopwatch. Why isn't he using it?

Sure enough, the first turn arrives and he's slowing his Titan, realizing he should have taken advantage of the straightaway when he could. But, hey, that's what practice is for. As he turns his Titan back toward his original starting point, I run my eyes over the track. The Gambini brothers built it six years ago, and the first race began a year after that. My dad says the older brother had an obsession with NASCAR and horse races and all things speed related. But it was the younger brother, Arvin, who envisioned the Titans. *That weasel's the one who pulls the strings*, Dad says.

The Gambini brothers have only one living relative, their grandmother. And that grandmother has pockets that run deeper than the depths of hell. It isn't money that the brothers wanted when they started the Titan Circuit, it was attention. When the cameras started rolling, and interviews started appearing, Arvin morphed into a man people envied. After all, plenty of people are wealthy. But not everyone has fame.

Arvin and his older brother may not need extra cash, but they certainly reap it on race days. Men travel from miles around and stomp heavy work boots through the forest to place bets on their favorite Titans. And the majority who lose their rears in a matter of minutes? Well, that dough goes into the Gambini account. Then there are the entrance fees too.

That fifty thousand dollars to enter your horse?

Straight to the Gambinis.

And the two hundred and fifty thousand dollars it takes to purchase a Titan?

A portion of that goes to the Gambinis as well, who hold shares in Hanover Steel Incorporated, the company and plant that produces them.

Of course, it's not as if the brothers don't have expenses. There are track designers to pay, and bet makers and bet takers. There are the engineers who build the temporary tracks as the summer weeks progress and the races become more challenging. And more dangerous. I've also seen billboard ads and heard radio announcements for the Titan Circuit. The brothers must pay for those too.

And then there is their entourage: a dozen employees who follow behind the brothers with bags of freshly pressed suits and makeup and hair styling creams in case of interviews. These people laugh at their bosses' jokes and smile only when Arvin and his brother are in good spirits.

Sometimes I wonder about the real horse track in Detroit, the one that's rumored to be three steps away from bankruptcy. Their undoing started before the Gambini brothers stepped in. After the recession hit, even the wealthy watched their wallets more closely, no longer visiting the tracks as they once did. Of course that left them bored. Bored enough to consider what the Gambini brothers pitched as a safe, new investment in technology, with all the fun that racing promised.

Horses that operated like race cars.

It would diversify their portfolios, the brothers said. And who knows engines and transmissions better than the people of Detroit?

They agreed. They shook hands. And soon after, the middle and lower classes were offered a new opportunity. Leave behind those champagne specials and cold stadium seats where you'll never truly belong, and join the party in the woods. A place where a man can hold a beer to his lips that he brought from home. A place where he can smoke and curse and impress his friends with a ten-dollar bet, paid in cash.

A place where he can be comfortable.

Where he can be king.

The police flocked to the Gambini brothers' track that first night, handcuffs at the ready. But then, their collars were the deepest shade of blue. After Arvin shook their hands and asked the Warren County police chief to fire the first shot for that opening race, and then pledged a hefty donation to the force, the authorities became more of an occasional sighting. More often than not, when you did see them, they were out of uniform, bet cards in tow. Arvin called them each by name, and made sure they got a good spot next to the fence before the races began.

As the jockey in blue brings his Titan around for a third attempt at hitting the corner in record time, I find myself slipping closer to the gate, just like those off-duty police officers. Magnolia hisses my name, but what does it matter?

The jockey takes off, and it's his worst run yet. I'm not sure whether to feel sorry for him, or to internally gloat. There's nothing to gloat about. It's not like I'll ever get the chance to race, or even touch a Titan.

Steel grinds against steel as the horse turns sharply and barrels toward the gate, running full speed toward me. I jump backward, and almost don't make it out of the way in time. The Titan slams into the space where my fingers were, and the jockey tears off his handkerchief and sunglasses.

"Practices are closed to the public," he snaps. He has blond hair that's tied back in a short ponytail, and dark brown eyes. He's not unattractive, but he's not particularly handsome, either. Not when he's scowling like that.

I casually turn my head from side to side. "Don't see anything that says that."

His hands grip the joysticks tighter and the Titan between his legs prances. "Go on, get out of here. I don't like being watched."

"It wasn't you I was watching," I retort, my gaze coming to rest on his horse.

Magnolia touches my arm, but her stance is rigid. She's ready to stand our ground if that's what I want.

The guy leans forward and shakes his head. "Titan fans. Such a pity that you'll never know what it's like to ride. You'll always be there . . ." He nods to me. "And we'll always be up here. So go ahead and watch every move I make from down there in the dirt."

Someone approaches from behind. I spin to see the old man staring past me at the jockey. If looks could kill, Handkerchief Boy would be eight feet underground. He doesn't speak, just glares at the jockey with a silent message I interpret as: *I may be old, but that means I don't have much to lose by burying you with my old man hands.*

The boy redirects his Titan and gallops toward the stalls.

"Well, that was rude," Magnolia says. Then, craning her neck, she yells, "Rude!" She glances at me. "That shade of blue on him is atrocious. All wrong."

I press my lips together and watch him ride away, fury burning through my veins. I'm upset because he's right. Compared to me, that guy will always have more. Even if the Titan is borrowed, it means his family has friends with influence. Friends who can pull strings and make things happen.

I'll never have the chance to compete in the Titan Circuit, yet I need that prize money more than anyone who rides this year will. That's how life works, though, right? The rich get richer, and the poor grow more resentful.

"Thanks for that," I tell the old man, but he only grumbles. "Seriously, you should go home. Drink some water and lie down. I've nearly fainted in this park too. It's the trees. The shade makes you think you're cooler than you are."

When the old man grinds his teeth, I hold my hands up in surrender and Magnolia and I take off toward home for egg salad sandwiches.

"Why'd you even help that guy?" Magnolia asks after he's out of earshot. "And why was he lurking around the track?"

"Same reason we were? And because I'm not heartless?"

"Why not?" she asks. "Being heartless is where it's at."

I laugh because I know she's not serious. But it's difficult, the laughing. Because even though the jockey and his Titan should hold my attention, I can't stop thinking about that obstinate man and his liver-spotted hands. He reminds me of someone that I don't need any help remembering. Because this person is always lingering near the front of my mind, and my heart aches something awful each time I think of him. It asks if I could have saved him, if I could have done something so that he'd still be here.

As Magnolia leads us through trees that grow denser, and foliage that scrapes against my bare calves, all I can think is—

I miss Grandpa.

CHAPTER FIVE

That night, my family sits at the table. We haven't eaten this way in months, and my hands sweat anticipating an announcement. This is how it happened when I was eleven. My mom offered a glass bubble of comfort in the form of chiles rellenos and ranchero beans, and six chairs positioned around a circular table.

Then they shattered that glass bubble with one swift hammer blow.

My younger sister, Zara, glances at me nervously. She's only ten, too young to remember the details of losing our place in my grandfather's home, but she recalls the emotions. The tears my mother cried, the silent shell my father built around himself. She knows there was a time of badness, and maybe she even remembers that it started with dinner as a family.

Dad stands near the stove, spooning Mexican rice onto plates while Mom rolls green chile carnitas tacos. This meal has been in our household rotation for as long as I can remember, one my mom learned from her mother, and one my dad tolerates. I take comfort in this meal. Nothing worrisome can happen when it's the usual on the menu.

Dani, my older sister, sits to my right, her legs spread wide, fingers frantic over her cell phone. The phone is from her most recent boyfriend, someone she's been with for over five months. An eternity, really. He doesn't like it when she's not available. I may be only seventeen, but that's old enough to realize that makes Dani's boyfriend a controlling jerk. Dani loves him, though, or so she says. And Mom and Dad aren't paying attention anymore.

I watch my dad now, working on our plates like his life depends on it. Everyone must have a perfectly fair portion. Exact measurements, that's his talent. At the electrical plant, he and Magnolia's father oversaw the production machines. If anything went awry, Dad could repair it according to code. And if that didn't work, he could envision an alternative solution in his mind and rig it so that it functioned again. Dad always said, *Machines work wonders, but you still need the human brain to oversee the machines.* I guess the plant disagreed, because now there are machines overlooking machines. I want to ask him about his interview today, but I'm smart enough to know that would be a mistake. If it had gone well, he'd have a glass of brandy in his hand, served over ice in a Green Bay Packers mug.

I glimpse an orange envelope in his back pocket and wonder what it is. Zara follows my gaze.

"What's in your pocket, Dad?" she asks.

Instead of looking at Zara, he glances at my mom. Her entire body clenches, and then I know, without a shadow of a doubt, that bad news is brewing. My dad tries to push the envelope farther into his pocket, but it only jackhammers in there, half hanging out as he distributes our plates and takes his seat.

My parents stand a mere five feet apart in our humble kitchen. But the Grand Canyon could settle itself nicely between them. There was a time when my father and mother were one entity, a united front against our sisterly quarrels and pleas for a backyard trampoline. They shared coffee in the morning, and lingering hugs after my dad returned from work. My mother would whisper in Spanish in my father's ear, and my dad would practically purr though he didn't understand a word of it. They were disgusting, really.

I'd kill to have that back.

My mom sits down, and we say grace. There may not be much to be thankful for, but Mom is from San Antonio, and her Catholic upbringing will never fade. Dad pretends to pray alongside us. And Dani never looks up from her phone.

Only Zara bows her head over clasped hands in earnest. My mother's daughter, through and through. As for me? I like the concept of my mother's God. But I'd rather rely on myself. Her God wasn't there the day Grandpa died.

But I prayed to him then, didn't I? I prayed awful hard.

"Dani, put the phone down," Dad says.

My older sister purses her lips, but continues texting.

"Dani," my mother adds softly.

When Dani still doesn't react, my pulse accelerates. I can feel the air change—a thick mustiness rolling in before a clap of thunder. My dad lifts his closed fist and bangs it once, twice against the dining table.

Dani slams the phone down. "What's your problem?"

"My problem is your mother and I made a meal you won't bother looking at," he booms.

"Tony, it's okay," Mom says, laying a hand on his arm.

My dad jerks away from her. "It's not okay. She and that boy are obsessed."

"His name is Jason," Dani sneers. "And I'm not obsessed with him. I'm *in love* with him." She flicks her eyes between my father and mother. "I wouldn't expect you to understand."

My dad grips his fork in one hand, and I'm afraid he might actually stab her with it. "You don't know what love is. And you don't get to judge your mother and me. Not until you've been through what we have and survived."

Dani averts her gaze and mutters, "Jason would never let us go through what you and Mom have."

Zara grabs my hand beneath the table, and the air in my lungs grows still. My mother doesn't move as my dad glowers at Dani. There are maybe three beats of silence. Then my dad's chair flies backward and clatters to the floor. The orange envelope from his back pocket flutters to the ground. When my mom sees it lying there, she clenches her eyes shut. But not before I notice the tears in them.

Dad grabs the envelope and crumbles it in his fist. He brings that same fist close to Dani's face and shakes it a couple of times, but words fail him. And as Dani ignores his outburst, my father storms from the kitchen and slams his bedroom door.

"Couldn't you have just gotten off your phone?" I bark, irritated with my sister.

She kicks back and gets to her feet. "Screw you."

Then she's gone too.

My mom rubs her hands together, and I study the dirt beneath her nails. I wonder how long until she abandons the table too. She'll tend to her gardens, and lose her worries to the feel of the soil between her fingers.

The answer: seven minutes.

She eats quietly with Zara and me for seven minutes, and then disappears. The front door clicks shut, and I tickle Zara, relieved that my family has mostly dispersed, though that can't be good.

"Come on," I tell a giggling Zara. "Help me with the dishes."

She rises, and I pop her gently with a towel to show my appreciation. In the end, Zara only watches as I scrub, rinse, and dry. Because I don't really need her help. Not with this, and not with anything else.

I just like her being close by.

CHAPTER SIX

Two hours later, I'm in the room I share with Dani. She slipped out the window Magnolia-style before I got there, off to see Jason the Glorious. Spreading out on my twin bed, I fiddle with the gears my father brought me over the years. He worked at an electrical plant, but a large space on the first floor was rented out to some guy who built customized parts for the Titans.

Titan 3.0s are built identical to one another, but there's a hefty demand for after-market products that don't affect performance. Pricey items, like sprocket covers engraved with the owner's initials that no one will ever notice. That's the kind of stuff this person made. When Dad realized it, he started bringing him vegetables from my mom's garden. It took three tries before he hit the dude's sweet spot.

Okra. He liked okra.

Dad never said anything when he left the parts on my bed, but I choked up every time. I wish my dad would say the important stuff out loud. I wish he'd tell me that what happened with Grandpa wasn't my fault, and that we'll never be as bad off as we were before we moved to the suburbs of Detroit. I wish he'd hug me and let me mourn. I wish he'd say he was proud of me, and that he's still happy being a father and husband.

But I settle for the Titan parts.

I twirl a lug nut between my fingers and inspect the diagrams I drew of last year's tracks. Cyclonetrack.com lists the basics from the previous season's winner—name, sponsor information, finish time. But I had more. I calculated the winner's turn ratios to the hundredth of a degree. I figured out his spin radius inside a particularly nasty jam, and the seconds he could have gained if he'd pushed closer to the slay zone.

I smile as I pencil a new set of numbers into my notebook, and draw a heavy box around an answer I've been computing for weeks. Then I return to the lug nut. Hold it up against the moonlight streaming through my bedroom window.

Does it need to be this heavy?

When the sound of my father's radio reaches my ears, I spring from bed. I know what he's listening for. It's the only reason he ever tunes in versus flipping on our box television set. I creep from my room and slip down the hallway. Another door opens, and I spot Zara grinning in my direction. I wave her toward me and hold a finger to my lips.

At the end of the hall, I peek around the corner. Dad's in his faded red recliner, the radio in his lap. I catch sight of Mom in the kitchen, knees covered in dirt. She's watching my dad the same way we are. If we're too eager, he'll send us running from the room. But if we advance like enemy soldiers, one silent footstep after another, he'll ignore us.

Dad lost what little money we'd managed to save since moving to Detroit on a Titan that never had a shot. It was before he got laid off, back when he thought a promotion was in the near future, and why not make two big things happen at once? Since then, he feigns hatred for the Titans and the drunken trouble the track brings so close to home. But he's as fascinated with the horses as we are. And so he only mutters his discontent as we crawl onto the floor, settle near his knees, and listen as the jockey delves into the latest news to come from the Gambini brothers.

"As all Cyclone Track fans know, this year marks the fifth year the Titans run. The winning Titan and jockey will be awarded the usual monetary prize of two million dollars, and will lead Detroit's annual Thanksgiving Day parade down Woodward Street. As always, all jockeys must complete the entire Titan Circuit, starting with . . ."

The man stops speaking and shuffles some papers. Within seconds, a female voice comes on.

"I've got it here, Jordan. All jockeys will start by registering their Titan 3.0s on cyclonetrack.com. That must be done by end of day next Friday. And that same weekend, the Titans run for the first time."

"That's right," the man interjects. "The sponsor race will take place on Cyclone Track so that companies, and those individuals who can afford the entrance fees, can be sure they're partnering with the best Titan and jockey. After the race, the jockeys and trainers will attend Travesty Ball to mingle one-on-one with sponsors. Once sponsorships are secured, and contracts have been signed, entrance fees will be paid and the official jockey/Titan lineup will be announced for the season."

The woman laughs lightly before adding, "Of course, then there are the preliminary races, the circuit races, the ad sponsorships to fulfill, and all the Cyclone Track gossip that jockeys have to contend with soon after."

"You enjoy that last part, don't you?" the man jokes.

"Guilty!" She laughs harder. "I buy every issue of *Titan Enquirer* I can get my hands on. You know I still believe Harding and Flynn had an off-course romance last year."

"Okay, before we get lost in that debacle, let's announce the big surprise the Gambini brothers have lined up."

"Oh, right!" the woman squeals. "I couldn't believe this when I heard."

Zara scoots closer, bringing me back to my parents' crowded living room. We're all packed together in there now: Mom sitting on the couch, Zara and I as close to my father as we can without him barking at us to go to bed.

"In celebration of the fifth year of Cyclone Track being opened, the Gambini brothers have decided that the first jockey to cross the finish line at the sponsor race will have their entrance fee waived."

My mouth falls open. No way. Someone will race this year for free? No fifty-thousand-dollar barrier? It could be anyone who got that free spot! It could be someone from Warren County, even. What if they won the derby at the very end? That kind of opportunity could save a family out here. It could set them on a different course for life, far away from poverty.

"It's so exciting," the woman says. "Of course, they'll need a Titan to enter."

My heart plummets, which is ridiculous. Even my dad turns off the radio at this last part.

"Who do they think they're fooling?" he mumbles to himself, ignoring the fact that we're here. "All they're doing is letting some rich chump hold on to cash he doesn't need."

"Yep," I mutter without thinking.

My dad's eyes connect with mine.

Uh-oh.

"What are you guys doing up? Off to bed. Both of you!"

I jump up with Zara, and my mom returns to the kitchen. As I head back to my room, I can't help sharing my father's resentment. I once heard that a cat is both drawn to, yet repulsed by, the scent of its own litter box. Maybe that's how I feel about the Titans. And about the celebrity magazines I hide beneath my mattress. They offer a glimpse into a different kind of life, one with excitement and security. I can't help but be drawn to something like that.

I also can't help but hate them for dangling a life that's unreachable.

CHAPTER SEVEN

Two days later, Magnolia is elbow-deep in a hair accessory project she won't leave alone. She begs me to come over and sit on her bed to watch her "genius in progress." I've been vegging out in front of the television for six hours, and need to take a break before my eyeballs roll out of my head. I tell her I'll be over after lunch, and decide to go for a walk around our neighborhood.

Where we live is nothing to get excited about—one-story houses with old siding and trash cans stinking by the curb. The homes are missing shutters, and their screen doors are torn. Mr. Reynolds has had a yellow couch on his front porch for as long as I can remember, and two houses down from there is a car parked in the grass.

Of course, most people's lawns are 100% all-natural weeds anyway. Don't want to wake to the sound of a lawn mower at 7:00 a.m.? Then we've got a place for you!

I smile thinking about my mother and these so-called lawns. Nothing in this entire world makes Mom more upset than people who don't maintain their garden beds. If they knew what she did to their properties as they chased sleep, they'd probably torch our house.

Or give her an award.

I walk five or six blocks before my footsteps falter. There's a man standing in his open garage wearing a welding mask, a machine between his hands. He's sliding something under the machine slowly but steadily, rotating the piece every few seconds. Orange sparks fly in all directions, and a high-pitched whirring reaches my ears.

The man straightens and places a hand on his lower back, stretching. Then he flips the hood up on his mask and curses loud enough for me to hear him from across the street. I can see his face clearly now, but I knew who it was all along. Both hands find his hips as he turns and looks in my direction.

"Nice vest," I yell.

He turns the machine off and squints. "You that girl from the track?"

"The one and only." I make my way across the street, drawn by the way he stands just like my grandpa, leaning too far back, shoulders raised toward his ears. I'm not sure how I missed the fact that he lived so close to Magnolia and me until now.

"What're you doing?" he says with obvious irritation.

"Preparing to catch you when you fall. It's hotter today than it was on Monday." I gaze at the material he has beneath his oversized power tool. It's a sheet of steel, which I've seen before, but the shade is darker. There's a subtle ripple effect that only the sun catches, and a sparkling sheen that lies beneath the surface. These things tell me everything I need to know. "Where'd you get that?"

"Get what?" The old man turns off the machine, and wipes his hands on a rag that could use a spin cycle or two.

"That's Titan steel."

He catches my gaze and studies me closely. "It's no such thing."

"Is too. It's got that ripple and sparkle and—"

"Kid, if you knew what you were talking about, you'd know this is much too dark to be Titan steel. Why don't you skip on back across the street and keep going wherever it is you were going."

He lowers his mask and stares at me like a serial killer.

I inspect the steel again, and my enthusiasm wanes. He's right. It's too dark.

Studying his cut lines, it's obvious he's off by three full degrees. Even if he does get the octagonal shape he's going for, it'll have unequal sides. I raise my chin. "I used to know someone like you, old man. Beneath all his grunting and frowning was a nice guy."

When the man raises a hand and flicks it toward me, basically telling me to *shoo*, my face reddens.

"You're off by three degrees." I point to the steel. "Maybe more." Then I turn to go.

"You think because you do well in high school math, you know about building things that run?"

"I know a bad line when I see one," I retort over my shoulder.

The man doesn't say anything else. I turn back once when I'm a safe distance away and see him holding the steel up to the daylight, inspecting his cuts. I smile to myself, imagining I'm right.

CHAPTER EIGHT

If I kept a diary like my idiotic older sister, I'd probably leave today's entry out. It starts on Sunday morning, at St. Joseph's Roman Catholic Church. Arvin Gambini has made an appearance, and it has the entire congregation humming with equal parts excitement and disgust. The priest must have been given advance warning of our visitor, because he preaches with incredible zeal, waving his fists and thumping his Bible for emphasis.

Zara sits between Dani and me, and my dad sits to my left. Mom has squeezed herself in next to Dani, and I wonder if it's to ensure her oldest daughter doesn't flee halfway through the service. I don't listen to most of the sermon. Instead, I concentrate on my father's arm pressing against mine. It's warm, dressed in a white shirt my mother ironed hours earlier. I stare at him from the corner of my eye, breathing in the scent of his Old Spice aftershave. He's running his tongue over his teeth, displeased by whatever our overweight, sweating priest is trying to drive home.

I glance around the room at the other dads. Most that are sitting next to their kids have their arms extended across the back of the pew. A church hug, if you will. Not my dad, though. His hands are clenched between his knees.

I wish he'd give me and Zara the church hug. He's got enough arm length to stretch behind the two of us. Biting my lip, I nudge closer to my dad. His eyes dart in my direction before moving his torso in the opposite direction a half inch. He probably thinks I want more room, but that half inch feels like a knife to the heart.

To shake things up, I turn my attention to the priest and actually listen to what he's saying. Suddenly, I understand my dad's tenseness. Father Tim is laying it on thick, talking about reaping the benefits of hard work. About how God loathes laziness, and awards those who toil for their Lord and family.

"Proverbs 13:4 says, 'The soul of the sluggard craves and gets nothing, while the soul of the diligent is richly supplied.'" Father Tim shows us his trusty Bible. "I say to you now, if you put your hands to work, be proud, for this pleases the Lord. But if you do not, I ask whether it is because work is truly unavailable, or because you are not willing to pick up a hoe and tend the fields." The priest holds up his index finger. "No work is beneath us, for the Lord does not discriminate between the field owner and the laborer. All are loved equally."

Dani, Zara, and I all turn slowly toward my father. His head looks like it's about to split open. He's actually quaking with anger. The priest couldn't be clearer in his message.

If you're out of work, it's because you don't want *work.*

After the congregation sings a half-hearted hymn, we file out. My dad glares at Arvin from across the room, cringing when the priest shakes Arvin's hand and thanks him for coming. With Arvin is another man dressed in a gray tailored suit. He's tall and dark-skinned with a smooth head. There's a cloth square, red as sin, peeking from his pocket. Arvin introduces the guy to the priest, and they shake hands too. Arvin's older brother, Theo, is nowhere in sight.

"That's who Dad interviewed with on Monday," Dani whispers to me.

My head snaps in her direction, unbelieving. "But Daddy hates the races."

"He hates them the same way he does brandy, with one hand on the bottle." She shrugs. "But he needs a job."

"It didn't go well?" I ask, afraid of her answer.

"Do Dad's interviews ever go well?" she responds, too loudly. "That man couldn't get a job if it hit him square between the eyes."

Zara nudges me and cocks her head toward Dad, who is glaring at Dani. When Dani sees him too, her eyes bug out from her head.

"Dad, I didn't mean—"

But he only brushes past her and storms toward the car, back muscles tight with anger.

I cast one last look at the younger Gambini brother before we head after Dad. Arvin is short and thick with too much hair on his head, as if he's mocking men who are balding. He smiles easily, but the gesture never reaches his too-small eyes. His ruddy cheeks remind me of Christmas and beautiful Michigan winters, but he's missing the authenticity to drive the resemblance home. The tall man by his side motions toward the exit, and Arvin wastes no time excusing the two of them.

This makes me smile, seeing Arvin jump when someone else instructs him to.

No one speaks on the way home, which only makes things worse. When our family argues, it's almost a relief. We're communicating. We're *trying*. But when everyone shuts down like this, it rattles me.

Discomfort crawls over my skin as my dad pulls our snot-green '02 Buick into the driveway and kills the engine. I'm afraid to breathe until Dani gets out of the car and slams the door. My mom goes after her, and then my dad charges after my mom. Only Zara and I remain. She's sucking on a peppermint she got from church and asking what Dani said that made Dad so mad. But I can't answer her, because my eyes have snagged on something that causes my heart to race.

Tucked into a small slot next to the Buick's steering wheel is an orange envelope.

I watch the house for any sign of my dad, and then I reach into the front seat and grab it.

"Was that the thing in Dad's pocket last night?" Zara asks in a whisper, though there's no one to hear us.

I turn away from Zara in case it's really bad, and open the flap. Out slides a thin piece of paper. I don't read much of it. I don't need to. The red, stamped words are the only thing I need to know.

EVICTION NOTICE

I crumple the paper in my hand and my breathing comes faster. Zara calls my name and tries to pry the paper from my fingers, but I've shut down. My body tightens and my eyes cinch shut and sweat pricks the back of my neck. It's happening again. My biggest fear will be actualized.

When I finally open my eyes, I find my dad standing outside the car. He sees the envelope in my hand and tears the door open. "This isn't yours," he snaps. Unlike Zara, he's able to rip both envelope and paper from my hand with ease.

I don't know where the anger comes from, but it slams into me like a hurricane. Great, heaping piles of anger so rich my mouth waters. "It's kind of mine, isn't it? And Mom's? And Dani's? And even Zara's? It's for all of us!"

My voice rises, and I know it won't be long before neighbors peek through their blinds for free early-morning entertainment.

"This is for me to figure out, Astrid. Go inside. Your mom needs help with lunch."

I shove him. I'm not sure what I hope to accomplish, but the mountain of a man hardly budges. "We're going to be on the streets, and you weren't even going to tell us. How much time do we have?"

My dad shakes his head like I'm overreacting. "I'm doing everything I can here."

"No, you're not," I shout. "You're looking for work, but what about us? We can help too. Mom could work. So could Dani and I."

"No," he says, his nostrils flaring. "I can take care of my family."

I drop my head to one side, the fight leaving my body in a rush. "But you're not, are you, Dad? If you were, you'd know we need *you* more than we need money. I forgive you for going to those races last summer. I just wish you could forgive *me*."

"What is that supposed to mean?" he asks.

I start to answer, but now Zara is getting out of the car and Dad is yelling at her to stay put. I turn my back to him and march toward Candlewick Park, tears streaking down my face. I don't want him to see me cry. But then again, I do.

I want him to chase after me and hug me to his chest and say that everything will be all right. That even if we lose our home, we won't lose each other. Not this time.

But we're already losing each other. We hardly speak anymore, and when we do, it's with biting words and venom boiling in our blood.

Our home is the only thing keeping us from shattering into five separate pieces.

And it's about to be gone.

CHAPTER NINE

I have my head in my hands, feeling nice and sorry for myself, when a voice interrupts my thoughts.

"You following me, kid?"

Glancing up from my picnic table, I see it's Old Man. "Go away."

I put my head back down.

The table rocks and I know he's sat down. "Maybe you need some water. Dehydration is dangerous."

He's teasing me, but it's the last thing I need. Realizing I'm not playing along, the man sighs. "Look, I'm not good at this kind of thing. So, can you help me out?"

I peek at him, thinking he must be joking. "What exactly do you need help with?"

"I'm trying to make you feel better. You're over here sulking, taking up my usual spot. Everyone knows that's my spot."

"So you want me to help you help *me* feel better?"

He grins ever so slightly. With the way his mouth turns down, even a smile looks more like he's indifferent. "When you put it like that . . ."

I stare down at my hands, my father's secret burning in my mind. How long has he known we were facing foreclosure? Did the letter come yesterday? A week ago?

"You know what I've found?" the man says.

"No."

"I've found you should say the thing that's bothering you outright." He holds up a fist and shakes it like he's strangling a large bird. "Takes away its power."

"My family is being kicked out of our house." I don't know why I say it. Maybe because it doesn't matter what this guy thinks. Or maybe I just want to sucker punch him for being nosy.

"Is that it?" He leans back. "Hell, I've been evicted a half dozen times if I've been evicted once."

"My family will fall apart if we lose our home. They won't make it."

"Yeah, they will. Now stop all this crying, kid. It shows weakness. You're not weak, are you?"

His words strike daggers through me. I've prided myself on having a stiff upper lip ever since we moved to Detroit, and this guy's calling me a child. Well, he doesn't know what I've been through. If he did, he'd feel bad about what he said. And perhaps that's why I open my mouth and spit out, "My grandpa died the last time we got evicted."

Old Man couldn't look less impressed with my horror story. "Yeah, well, that's what grandpas do. They die."

I wince. "You know, you're a real piece of work." I start to stand up, but the man's face softens and he holds up a hand to stop me.

"All I mean is, your grandpa isn't here anymore. So that has nothing to do with what your family is facing now."

My head lowers, and though it angers me so bad I could spit, my bottom lip trembles.

"Oh, man." The old guy runs a hand through his wild, white hair. "You're one of those, huh? Got it in your head that you somehow killed the man, don't you? I heard kids do that. Find a way to take ownership of tragedy."

"If I'd been there, he'd still be alive," I say in a whisper. It's the last thing I can say about it. No matter what he comes back with, no matter how upset he makes me. Not one more word about me and Grandpa and *that day*.

The man stands up, and gazes toward the sun, then back at me. "You can call me Rags, I s'pose."

I wipe the back of my hand across my eyes. "Wh-what?"

The old man scrunches his face like he's trying to figure me out. "You were right about those cuts. I was a few degrees off." He points at me, and his tone hardens. "But it wasn't no three degrees. It was two. Maybe less."

"It wasn't less than two," I respond.

He shoves his hands into jeans that sit too high on his waist. "No. No, I guess it wasn't." When I don't respond, he stands up. "You gonna keep crying after I leave?"

"I'll cry if you don't leave."

That does it. The man—Rags—laughs. It's more a bark than anything else, but it makes me smile. He squints in my direction. "You really that good with math and all that?"

I square my shoulders. "I am."

"Well, come on, then." He turns on his heel and walks away.

"Am I supposed to follow you?" I yell.

"Can if you want," he responds without looking back. "No one's making you."

I glance in the direction of my house and wonder if I should go back home. Zara must be confused as to what's going on, and I hate to think of her worrying. But Rags's orange vest is like a beacon of hope against my future, and I find myself trudging after him.

Magnolia would flip out if she caught me following this dude through the woods. But we aren't in the woods long, thank goodness. Rags leads me on the same route I walked a few days ago, and soon we're stopped in front of his house. He fidgets,

41

and I realize he's nervous. This makes *me* nervous. What the heck was I thinking? The first thing my mother ever taught me was a lesson about strangers and not going with them.

"I'm thinking I might show you something in my work shed," he says.

"Welllll," I drawl. "If that's not the creepiest thing anyone has ever said . . ."

He rubs the back of his neck. "Can you keep a secret, kid?"

"My name is Astrid, and I'm really thinking this is the part where I run home and call the cops."

He ignores my commentary and instead stomps between his house and the neighbor's house, muttering the entire way. I stay rooted in place, watching him go. Craning my neck, I make out a shed in his backyard, cream colored with blue trim. It's the size of a one-car garage, with a tired roof. He pulls a key ring from his pocket and unlocks the door. Only when he's taken a couple of steps inside does he holler, "You coming?"

"Nuh-uh," I reply.

Rags glances around to check if anyone's listening and then says, "Astrid, I'm never going to make this offer again. Not to you. Maybe not to anyone. So you can come and have a look, or you can go home. It's no sweat off my back."

Dead bodies. There has to be dead bodies in there. Or maybe a lifetime supply of orange vests, lightly splattered with inconspicuous blood for good measure. I'm not sure what's in his work shed, but I do know fifteen minutes ago I felt like the world was ending. And now my lungs are pumping and my blood is warming and I'm walking toward the thing he's motioning to.

He steps all the way inside, and I follow him in. After he flips the light switch, I make out a lumpy figure on the dirt floor, covered by a burlap blanket.

Yep, dead body.

"Can I trust you?" he asks.

"Can you trust me?" I repeat. "I'm standing in your Creep Dungeon staring at what looks like neatly arranged corpses. I think the question is whether I can trust *you*."

He shakes his head. "I'm an idiot for doing this, but I'm getting too old to stand still."

He bends down, knees creaking, and pulls back the blanket.

I gasp when I see what he's revealed. A Titan like I've never seen before, with smooth black steel and silver hooves dirtied by years of neglect. The animal's legs bend at awkward angles, and its head is thrown back as if in pain. Though its eyes are closed, soft faux lashes encircle the sockets, giving the horse a kind appearance despite its intimidating black coat.

I circle the creature, and my eyes land on the control panel at the base of its neck. The dials are different from today's Titans, but I could figure them out.

I could figure them out.

That's how quickly I go from studying this broken-down Titan to thinking about the one rider who will be allowed to enter the circuit this year, free of charge.

I could figure them out.

I could race in the Titan Derby.

I could win and save my family's home.

I can hardly keep my legs beneath me when I look at Rags and utter, "Are you going to race this thing this year?"

"Me?" He shakes his head like that's preposterous. "No way. I'm an architect, not a jockey."

I swallow the lump in my throat, and ask the question I'm terrified to ask. "Can *I* race it?"

43

He hesitates. "I'm not even sure this model would qualify."

"Course it would," I argue. "It's clearly a Titan."

The old man teeters on the edge of indecision. Though why bring me here if not for a reason? So I give him a nudge.

"I could win," I whisper. "No one would want it more than I would."

Rags scratches his chin. Looks at me. Looks at the Titan. "Okay."

"Okay?"

"That's what I said."

I slap my hands together and jump a foot off the ground. "No way! This is not happening. I mean, it is. But what are the chances?" I run a hand through my hair, struggle to pull in a deep breath. "How do you even have this machine? Don't they cost like a quarter of a million bucks?"

"Do you really care where I got it?"

Nope. Not really. My mind is racing so fast that I don't care enough to concentrate on anything except the Titan. I mean, if he stole it, I should probably know so I can fully appreciate what I'm getting myself into. But it doesn't look like he wants to share this information, so instead, I say, "So, what first?"

"First? First you get out of here and let me think on the poor choices I'm making and how much bail money I'll need."

I try to contest his backtracking, but Rags won't hear it. He all but strong-arms me out of the work shed and into the street. But that's okay, because he says I can return in two days. I can't feel the asphalt beneath my feet on the return trek to my house. I can't remember the tears I cried earlier today when I learned my family was losing their home. Because now there's a chance I can do something to help. Something big.

Dad may believe this problem is his to handle. But I've learned a lot from watching my silent, brooding father over the years.

Don't let others do for you what you can do for yourself.

I head straight home from Rags's house and locate Zara.

I tell her everything will be okay.

I'll make sure of it.

PART II
THE LONG SHOT

CHAPTER TEN

As Magnolia and I walk toward Rags's house, she lists the reasons my riding a Titan in this year's circuit is a terrible idea.

"You're only seventeen."

"Entry age is seventeen and above," I retort. "As long as my parents don't mail an objection form, I'm cool."

"Your dad will kill you."

"If he finds out."

Magnolia gives me a look like I'm crazy. "How would he *not* find out?"

"I can do this, Magnolia," I say, as if that's an answer.

"Of course you can. Astrid Sullivan can take on the entire world as long as she doesn't have to rely on anyone else to help her."

I grin. "What can I say? I work better alone."

"It's kind of gambling, isn't it?"

I halt in place, because she's broached the one subject we both avoid. I want to dismiss what she said, but she's right. My grandfather's gambling cost us our first family home, and my dad's addiction will soon cost us our second. Magnolia and I loathe gambling, and everything that goes along with it. Yet here I am, ready to involve myself in the tracks—the same thing that led to the biggest loss in my father's habit.

"This is different," I mutter.

Magnolia nods, recognizing that I don't want to discuss this. Instead, she adjusts the bumblebee hair clip she made from wire, yellow spray paint, and glitter, and motions for us to keep walking. "Well, you'll need me for moral support. And for fashion advice. If you go through with this, you'll need a glam squad. That's what celebrities have, Astrid—glam squads. I know these things." As we walk in silence, she sobers. "What about the guy we saw fall off his Titan? The one who—"

"I know the one." How could I forget? We were only thirteen, and the man couldn't have been older than thirty. I can still see the surprise on his face as he tumbled from his horse. Still hear the way the crowd screamed as one throbbing mass as the other Titans trampled his body.

"There have been others too," she says quietly.

I don't answer. Because I know she's right. But I can't think about them. I have to think about the winners. That's where my focus must lie, never wavering.

Rags is waiting at the end of his driveway when we arrive, one hand on a brown pickup truck that looks like it was built in the eighties. He's already shaking his head. "No. No way. I'm not dealing with two of you. One teenage girl is more than enough headache."

"Hi, Rags!" Magnolia waves cheerfully. "I brought muffins."

"I don't like muffins," he grunts.

"You'll like these," she replies.

Rags looks at me. "Why is she here? I asked if you could keep a secret."

"I can," I say. "But not where my best friend is concerned."

Magnolia shoves a cranberry-orange muffin into Rags's hand after we cross the street. "Don't worry. I'm like a vault. Whatever you put in this thing ain't coming out." She taps her temple.

Rags studies my face before rolling his eyes. "This is strike one, kid. If you cross me again, I'll toss that Titan in an incinerator and be done with this harebrained idea."

"So we're still on?" I ask, all business.

In response, he walks toward his work shed. "The first thing we gotta do is get you registered, and don't be surprised if the Gambini brothers shut us down then and there. They'll be looking for any reason to keep us out of the race, and we're going to give them a solid one."

"Why?" I ask. "Because our Titan isn't—"

"Even if we can get you registered, you'll have to ride well enough to compete in the sponsor race. At the very least, we have to keep you in the saddle."

"She can do more than stay in the saddle," Magnolia interrupts. "She rode my brother's skateboard like a pro. He said so himself."

Rags rubs his forehead. "A Titan isn't a skateboard."

"How is it not?" she contests. "Four wheels. Four legs. Both unstable."

"Why are you here again?"

She holds up the muffins. "Munchies."

Rags tosses the muffin into an ivy patch my mother would detest, and stomps the rest of the way to the work shed. "I've been working on him ever since you left."

"I think you were working on him even before that," I reply, patting Magnolia on the back, none too happy about her disgraced muffin.

Rags doesn't respond. But when he gets to the door, he turns with a glint in his eye. "He's prepped for transport, but I'll need help rolling him to my truck and loading him in." He unlocks the door and pushes it open. Inside the shed is what appears to be the largest coffin I've ever seen. It's painted black with yellow trim.

"It looks pretty morbid," Magnolia mumbles.

"It looks wicked cool," I say.

Rags motions toward a flatbed with wheels, and together, the three of us manage to get the covered Titan onto it using ropes and pulleys that Rags configured. After we roll the Titan coffin next to his house, and struggle to get it into the truck bed using a ramp, Rags slams the tailgate closed. "You can ride with me," he says, ignoring Magnolia.

"And where will Magnolia ride?" I ask.

"She can ride her skinny rear back to her house."

I cross my arms, and he growls deep in his chest. "You know I could find a hundred different people to race this Titan."

I remain fixed in place.

"Get in the truck," he says, tossing an oddly shaped bag into the back. "Both of you."

"Wait," I say, realizing I'm missing the bigger point here. "Where are we going?"

"To my friend's place south of the city. He's got a track." Rags rounds the truck and gets behind the steering wheel. When Magnolia and I slide inside, he glances over at us. "Your parents going to put an APB out on you two?"

"My mom's working." Magnolia bites into a muffin. "And Dad's looking for work."

Rags glances in my direction.

"They won't be looking for me," I say, staring ahead.

"All right then." He starts the ignition. "Let's waste some time."

....

The two-story white clapboard house sits so far off the road it's as if Rags's friend is hiding something. Turns out, he is. The course that winds between the trees near his home is a close replica of Cyclone Track. I wonder why he has it, but Rags instructs us not to ask him stupid questions before we get out of the truck.

"Barney," Rags says with an honest-to-goodness smile.

The man, Barney, moves toward us. He's as bald as the day is long, with short legs and arms that swing as he waddles. A white beard sweeps across his face, and his blue eyes dance as he clasps hands with Rags.

"Thought you said you might bring a girl by," Barney says. "As in, one."

Rags nods. "You know how girls are. Takes two of 'em to use the toilet."

"Excuse me?" I say.

Barney looks at Magnolia. "What's that you're holding?"

She purses her lips, but holds out the basket. "Muffins."

Barney looks at Rags and then back to Magnolia. "Anyone who brings food is welcome in my book."

Magnolia smiles.

"You sure we can use your track?" Rags asks.

"I said you could," Barney responds, already reaching for a second muffin though he hasn't eaten the first. When he finishes his breakfast, he helps Rags unload the giant crate and rolls it a good distance from the truck. Rags reaches down and messes with a padlock. It takes him several minutes before it unlocks. So long that Magnolia makes a joke about him packing an atomic bomb in there instead of a Titan.

"That thing *is* an atomic bomb," Barney says.

"You built him," Rags says as the lock pops open. "Don't judge too harshly."

Barney belly laughs. "That's *why* I judge so harshly."

"You built this thing?" Magnolia asks the portly man.

Barney salutes her. "Titan 1.0 Senior Engineer at your service."

My eyes dart to the box, a chill rushing over my skin. A Titan 1.0, he said. The very first model ever designed. They never even made it to the track, and there's no mention of the machines on cyclonetrack.com. The only thing I ever found about them was a single blog post by a Titan enthusiast, who said the first model was quickly discontinued because of *jockey/Titan misalignment*.

"This is a first edition?" I ask, my voice breaking.

"The most advanced version created," Barney responds. "It was all downhill from there."

I doubt that's true. Otherwise, why wouldn't Hanover Steel still make them? Before I can think more on this, Rags lifts the lid. I stare in wonderment at the machine—the steel a shade too dark, its hooves a touch too bright. Other than the color difference, I can't see what makes this model a 1.0, and the others I've seen 3.0s. What am I missing?

Rags slips off a key from his ring and inserts it into the horse's control panel. At first, nothing happens, but after Rags pushes a few buttons, and eventually slams his open palm against the machine's side, a soft whirring sound begins.

"Holy cow," Magnolia whispers.

"After all this time," Barney says at the same time.

As for me, I stay quiet. But a spark of electricity shoots from my feet, up my torso, and down into my fingers. And when the Titan stirs in its black and yellow coffin for the first time—a simple twitch of its head—my heart jackhammers in my chest.

I lean forward, my pulse thrumming in my ears, and inspect the Titan.

"Careful," Rags says.

I stretch out a shaking hand, my mouth painfully dry, and lay it ever so gently on the machine's neck. Cool metal rumbles beneath my fingers for only a fraction of a moment.

And then its eyes flash open.

The entire coffin rocks and the machine thrashes from side to side. Magnolia releases a small scream, and Rags grabs me and yanks me backward. As the four of us look on, the horse continues to flail until finally, finally—

The Titan rises to its feet.

CHAPTER ELEVEN

I can't think past anything besides the Titan stepping out of the crate and moving toward me. Rags tries to block the machine's path, but I won't budge. I'm too busy studying the creature's nostrils flaring, and its eyes fluttering. I'm too preoccupied with the sleek black steel that's in desperate need of a good polishing, and the screeching sound its body makes as it moves. I can't stop staring, and so when the horse is just a hand width away, I forget to be afraid. Until it stops. It's a machine, after all, weighing in at eight hundred pounds. And the way it's looking at me isn't comforting.

The Titan bends its head and sniffs my tank top. Then it blows out through its nose like it's not at all pleased with what it smelled. Realizing we've got to get things moving, I lift my hand a second time so it can get a good whiff of my scent. Don't animals like that? Smelling things and such? Only when I do this, the Titan throws its head back in irritation.

And then it bolts for the woods.

"He's on auto!" Barney yells, running for Rags's truck. Rags sprints after him, telling Magnolia and me to stay put. But there's no way I'm leaving my only chance at a new life running through the woods without following it. Magnolia and I jump in the bed of the truck, and though Rags yells something vulgar over the growling engine, he doesn't take the time to toss us out.

The truck kicks up dirt and barrels toward the fleeing Titan. Magnolia and I hang on as we fly over large rocks and hit dips in the field surrounding Barney's house. Before long, we're blazing between trees, and I catch sight of the horse dashing ahead. A thick branch flies toward our heads and I tackle Magnolia moments before it would have hit her.

I get on all fours as the wind whips by and breathe in the smell of soil and sugar maple trees. The truck jerks to the right, and though I've braced myself, I roll to the left and smash into the side. Almost immediately, the truck slams to a stop. At first I think it's because Rags and Barney heard us rolling around in the back, but when I peer over the side, I see the real reason.

The Titan is on the opposite side of a creek, tangled in vines and whining frantically. I'm struck dumb for a heartbeat, surprised to hear the animal produce such a sound. Then I'm flying over the side, Magnolia hollering at me to keep my distance. But she doesn't understand that when I see the Titan, I see that eviction notice. I see my grandfather dying. My family falling apart.

I see myself alone.

Rags and Barney are out of the vehicle now too, but they won't reach the Titan as fast as I will. I dive into the creek— frantic from the race through the woods—and trudge across the waist-deep water until I reach the machine. The vines are wrapped around its neck and back legs, and the horse is hysterical with fear. But that can't be right. It's a robot. An intricate system of parts and gears built for entertainment. How could it possibly be afraid?

I approach slowly, my hands outstretched to show the beast I don't mean any harm.

"Leave him," Rags yells. "Don't touch him, Astrid."

But I'm afraid that if it continues jerking around, the animal will suffer irreparable damage. I can't let that happen. So I grab the first vine and pull.

The Titan goes ballistic.

I almost fall beneath its stamping feet, and I swear on my sketchpad that the Titan nips me on the shoulder. Gritting my teeth, I lunge for the vines again. This time I'm able to tear one away, and then another.

Rags reaches me as I rip the last of the vines away. When the Titan realizes it's free, it raises up on its back legs and hooves the air. I fall back, transfixed by the machine's size, glimpsing my reflection in the black steel. When it touches back down, it sniffs me again, but with interest this time instead of anxiety. I don't move a muscle, just gaze into those two black eyes staring back at me.

Rags tosses himself over the Titan's side, pulling himself up with the faux horse hair falling down the machine's neck. The second he lands on the horse's back, the creature loses its mind. Bucking, the Titan takes off down the side of the creek. Rags hangs on with impressive agility, and after he runs his fingers over the control panel, the horse lurches to a halt. Breathing deeply, he turns the horse back toward us and leads it into the water. I wade after him as Magnolia and Barney cheer from the other side.

"You still got it," Barney crows.

"Without a saddle and everything." Magnolia claps her hands in appreciation of Rags's performance. When I show up on the opposite side of the creek, dripping water, Magnolia clears her throat. "Oh, uh, you did well too, Astrid. Way to snap the vines like a champ."

The Titan remains in place as Rags reaches into his truck and withdraws a set of reins used on real horses. He threads it through the Titan's mouth and pulls the thin leather straps over its neck. The horse heaves as he does this—a false animation I've never seen on a Titan 3.0.

"What's wrong with that thing?" I ask as Rags dismounts. "Why did it take off on its own like that?" I'm soaking wet and infuriated that this day isn't going smoothly. The sponsor race is next weekend, and we've wasted precious time chasing this psychotic thing through the woods instead of practicing.

"I forgot to turn off the autopilot function," Rags says gruffly. "I didn't know he'd be so rambunctious after lying dormant this long."

"Rambunctious?" Magnolia says, voicing my exact thought. "Titans can't be rambunctious. They can't be anything. They're machines."

"Oh, you didn't tell her?" Barney slaps the outside of his thigh, belly shaking with laughter.

"Tell me what?" I ask.

Rags leads the Titan away.

"Hey, Rags. What are you not—?" But I don't finish the thought, because the answer comes at once. "Oh, man. No way. This is not happening."

"What?" Magnolia says.

Rags guides the horse into the back of the truck, and turns back to us. When he doesn't respond, I glance at Magnolia.

"That thing has, like . . . thoughts or something."

"Emotions," Rags corrects.

"*And* thoughts," Barney says. "Don't cut yourself short, Rags."

I take a step toward Rags and stare him down, orange hunting vest and all. "Wait, you created this thing? This was your design?"

"He was the senior architect on the project," Barney answers for him. "Not as important as the senior engineer, but you wouldn't know it with how those architects tout their own work."

Rags glowers at his feet as if I've caught him doing something deplorable. But it doesn't matter, does it? In fact, it's fantastic that we have these two guys on our side. If something goes wrong with our horse, he and Barney can make the repair. When Rags can't avoid my gaze any longer, he mutters, "That's how Barney and I met. We worked at Hanover." Rags's brow furrows and his expression changes to one of frustration. "What does this matter anyway? Let's go back and get started."

I follow after Rags, and Magnolia and I squeeze into the backseat of the truck. During the entire return trip to Barney's place, the two of us face the truck bed, watching the Titan. It lies down, four legs folded beneath its body. Even when Rags rolls over bumps and ditches, the creature doesn't move.

It's a far cry from the savage machine I witnessed galloping through the forest.

CHAPTER TWELVE

After we return to the outskirts of Barney's track, Rags says it's time to teach me the control panel. He punches some buttons and the Titan lies down, sniffing at the grass. Once Rags has my attention, he launches into an explanation of how everything works. First, he points to the handlebars situated on either side of the board. "If you're ever riding, and something goes wrong, grab on to these and hang on. Understand?"

I nod, and he points out the ignition slot that's currently engaged and self-explanatory. The key turns the Titan on. Next is a black turbo button. It's covered by a silver flap that I can flip up with my thumb, and Rags explains that it's covered for a reason.

"This button is what triggers the Titan's racing capability," he says. "Push it when the starting gates open and the horse will enter manual transmission."

There's a smaller black button above the covered turbo one, so I ask, "This is what turns on the Titan's eyes, right?"

"You got it," he replies. "That sends a signal to the Titan to ready itself to race. Then the turbo button is like a detonator."

"So many buttons, so little time." Magnolia leans against Rags's truck, chewing a lengthy blade of grass like she's a prairie girl born and raised.

Rags ignores her.

"What's this?" My eyes take in a small silver switch in the top right corner of the panel. Like the black button, it has a cover, but its cover is made of plastic instead of metal, so you can see through to the switch beneath.

Barney gazes over Rags's shoulder. "That's what this old timer forgot to turn off before he started the Titan's engine."

Rags chews the inside of his cheek like he's not sure he's ready to cover that part of today's lesson. Eventually he shakes his head like, *What does it matter?* and says, "That's perhaps the most important part of the Titan 1.0. This is what the Gambini brothers were afraid of."

"It's what threw Arvin on his rear!" Barney chokes on laughter.

"Arvin rode this model?"

"Not for long." Rags waves his hand as if dismissing the subject. "All Titans can be placed on autopilot if their dashboard blows."

"If the Titan is pushed too far past the slay zone," I offer.

"Exactly, but don't worry too much about his control panel. The only thing that could take this baby down for good is a blown engine." Rags runs his thumb across the clear, rectangular autopilot cover. "This Titan can run on autopilot like today's Titans can. But because it experiences emotions like fear, and even a sense of competitiveness, it can make the machine more . . ."

"Unpredictable?" Magnolia's voice is thick with anxiety.

Rags furrows his brow and says too fiercely, "No, not unpredictable. Just different, that's all."

I don't believe him. Magnolia pegged it when she used that word. Even if today's Titans run on autopilot, they're following a set of programmed backup responses, and the way it would run would most likely be less risky than what a jockey would have the machine do. But autopilot is a last-resort scenario, and there's no reason to believe the control panel would ever malfunction.

Rags pats the horse on his back. "We'll eventually need you to learn how to ride using both manual and autopilot in combination. Certain tracks will require your use of cognitive thinking, particularly that math you think you're so good at. While other times, especially for off-track sprints, it'll be best to let him go on his own."

Nope.

There's no way I'd ever trust this thing to run on its own, but I don't need to tell him that.

We then move on to the stopwatch, which looks archaic compared to the digital ones installed in Titan 3.0s. He shows me the gear sticks on either side—positioned above the handlebars—that navigate the horse from side to side, back and forth.

Finally, he shows me the performance gauge.

When I run my fingers over it, the hairs on the back of my neck rise. The gauge resembles a speedometer, but instead of numbers, it includes a length of green arching from the bottom left to the very top. After that is a stretch of yellow—the caution zone. And then there's the slay zone; a small length of scarlet red that extends from the yellow strip to the bottom right-hand side of the glass circle. The slay zone, more than anything, is what takes down Titans. Jockeys get too greedy for the win, and forget about the permanent damage they can inflict on their machines.

Running your horse in the slay zone is also dangerous to the rider, like racing a four-door family sedan down a major interstate at a hundred miles an hour. A standard vehicle isn't built for such things, just as a Titan isn't built to be pushed past its limits. A flash of the jockeys who have died crosses my mind once again. I can see their faces, all of them, in succession. So far, the Gambini brothers' race has cost Detroit four of its citizens' lives.

At some point during my lesson, Barney and Magnolia come out of the house with iced tea, and cucumber and cream cheese sandwiches that I'm sure Magnolia made. We eat like champions, and after I wipe my mouth, I return my attention to Rags. Tired of listening versus doing, I ask him, "Can't I please just ride it? I'll learn a lot quicker that way."

"First, no, you can't just ride it. Second, stop calling the Titan an *it*. It's a *he*, and he'll respect you a lot quicker if you treat *him* with respect."

I laugh. I can't help it. "Okay, let's get real. You may have designed the thing to include some sort of canned emotions, and maybe a computer programmer made it so the horse mimics human reactions with a prerecorded set of responses, but that thing"—I jab a thumb at the Titan—"is a machine. That's it."

The Titan snorts.

I give it a confused look as Rags grinds his teeth. "Call it a *he*."

"It," I say.

"Astrid," he growls.

"Iiiiit," I respond, knowing I'm being childish.

Rags turns toward his truck. "This is never going to work."

"Ah, come on, Rags," Barney says. "It was hard for the Gambini brothers to believe at first too, remember?"

Rags opens the door to his truck. "Get in."

My heart plummets. "What? That's it?"

The old man slams the door and stomps toward me. "Look, this isn't your normal Titan. In order to ride him, you'll have to form a connection. And the first step in that process is acknowledging that he's not simply parts and pieces and coded instructions. He has . . . he has *understanding*."

Because I don't want to lose this opportunity, I keep my remarks to a minimum. Instead I say, "Can't I just turn off the autopilot like you did today?"

"That doesn't shut off the Titan's emotions. Nothing can do that. Not with the EvoBox Rags designed functioning inside him," Barney chimes in. "Besides, only using manual transmission means he's not operating at his full potential. It's like a human on allergy medicine. The kind that makes you drowsy, ya know?"

Rags straightens to his full height. "Can you learn to trust this creature, Astrid? I mean *really* trust him? Because if you can't, this will never work."

I glance down at the hunk of metal and ask myself if I could. The answer comes swiftly—no. I trusted others once before, and it was the worst mistake I ever made. But I trust *myself* enough to know I can operate any piece of machinery if it means staying off the streets.

"I can," I reply softly.

"Okay, then." Rags puts his hands on his bony hips. "Then give him a name."

"Ooh, ooh!" Magnolia hops from one foot to the other. "Let me. I'll name it. Prince! Or, no, how about Channing Tatum . . . Tatum for short? Or, oh, let's call him Sparkle Foot."

All three of us look at Magnolia after hearing the last one.

"Because of his silver hooves," she explains meekly. "No?"

Rags sighs. "Name him, kid. Take ownership. Show me you'll treat him as a partner, and not as a means to an end."

I bite my lip. This should be easy. Just pick a name. Any name. Who cares as long as Rags buys that I'm playing along? But when I open my mouth, what comes out is a defiant "Horse."

Rags points to the truck, and this time, I march toward it. I need a break from the old man anyway, and if we stay much longer, our parents will wonder where we've gone off to. So I climb inside the vehicle. Magnolia waves good-bye to Barney and follows after me. Then my best friend and I are alone in the front seat as Rags rounds the truck.

"Why couldn't you just name it?" she asks.

I tongue the inside of my cheek and look back at the Titan. "Because it's stupid."

But that's not the real reason, and we both know it. It's just that I don't want to open myself up to anything or anyone again. There's also the simple fact that I don't need a relationship with the dang thing to win, regardless of what Rags and Barney believe.

When Rags gets in, I turn back and look at the Titan.

"You're just leaving it here?" I ask.

But Rags doesn't respond. I don't blame him, I suppose. Still, I watch the Titan as we leave, and so I see when the horse clambers to his feet and tosses his head in agitation as we pull away.

As if it knows that it's being left.

CHAPTER THIRTEEN

As we drive home from Barney's place, Magnolia lays her head against the window. It isn't long before her breathing deepens. It's awkward being the only conscious one in the truck with Rags, so I break the silence, despite our earlier head-butting.

"Can I ask you a question?" I say quietly.

Rags adjusts his weight in the seat, which is the closest I'll probably get to him saying, *Sure! Fire away, pal.*

"Why me? You must have had that Titan for a while. Why didn't you race it before now?"

The truck accelerates, as if Rags is eager to get home. "It was the right time."

"Why?"

"Because I know some things about Arvin Gambini and his dealings. And because I'm tired of watching and waiting."

"You don't like Arvin, do you?"

Rags grips the steering wheel so tightly I'm afraid we'll careen off the road. I elect to move past that subject and revisit my original question. "You haven't said why you chose me to ride the Titan."

"Because you were in the right place at the right time," he grunts.

I smile, because I know that's not all there is to it. Just like I know he and Arvin have a history I haven't fully learned. I *do* know Rags and Barney worked for Hanover Steel, of which the Gambini brothers own a healthy share. And I'm guessing they got laid off. But I wonder what Arvin had to do with that. Did the three men clash on the Titan 1.0 project? As a large shareholder, Arvin would probably be able to fire them over whatever he wanted.

Look at me applying all my learning from Ms. Shimoni's finance class.

She and her cat sweaters would be most proud.

....

On the walk home from Rags's house that night, after I say good night to Magnolia, I spot a woman in the shadows. She's moving with impressive stealth from yard to yard, pruning shears in her right hand. Anyone else would assume she's about to commit a heinous crime, tiptoeing across people's properties like that. But I know better.

"Hey, Mom." I wave hello, and she holds a finger to her lips.

Making her way toward me, she whispers, "You been at Magnolia's all day?"

I shrug so that it's more a lie of omission. "What are you working on tonight?"

Mom points up the road to Mr. and Mrs. Wright's house. They have a rosebush that's been mistreated far too long. It now grows into the lawn itself and is infested with weeds and browning buds. "It needs a good pruning. If they won't take care of it, I will."

My mother, Horticulture Superhero, saving our neighborhood one snip at a time. I squeeze my fingers over my thumbs and ask the question I'm afraid to ask. "Mom, did you know about the eviction notice?"

She drops her gaze and twists the gold band on her ring finger. "'Course I did. But I was hoping we could keep it from you kids until your dad could figure things out."

"We can't just rely on Dad to help our family. We're in this together."

"He's the head of our household, Astrid, and I'll stand behind him the same way I have the last twenty-two years."

Hearing her words frustrates me to no end. What is this? The 1950s? "You can do what you want. Stand by and pretend Dad will magically fix everything even though he's the reason we're in this mess. But as for me? I'm taking action."

I turn on my heel and head toward our short-term home. My mom calls my name three times before I glance back. She raises her hands like she's helpless in all this. Eventually, she says, "Help me with this rosebush, mi amor."

I sigh, because my mother is who she is. She'll always be the woman who is bold only when others are asleep in their beds. That way no one can challenge her head-on, and she'll never have to deal with confrontation. But because she's my mother, the same woman who made a "If my daughter were a dinosaur, she'd be a Mathosaurus" sign before a math competition in middle school, the mother who told me I was born a shooting star—my frustration lessens. "No, Mama. I'm going to bed. But you have fun."

She gives her wedding ring one last twist, and heads toward our neighbors' yard.

CHAPTER FOURTEEN

I show up at Rags's house early the next morning, a sleepy Magnolia by my side. She insisted I wake her when I was heading over because "my battle is her battle." My chest warms remembering the way she looked at me when she said this.

Magnolia is my best friend, and so it doesn't surprise me that she's committed to helping me compete in the Titan Circuit. But she doesn't know that if I won, somehow, a part of that money would go to her. I don't know how Rags would split the hypothetical winnings between us—he being the one with the Titan and knowledge, and me taking the risks out on the track. But Magnolia's family has struggled as much as mine has, and I want to make sure they don't end up with their own eviction notice in hand.

Rags is loading two bags into the truck bed when we arrive, and this time he doesn't even complain when he sees Magnolia, other than mumbling a quick "Why is she here?" I hold my breath, afraid he'll tell me it's over since I didn't refer to his precious Titan as a *he*. But the old man only waves toward the truck and retrieves a thermos of coffee from the hood. I sigh with relief and Magnolia and I jog to get in.

When we're safely inside, Rags gets behind the wheel and says gruffly, "It's Wednesday. The sponsor race is this Sunday. No more messing around when we get there, understood?"

"Understood," Magnolia says.

I smile at her, and then look back to Rags. "I understand."

With a slight nod of his head, we travel toward Barney's house. It's a quicker trip than it was the day before, and when we arrive, Barney is already outside his house. His eyes move immediately to Magnolia's empty hands, and the man deflates.

"Next time," she says. "I promise."

Barney shrugs. "You can't go gettin' a man's hopes up. You bring muffins one morning and there's a certain amount of expectation after that."

The Titan prances when it sees Rags approaching. In anticipation of riding, I wore jeans and my favorite lime-green sneakers, and I'm hoping my preparation isn't for nothing. Rags opens the Titan's engine flap, glances inside at the parts within, and closes it. Then he pats the Titan on the neck and scowls at me. "Today, you ride."

Goose bumps rise on my arms.

Rags strides toward his truck and withdraws the larger of the two bags. Inside is a standard black leather saddle I've seen other jockeys use. He walks toward the Titan and then tosses it over the creature's back.

"With a real horse, we'd put a saddle blanket down first so the leather wouldn't rub. No need for that here." He grabs a knob-like thing at the front of the saddle. "The saddlehorn is typically used to mount, dismount, and to keep from falling off if the horse ever bucks. Since you have the handlebars on the dash, you won't need it for stability. But you'll still use it to mount." Rags holds up the stirrups that fall on either side of the Titan's middle. "You'll use these to mount and dismount, but also to lean forward and backward depending on the track. If you're going downhill, lean backward to take weight off the Titan's front legs. If you're going uphill, lean forward. This'll help him maintain top speed during the race."

I know most of what he's telling me, but I don't interrupt.

And when he says it's time to mount, I decide this is my reward for being attentive and patient.

"One foot in the stirrup. Always mount him from the left side." Rags stands ready to help me. "That goes back to ancient times when soldiers holstered their swords on the left. They mounted on this side so they didn't accidentally sit on their swords."

"Is that true?" Magnolia asks.

"All Titans are designed to tolerate being mounted from that side because of that," Barney answers her. "We liked the idea of keeping to tradition."

I look at Rags, impressed that these two had a hand in minor details that are still in place for Titan 3.0s. Rags gestures for me to go ahead, and my heart flutters as I slip my foot into the stirrup, grab on to the saddle horn, and pull in a breath. The machine turns its head and gives me a good, curious sniff like a real horse might do. It's startling, but I remind myself it's only an artificial response to mimic emotions. Not real ones.

I return to the moment. A moment I've thought about since I was twelve years old. Since I first heard about the track being constructed and glimpsed those steels gods being rolled into the forest.

I ease my foot into the stirrup and stretch until my hands find the saddle horn. Pulling in a deep breath, praying I don't make a fool of myself through mounting alone, I hoist myself up.

My opposite leg swings over the top, and every nerve ending in my body fires at once. I'm on a Titan. I'm sitting in a saddle . . . on a Titan.

"You look like an empress," Magnolia declares.

"An empress who's going to fall on her rear if she doesn't grip those handlebars tighter," Rags says. "Are you ready to ride?"

I answer him without speaking, because somewhere between the ground and this place above the rest of the world, I've lost my voice. After a few moments, I find it long enough to say, "I'm sorry about being difficult yesterday."

"Yesterday is gone," he replies, adjusting the stirrups. "Let's take him out."

CHAPTER FIFTEEN

There's only one starting gate stall, and the Titan and I are in it. The horse stomps its feet and bangs its back end against both sides, anticipating its first track run in who knows how long. Maybe its first track run, ever.

There I go again, thinking of *it* as a thing with feelings.

"I'm not going to give you any instruction other than to keep the horse in the safe zone," Rags says. My eyes fall on the performance gauge, and the stretch of green I have to play with. Fair enough. "Don't worry if you have a hard time getting him to accelerate or turn or whatever. Just get a feel for what it means to stay in the saddle. If at any moment you get afraid, push the brake bar up slowly. *Slooowly*."

I can barely hear him above the blood thrumming in my ears. The Titan slams against the starting gate, and I can't help but agree. It feels like I've been back here an eternity, like I've spent my whole life in this exact spot, waiting to feel the breeze off a track slice through my hair.

When Barney's hand closes over the steel rod to open the manual gate, I close my eyes. Breathe in, breathe out. Try to quiet the voice that says I won't be able to do this. I lean forward in the saddle and hear the leather adjust to my weight, smell the scent of polish Barney applied this morning. Then I push the smaller black button to ready the machine. When a faint red light grows in color, signaling the Titan's readiness, pledging power and action, I lose my mind with excitement. I touch the gas bar, and the Titan produces a low whirring sound.

Everything falls away. My best friend is speaking, but I can't hear her. Sparks are flying off the Titan as it clashes against the gate, but I don't feel a thing when they hit my skin.

Rags provides one last nugget of advice. Something about staying in the saddle.

But all I see when I look ahead is my grandfather standing in the distance. His face is the same ashen color it was when I returned home to our apartment, the day my family failed me. The day I failed my family. Grandpa is trying to speak, but can't. I'm fumbling for his heart pills, something Dani should have remembered, but I know it's too late. I know he's dying, but there's nothing I can do to help. There's nothing I can do.

But when that starting gate slides open, it's as if that old, helpless Astrid slides away with it.

Now I am Astrid with a Titan beneath her.

I am invincible.

Unstoppable.

I push the black turbo button—*Manual transmission. Go!*— and the Titan runs. He's slow to start, much different from the same horse I saw yesterday running on his own. But a quick push of the accelerator, and he's off, gaining speed. His head jerks up and down with the pounding of his steel hooves. He's not even a fraction into the safe zone, and it feels like we're flying impossibly fast. The landscape whips by. The trees and ground blur into a brown mass. There's a turn coming up, and I grit my teeth, terror swimming through my veins. We won't make it. The Titan will skid out, flip, and I'll go flying.

My right hand pulls away from the handlebars and shakes above the brake lever. I have to slow down. I must. But as we barrel closer to the turn, I think back to the races I've watched. Those Titans were going three times as fast, maybe more, and they closed those turns with ease. At the last minute, I push up on the accelerator and ease the joysticks to the left, leaning away from the turn like Rags taught me to do.

The Titan leans too.

Tears sting my eyes when I see the ground racing past, so close it's as if I could reach down and touch it. Feel the skin rip away from my palm. But I hold tight and lean, lean, *lean*. Then we're upright, and the Titan is off again. We race down a long straightaway and take two more turns. Each time, I accelerate into them, though it's the opposite of what I've seen on the cyclonetrack.com replay videos.

The Titan rolls with my punches, lapping up each degree in acceleration with an eagerness I envy. As for me, my hands are sweating, and I can barely keep a grip on the bars. This wouldn't bode well in an actual race. I need my hands to switch gears, to turn the Titan with precision. But the only thing I bring to the table now is my mind.

Each new twist I discover in the track is a calculation waiting to be solved.

Thirty-five-degree turn.

One sixteenth of a mile.

Traveling at twenty-nine miles an hour.

Wait . . . wait . . . *Now!* I accelerate and lean, and the Titan leans against me. We arch toward the track in a dangerous dance before pulling upright again. Knowing Rags will kill me if I go too much farther, I snap my teeth together, bear down in the saddle, and look at the performance gauge. Nowhere near the caution zone. A light-year away from the slay zone.

Nothing to lose.

"You wanna go faster?" I yell.

The Titan neighs, surprising me with the realistic sound. I laugh against the fear and imagine the Titan actually comprehended what I said. Kicking my heels lightly into his side, I nudge the accelerator bar. And then I nudge it again.

Perspiration beads on the Titan's body, and tremors shake my arms.

It feels as if we're going so much faster than forty miles an hour.

I'm not sure my mother has ever driven our busted-up Buick this fast before. The wind tears through my hair the way I always imagined, whispering for me to close my eyes, but I won't. I don't want to miss a single second of this. I've never felt so free. So fast. So bold. So beautiful.

I've never been this critically close to the grave.

I don't know where the last thought comes from, but once it's there, I can't shake it loose. My eyes snap to the ground and I realize how much damage we'd both incur if we crashed. The difference is the Titan is made of steel. I am soft skin, fragile bones.

I push up on the brake bar. The problem is I also push up on the accelerator. I panicked and punched both, and now the Titan is jerking from side to side, blazing into the grass on the edge of the track and back onto the dirt path. He doesn't know what to do and I can't remember which is the brake bar and the horse is on a crash course with a tree that has no mind to move aside.

My hands fly across the control panel, searching for anything that will get him to turn. I catch sight of the performance gauge. We're in the yellow. Rags is going to kill me. I'm going to be flattened by this tree, and then the old man is going to finish me off.

I hit the black turbo button repeatedly, but that only causes the scent of smoke to touch my nose. Maybe that's what brings me back. That smell. The tree is maybe four feet away when I take the joysticks in my hand, turn gently to the left, and then push the brake bar forward. The Titan swishes away from the tree, but I still duck to keep from having my head taken by a limb.

Once we've bypassed it, I bring the horse back into the center of the track and slow him to a stop. My hands are shaking and sweat drips down the back of my shirt. I hear Rags, Barney, and Magnolia yelling in the distance, but it does little to calm my nerves. Sliding off the horse, I fall to the ground, landing hard on my left hip. The Titan turns its head in my direction.

Then it gives me a *look*. I kid you not; the horse looks at me like I'm an idiot. Maybe I'm hallucinating, and my pride is so injured that I'm seeing laughter in a steel horse's eyes. But something tells me I'm not imagining this.

The threesome is still running toward me when the Titan takes a step in my direction. Then another. My heart hammers in my chest seeing it venture so close. I'm laid out on the ground, my hip singing with pain, and here is this metal monster looming over me.

Maybe it does have a mind of its own.

Maybe that mind is telling it to stomp on my skull.

The red light fades from the creature's eyes, and it lowers its muzzle. I flinch when warmed steel touches the outside of my arm. The horse nudges me. Then it nudges me again. When it pushes its head under my arm and lifts, I realize what it wants me to do. I grab hold of the silky steel threads that serve as hair, and swing the opposite arm around its neck. Slowly, the Titan lifts me to my feet.

As soon as I'm upright, the Titan jerks its head away and pins its ears back. The machine's message is crystal clear.

I helped you up, but you're still an idiot.

And that's the first moment—with my chest still aching from adrenaline and fear, and Rags hollering who knows what— that I smile at the Titan.

CHAPTER SIXTEEN

I've had three days of practice since my first epic fail. And I'm getting better. Even Rags will admit as much. He says I take the turns too quickly, that only a madman would accelerate through them. He also scolds me about never utilizing the autopilot function. *If you'd only used it that first day, the horse would have turned on his own and kept running at the same speed you'd set on manual. No near collisions with trees. No worries. Stop being so hardheaded, Astrid.*

But I relish the control, knowing I'm setting the pace, calculating the angles, letting up only after I've pushed the two of us past the safe limits and into the caution zone. Barney warns me about the slay zone. *Don't get too cocky.* And Magnolia tells me on the way home from Rags's house each night how she worries about my getting hurt.

What no one says, though, is that I *have* to push the Titan. And I have to push myself. Because the sponsor race is tomorrow. Will the other jocks keep their Titans in the safe zone when the clock strikes midnight? Will they shy away from the caution zone?

No. Not when every sponsor is there watching. Those company representatives seeking to invest in a jockey and Titan 3.0 as part of their annual marketing plan. The races may only last the summer season, but having a winning jockey adds celebrity value to a brand, and it moves products off shelves in Detroit retailers. *Sparklet Root Beer* isn't that glamorous. But when the face of the 2015 Titan Derby winner is smiling at you from the bottle, suddenly it is. There will be a few individuals looking to sponsor horses too, of course, but there may be only one or two of those a year, if any. Those few seek an ultimate gamble, front-row seats, and a way to impress their friends.

Only one jockey will win a free place in the circuit.

So, yeah, what no one mentions is my being reckless is our only shot. No sponsor will want an old, discontinued Titan model or a seventeen-year-old spokesmodel who can't compensate with stunning good looks unless I push farther than the other jockeys are willing to go.

They have experience; months and months of training, if not years.

I have everything to lose.

I finish another lap and slow the Titan to a stop in front of Barney, who's holding a tin bucket. Rags and Magnolia are out of sight. Barney lifts the bucket. "Time to clean him up."

"Seriously?" I ask, but I'm already reaching for the handle, because a break from racing sounds glorious. It's early June in Detroit, and as fiery as my father's temper. The skin on my forearms is red from the sun, and even the Titan has perspiration across its coat from the engine's cooling fluid. So when Barney tells me there's a water hose at the back of the stable, in the *shade*, I practically sprint toward it. When the Titan doesn't immediately follow me, I turn and give a frustrated *come on* wave of my hand.

Barney chuckles as the horse clops after me, taking its sweet time, stopping to sniff dandelions as if it can enjoy such things. When we arrive at the barn, I duck inside and search for anything else I may need to wash the thing. I find some brushes, soap, and a couple of dry towels near a dusty full-length mirror. I'm about to holler for the Titan to move its rear when it trots toward the end of the barn, stopping short of the hoses.

"Hey, no," I say. "I have to clean you. You can't go to your stall."

I stop when I see another horse, a real one, reach its head out and nuzzle the Titan. The mare is gray in color, with a white face and mane. The Titan meets her nose and nods his head up and down. The mare matches his enthusiasm, coming off her front legs a few inches and touching back down.

"Oh my gosh. Does the Titan have a girlfriend?" Magnolia strides in, a plastic bottle in her right hand, and two sodas stacked in her left. "If that machine develops a real relationship before I do, I'll just die."

I laugh. "You have a different boyfriend every month, Mag."

"My point exactly. They come and go so quickly."

"Because you show them the door."

"Because they bore me." Magnolia smirks. "Besides, didn't you break up with Dave?"

"Not exactly," I mumble. Dave and I dated for exactly three months during my junior year. I know, because he gave me a box of dried, chalky chocolates to commemorate the day, and then promptly dumped me for Misty Gamin. I never knew quite how to take that.

"What did I tell you?" Magnolia hands me one of the sodas. "If you believe you dumped him, others will too."

"I don't care that he dumped me," I say.

"Riiight." Magnolia juts her chin toward the back of the barn. "Rags said you're going to clean him. Want help?"

"If you're offering."

I give Magnolia my elbow and she takes it, smiling.

CHAPTER SEVENTEEN

After Magnolia and I wrangle the Titan away from the mare and into the back, I turn on the water hose, point it toward the horse, and prepare to spray.

The Titan snorts.

"You think I won't do it?" I say.

The Titan gazes over my head, searching for the gray mare. Realizing it's ignoring me, I squeeze the lever and water shoots from the nozzle. It hits the Titan square in the chest and causes a fine mist to float over Magnolia and me. Magnolia squeals and the Titan rears up on his back legs, surprised that I actually did it.

The steel horse makes for the front of the barn. Feeling brazen, I step in front. The horse halts and tries to get by on the other side, but I'm there, spraying away. Dirty water washes in rivulets down the horse's legs. When the horse tries to escape for the third time, I hold up my hands to shush him.

"It's okay, horsey," Magnolia says between sips of her soda. "We all gotta bathe. If you want to impress that girl of yours, the first step is good hygiene."

When I turn the water back on, I don't squeeze the lever as hard. This time, I start with his silver hooves and work my way up slowly. Even though the water is far from its head, the beast holds its nose so high in the air I can't help but giggle. The Titan eyes me laughing, picks up a long, glittering leg, and brings it down into a puddle of watery mud.

Dirt splashes across my shins.

"Oh!" Magnolia exclaims. "Did he do that on purpose?"

I press my lips together because, yeah, I think it sure as heck did. "You want to play that game?" I level the spray gun at the horse's face, count to three, and squeeze. As the water hits it, the Titan stumbles backward until its rear slams into the back of the barn. I stop spraying at once and rush toward the creature.

"Are you okay?" I ask. "I didn't mean to—"

The Titan lifts his right leg.

Oh, no.

I turn to flee, but before I can, water and mud spray across my back. Magnolia holds her stomach with laughter for several seconds, but when the Titan kicks more and more mud onto my clothes, she makes for the barn door, yelling that I'm on my own.

Refusing to be bullied by a computer, I continue spraying the horse. And the horse continues spraying me. In the end, one of us is very clean. And one of us is covered in muck. I glance down at my shirt and jeans, my shoes and socks and bare arms. I'm wet. And filthy.

And cool despite the summer heat.

And having fun, though I hate to admit it.

I shake the nozzle at the horse. "You're an ornery piece of scrap metal, you know that?"

The horse huffs, and I laugh. The sound startles the Titan. Its ears circle forward as if it's surprised to hear this sound from me.

"Can I wipe you down?" I grab one of the towels, feeling loony for asking permission from a machine.

The Titan turns its face away, but I take a determined step in its direction. "Come on. Let me dry you off. Please?"

The Titan looks at me and—I swear on my grandfather's gambling addiction—it sighs. As if it's conceding. As if it understood my request. I dry it off using firm pressure and a circular motion, and when I get to behind the Titan's ears, the beast leans into my touch. I have to bite down to keep from giggling.

Spotting the plastic bottle Magnolia left behind, I pick it up. After seeing that it's some sort of Armor All for Titans, I grab a clean rag and work in the white cream across the horse's body. Finally, I wring the used towel and pull it backward like I did a few nights ago when Zara and I cleaned dishes. Except this time, my target realizes what's coming. I pop the horse lightly on the thigh, and in return the Titan noses me roughly in the back. I stumble forward and catch myself on the stall. Gazing ahead, I see that the gray mare is watching.

"Your boyfriend's aggressive," I tell her. "You could do better."

I turn around and take in the Titan in all its clean glory, but it's too dark in here to appreciate my handiwork. So I motion for the horse to follow me, and after the Titan pauses at the mare's stall for a few seconds to prance, it obeys. I stop the creature at the front of the barn and wave my hand toward the mirror until it gazes over and sees its reflection. Almost immediately, the Titan jerks its head upright, chest puffing out.

The horse turns from side to side, nosing the mirror and then lifting its chin. I suppose I can't blame the mechanism for accessing its preprogrammed *vain* emotion. The Titan looks good—black steel shining, threads of steel hair smooth against its back, silver hooves glowing in the dying sun. Even its false lashes appear longer. Standing back, I swell with pride that this is the machine I'll be riding in tomorrow's sponsor race. It no longer looks like a broken-down engine stored in an old man's work shed. Today, it looks like a champion. Not a first edition that's been twice replaced, but the edition that got it right.

My heart fills with something I can't name, and before I can dwell on it, I toss the last of the used towels over the horse's prideful head. Then I stride out of the barn and into the summer evening. Magnolia is perched on Rags's unfolded tailgate, legs dangling beneath her. She covers her mouth and laughs into her hands when she sees me. And when Rags and Barney round the vehicle, they laugh too.

I guess I look worse than I thought.

"That horse is a menace," I mutter.

"That he is," Rags agrees. "But he cleans up nice; huh?"

We all turn and inspect the thing strutting outside the barn, never venturing too far from the full-length mirror.

"He's a good Titan," Barney says. "Strong, with potential we never fully explored. We might just have a shot tomorrow."

Barney is saying what we want to believe. But the truth is the odds are stacked against us. Four days, I've been riding. Yes, I've studied every aspect of the Titans for the last five years. And maybe I've got a knack for racing like Barney says. But those other jockeys will have studied their Titans too, probably for much longer, and with better resources behind them.

I brush the drying mud from my jeans and avoid Rags's gaze. "I thought of a name for the horse."

Rags, Barney, and Magnolia stare at me. I roll my eyes. "What? It needs a name, right?"

Rags smiles like my grandpa used to after downing a mint julep. It's infectious, that smile. And I find myself mirroring the emotion. The old man slaps his leg and jogs to the front of his truck. When he returns, he's holding an envelope. He gives it to me, and after I take it, he shoves his hands into the pockets of his orange hunting vest and rocks back and forth on his heels. He doesn't look so old in this moment. Just the opposite, really. I can almost glimpse the young man behind those hooded blue-gray eyes. A man with a mischievous grin, a brain that sizzled, and dreams so big only a blueprint could capture them.

I open the envelope and shake my head with disbelief. Because there's my name, and the serial number for our Titan 1.0, and race dates and legal jargon and signatures on clean, crisp lines. Only two spaces are empty, in fact; one where I'll sign, and another where I'll fill in our Titan's call name.

"Our registration papers." I hold them to my chest and glance up at Rags. "I almost forgot."

"Good thing I didn't." He practically dances as Magnolia leans over my shoulder, saying she wants to see.

"Get her a pen," Magnolia orders.

I gaze at her, my best friend. My rock when the ground beneath my feet trembles. Is there anything I wouldn't do to keep her in my life through the years? "Thank you, Magnolia."

"For what?"

"For believing in me," I reply. "For being my friend."

"This whole thing still makes me nervous."

"But you'd do it too," I say in almost a question, wondering if she's ever upset that Rags gave me this opportunity instead of her.

"Heck, yeah," she says. "Sometimes I pray you hurt yourself *just* enough so that I can step in and save the day."

I chuckle at her honesty, and when Rags returns with a pen and offers his back as a place to sign, I move toward him. Laying the white paper between his bony shoulder blades, I hold the pen above my signature spot, and write my name with intention. Thick letters so the Gambini brothers know I mean it.

Then I move the pen to the Titan's call name. I glance once more at the horse strutting in the field outside the barn and shake my head. I remember the way Rags transported him in that jumbo coffin. And how the Titan rose to his feet from his dark prison within seconds of that lock being removed. How he ran to stretch his legs, to breathe the air and feel the soil beneath his hooves. It's like he'd waited a lifetime for that run. Like he was trapped for years without an outlet. And then, suddenly, he was free.

I shake the pen a couple of times, and I write his name.

Padlock.

CHAPTER EIGHTEEN

After church the next morning, I pack a small bag with an extra T-shirt, a clean pair of socks, and a stick of deodorant, planning to sneak out of the house for the day. In previous years, the lineup for the sponsor race was announced the morning of. But since my father didn't come in to kill me in the middle of the night, and didn't say anything this morning, I have to believe the list has yet to be revealed.

And I can't be here when it is.

Zara stops me on the way out the door, a pout on her face. I sling my backpack over my shoulder and glance down the hallway to ensure my mom or, more importantly, my dad, isn't coming. "You're leaving again?" she whispers.

I grab her shoulder and give it a friendly shake. "I'll be back soon enough."

Zara pulls away, igniting a painful ache in my chest. "You're gone like Dani is now."

"That's not true."

Or is it?

Zara kicks at a pinkish stain in our dingy carpet and doesn't reply.

"Look, how about tomorrow you and I hang out all day?"

She shrugs. "It's weird around here. Dad yelled at Mom last night, and then she left with her garden stuff. She didn't even come in to tell me good night."

"She was gone that long?" I ask, surprised. Mom usually stays out late when she goes on a Garden Rescue Mission. But we're allowed to stay up late during the summer. Late enough so that Mom always pokes her head in to say good night as we're nodding off, dirt smudged on her cheeks.

I quickly hug Zara to my chest. Then I reposition the backpack and repeat that I have to go, but that I'll be sure and stick around tomorrow. And to not worry about Mom and Dad. Parents fight. It's normal.

But it's not normal. The amount of yelling that happens behind my parents' bedroom door lately is *not* normal. And I know that what Zara is really afraid of is the same thing I am. That it's getting worse. That everything in our house feels brittle. Like there's only a thin layer of ice beneath our feet . . . and man, is it getting hot in here.

"Things will get better," I say quietly to my baby sister. "I promise."

Then I turn and walk out the door, determined to keep my word.

....

I take Padlock out several times that day. We run two furlongs— a quarter mile—and Rags announces our time. I'm improving, but it's not good enough to beat previous jockeys' times, which I've memorized. The horse and I do better on the half mile. Even better on the mile. But it isn't until we reach the three- or four-mile sprints that we excel. All those fractions of a second on turns add up. I know how to hug the curb, and I know how to lean to ensure my Titan is stable.

Numbers tick through my brain until I'm afraid my head will burst. Our only shot is to have a long race tonight. Three miles or more would be best. Two is a must. History doesn't tell us anything. The other four sponsor races don't contain numerical trends, though most have been longer than a furlong to give sponsors enough time to make judgments.

I can tell Rags and Barney have the same concern I do. Eventually, Magnolia calls the elephant for what it is.

"So we need a long race tonight, right?" she asks.

"Unless someone has an extra fifty grand on them." Barney scratches his belly and inspects Padlock.

"They'll do fine either way," Rags says. "You never know what race night will bring. That's what makes the Gambini brothers rich. People match jockey strengths to track lengths and place bets accordingly. But that doesn't always work or they'd always win." Rags meets my gaze and says again, "You don't know what race night will bring."

I dismount Padlock and stretch. Instead of revealing the nerves blooming in my stomach, I mutter, "I'm starving."

Barney holds up his finger. "Pre-race dinner! Let's hit up the Sugar Shack."

Rags groans, but Barney insists. And Magnolia and I are curious. So we pile into Rags's truck and head toward a restaurant that looks like it was built by the blind. The three of us are escorted to a red booth near the back and handed sticky menus featuring culinary delicacies like mozzarella sticks and potato skins. In other words, I'm in heaven.

After ordering a Pepsi, I glance up, delighted to have the best view of the lone mounted television. So I'm the one who spots it first. The one whose face changes, causing the others to turn in their squeaky vinyl seats and gape at the screen.

I can't hear what the local news anchor is saying, but I don't need to. Our names are rolling across the bottom, one at a time, and—*oh, there we go*—now they have the full list up on the screen. A shiver works its way down my spine, and Magnolia watches as she chews her straw, knowing exactly what it is that's freaking me out.

I have the best view of the jockey lineup at the Sugar Shack that evening.

My question is—

Who has the best view in my parents' home?

CHAPTER NINETEEN

I do my best to forget that my family may now know what it is I've been up to these last few days. I'm seventeen, it's summer, and they have bigger issues to deal with than where their child is spending her free time. But if they find out I'm racing, a good grounding will be the least of my worries. Jockeys as young as seventeen can register, but if a guardian submits an objection form, I could be barred from competing.

I can already picture the look on my father's face if he knew.

The things he would say.

It was gambling that put our family in debt, Astrid. And it was that same debt that put stress on your grandfather's heart. Have you learned nothing?

What he won't say is the second part. How my grandfather was so addicted that it made the habit enticing to his only son, who knew all too well the risks it carried. My grandfather taught my dad how to properly hold a screwdriver. He taught him the words to whisper in my mother's ear so that she'd allow him a kiss at the night's end. And he taught him that the only thing more important than family was dealing cards around a green felt table. If my father didn't lose his hard-won savings, and Dani's only shot at community college, on that horse last summer, we might never have been served that eviction notice. He'd still be under pressure to find a new job, but we'd have a little more precious time.

If Dad never learned to gamble, he might not be so angry.

And I might not be here.

Even as I think these things, a small, stupid part of me hopes my father does find out. Would he come tonight? Would he stand outside the chain-link fence as I've done in the past and watch as his middle daughter rides to save their home?

As Padlock and I barrel down the track, I envision the wrath on his face replaced by something else. Bewilderment, maybe. No . . . *pride.* In my mind's eye he raises his fist half-way through the run and shakes it with growing excitement. "That's my daughter!" he bellows, tears stinging his eyes. "That's my girl!"

I swallow a painful lump in my throat and concentrate on the fact that we're pulling into Cyclone Track. Magnolia and I sit in the back without speaking, and every few seconds I wipe my hands on my knees. My stomach twists from nerves and the bacon-cheddar fries I shouldn't have eaten. Even watching the medics readying their equipment near the track doesn't soothe my nerves. In fact, it only causes me to imagine them using that same life-saving equipment on me, and brings to mind them using it on unfortunate jockeys from seasons past.

When we come to a stop, I glance out the window. We've parked behind the stables, and although there's an hour until the race begins—the night accentuated with thick humidity and a full moon—I can still make out the crowd in the distance. The bodies sway together like a swarm of ants, muddied colors and constant movement.

Rags and Barney approach the bed of the truck and tear the blanket off the open coffin, which we brought because Magnolia swore it'd make for the ultimate accessory. After the two men roll him onto the ground, Rags inserts the key into his ignition and the horse springs to life.

As soon as Padlock sees where he is, and hears the rumbling of the crowd, he grows agitated. He twitches at the smallest sound and pins his ears back. I approach him slowly and speak in a soothing voice. The last thing I need tonight is another nervous party, whether that nervousness is falsely animated or not.

Rags loops reins around the horse's head, and Padlock takes the leather in his mouth without the use of a bit. Handing the reins to me, Rags says, "Let's lead him into the stables. It'll give him a chance to relax before things begin."

"When do we find out the race length?" I ask.

"For the tenth time, Astrid, it'll flash on the board before the starting gates open."

"But don't they want the bettors outside the gates to know what they're betting on?"

Rags shakes his head. "No bets tonight, you know that."

The betting is the only part I never really paid attention to, because it hurt too much to envision my father salivating over his own bet cards. But now I wish I had. Rags says something about bets only getting upped in the last sixty seconds before the race starts, not changed, and I nod along as odds and percentages about me and Padlock and the length of this race swirl through my head.

Swallowing my anxiety, I follow behind Barney, who holds a large and a small bag. The bigger of the two is Padlock's saddle. Not sure about the little one.

The bustle inside the stables is even louder than it was outside. Trainers jog past, headed to their vehicles, and jockeys throw fits to anyone who will listen, over every little thing. The floor is made of smooth concrete, and the soaring wooden roof makes those shouting voices thunderous.

When I pass by the first occupied stall, I spot an older woman dressed in the standard jockey uniform—calf-length breeches, boots, and silks. When she sees Padlock, her jaw drops. She stops talking to the man in the stall with her and walks to the front of her stable to gape at my Titan.

Ignoring the burning in my cheeks, I lift my head and continue down the path, seeking an empty stall in the largest stable in northeast America. With each one I pass, I accumulate more weary eyeballs and surprised gasps. Padlock doesn't look that different from the other Titans, but I guess the details are enough. His black coat, his silver hooves, his nostrils flaring and the flutter of his lashes—it's throwing an unknown into the jockeys' well-planned wins tonight.

Rags searches for a stall with my last name, but comes up empty. All the other stalls are marked. Why not ours?

"Don't worry," he says from between clenched teeth. "I'll talk to the track manager about getting you a permanent stall for the season."

If I win this sponsor race, you mean.

Rags stomps away as Barney locates an unlabeled stall near the back and ushers us forward. Magnolia trails behind, digging her right hand deep into her pocket. I wonder if she brought along her playing cards for luck.

"You okay?" I ask as we file into the stall.

She beams. "My best friend is riding a Titan today. Right now I'm ten feet tall and bulletproof."

Before I can stop myself, I throw my arms around her. "Thank you for being here."

She pats my back. "Oh, you're totally going to eat it out there. But I'm here when you do."

I know she's joking, but I still pull back and say, "There's no way I can win this. I don't even know why I—"

Magnolia takes my face in her hands. "You listen to me. Don't worry one bit about winning or losing. When you go out there, I want you to remember the first time we saw the Titans run." She lightly punches my shoulder. "Remember how on the way back we rehashed every second of that race? We never thought we'd be given the chance to touch a Titan, much less ride one."

A lump forms in my throat.

"Let that same little girl have fun riding today, okay?" she says. "That's it."

I nod, noticing she didn't say I could win, and hating myself for noticing. Why must I always focus on the negative when my best friend is giving me a reason to be grateful? When I find my voice again, all I manage to say is, "You were right when you said this is gambling. My grandfather risked our home. My father risked every cent we'd saved. And now here I am, risking my safety to win it all back. This is no different than what they did."

Magnolia opens her mouth to respond, but is cut off when Barney interrupts.

"If you girls are done with your mushy moment . . ." He unzips the smaller bag and swings it off his shoulder.

When I see what Barney pulls out, my concerns fall away. All that remains is my heart, leaping with excitement.

CHAPTER TWENTY

Barney holds a black pair of breeches, black riding boots, and a bold yellow silk. He turns the silk around and I nearly lose control of myself when I see my last name, SULLIVAN, across the top.

"From all of us," Barney explains. "They're used, and Magnolia had to iron on the lettering, but it'll work for today."

"There's this too." Magnolia reaches into her right pocket again. This time she produces a black-and-yellow headpiece I can't quite figure out. She walks around behind me and pulls my dark hair into a ponytail. "The bumblebee covers your hair band, with its wings at the top, and then this gold tail wraps around your actual pony, down to the very tip." I feel her secure the bumblebee around the base, and then use the flexible gold wire to wrap my pony. "It's like my pin, only a hundred times better."

I touch a hand to my hair, amazed by friend's talent. "I can't believe you made this for me."

"Uh, you're a jockey in the sponsor race. This is publicity for my work at its finest." She bites her lip. "Besides, my best friend training to race has been the most exciting thing to happen to me. Not to mention the best distraction, ever."

I want to ask Magnolia what she needs distracting from, but Barney is motioning me to get dressed, and shoving a heavily scuffed helmet into my hands. The two of them start to leave, but Magnolia stops before rushing off. "You could have won this race when you were thirteen years old," she says evenly. "Those other jokers don't know what it means to hunger."

Her words ring through the stall, snaking around my rib cage in a firm embrace. Then it's only Padlock, who's been saddled, and me, whose knees are shaking. All around is the sound of unfamiliar voices. Some call for equipment, others whisper strategies with their managers. The smells of fuel and wax and sweat mingle in the air, and though it's not a pleasant scent, I breathe it in, exhilarated to be inside this stable for the first time.

When I notice that Padlock is hovering near the back of the stall, I'm struck by guilt. All this time I've thought of only my fears, my doubts. But Padlock was programmed to have these emotions through his EvoBox, wasn't he? And whether they're real or not, they must feel real enough to him. Ensuring no one is watching, I slip on my riding gear and approach Padlock. I hold my hand out, and he sniffs the pink of my palm.

Stepping closer, I bring my lips to his steel ear. "Did you hear what Magnolia said? We should just have fun."

Padlock snorts, and I smile.

"I know what you mean," I say. "I want to win too. It's our only chance of continuing. No one will want to sponsor a poor girl from Warren County and a late edition Titan. Even though . . . even though I think you look pretty legit."

Padlock pushes his muzzle into my hair tentatively, like he's afraid of how I may react. Taken aback, I suck in air from between my teeth, and then slide my hand through his steel-threaded hair. The horse releases a funny neigh as I give him a good scratch.

My Titan is really getting into my affection when Rags jogs up to the stall, red-faced and out of breath. "Hey, listen." He glances over his shoulder as if someone might be watching. "They're going to have the horses line up soon for parts check. If they try and stop you from proceeding, steer Padlock by them, okay? Don't stop. Just get to the starting gate."

"What are you talking about? Why would they stop me?" Understanding dawns on me. "They don't want a Titan 1.0 running. Did the registration papers not get approved? They listed my name last night."

Rags clutches a roll of papers in his hand. He smiles and slaps them against the side of the stall door. "Just get to that starting gate." He turns to leave, but then glances back, admiring the used silks he, Barney, and Magnolia surprised me with. "You look good, kid. Like a real Titan rider."

Then he's gone.

Just as he predicted, a few moments later I hear the booming voice of a woman with authority. When I peek my head out, I notice she has a clipboard in her right hand and a walkie-talkie buzzing on her belt. My blood pounds in my ears as I turn and pull myself into Padlock's saddle.

Bending toward his ear, I say, "Listen, horse, we might have to run earlier than the rest of the Titans, but don't panic."

Padlock stomps his foot.

After kicking the stall door open, I return my boot to the stirrup and watch as the other jockeys lead their Titans into a neat line. The woman at the front, who has purple-framed glasses balanced on the tip of her nose, searches intently inside a Titan's engine flap, then checks something off before the horse is allowed to leave the stable.

I ensure Padlock and I are in the very back, and by the time our turn comes, I have a dozen half-fleshed-out excuses for whatever argument she may provide. Or maybe I'll go with Rags's plan. Just bypass her and act like I can't hear what she's saying.

When we're two steps away, I can hardly pull in a breath. The woman looks up like my being there is a surprise. When her eyes fall on Padlock, I know my earlier suspicion was accurate.

Rags never got full approval for me to race a Titan 1.0 model.

I open my mouth to say something, anything, but Padlock beats me to the punch. Kicking out with his back legs, he neighs and whines. The woman spreads herself against the wall, and as Padlock throws his head, I yell, "Sorry, I think there's something wrong with him."

She points her clipboard at us. "That's not a 3.0!"

I don't respond. Instead, I hang on as my demon horse races away and heads toward the starting gate, like he already knows where it is. The woman shouts from behind us, but her complaints are soon drowned out by the crowd. The crowd that knows this is it. We are all here. Not all of us will secure a sponsor and race in the circuit, but that doesn't matter just now. What matters is these are the contenders.

Among this group of forty-two Titans is this year's champion. And everyone is waiting to see if they can pinpoint that champion after the first run.

The stalls are open from the back, but within seconds someone is sliding the gate closed, locking us in. I glance around, attempting to see through the bars to the other jockeys. But I can't make them out in detail. Only that they are staring forward, studying the track, as I am studying them.

The Titans stamp the dry dirt, and already my mouth and tongue feel gritty. With trembling fingers, I reach down and push the smaller of the two black buttons. A small click, and then Padlock's eyes blaze red across the front of our stall. His sides grow warm beneath my legs as his engine prepares to race.

Nerves fire through my body, making every sense sharp as a blade. Sharp enough to cut through the night sky and cause the stars to rain down. The crowd roars, feverish, as the digital scoreboard flickers to life. Our last names ping across the top, and I see my own name appear.

SULLIVAN.

My heart thunders at the sight, and I wonder if Magnolia feels the same way I do in this moment. Terrified. Exhilarated. Hopeful, though it's ludicrous.

I lean forward, keeping one hand firm against Padlock's side, and watch the RACE LENGTH output. It flickers on and off, on and off. And then a zero. And then, finally, the actual length—

TWELVE FURLONGS.

Padlock rocks inside the stall with impatience as my mind reels. A mile and a half. A half mile less than I need to have any confidence at winning. We can't beat the others this way. I know this. I'm the girl who spent every spare second she had studying cyclonetrack.com. Many of the previous jockeys I understand better than my own family. Their successors will beat me here today, and I'll lose my shot at entering the summer circuit.

So here's what I do.

I let go of the dream and remember what Magnolia said.

I lean forward, wrap my arms around my steel horse, and whisper, "Let's do this, Padlock. Not to win. Not to place. But to remember this moment as the time we ran with the Titans. Because you *are* a Titan. And tonight, I am a rider."

Padlock kicks the front of the stall with aggravation, eager to put my words into action, or so I'd like to believe. I breathe evenly, letting my fear slip away. In its place is wonder for this machine I've mounted. I gather his hair between my fingers, and rub the place behind his ears. Then I grab the left joystick and place my right hand above the turbo button.

A man runs toward the starting gate and the crowd cheers. He motions to another man, who has a gun pointed at the moon. They share a hand signal, and I fill my lungs.

The starting light flicks on.

Red.

The stalls shake from the steel horses, but my own horse, Padlock, settles.

Yellow.

Yellow.

Yellow.

The first man approaches the starting gate and places his hands on something I can't see. A mile and a half. Not long enough to win. But long enough to be remembered.

"You ready, Padlock?" I yell, the moment working me into a state of madness.

The horse snorts once, loudly, but keeps his eyes steady on the track. Steady. So eerily steady with his red, apocalyptic eyes and his black-as-death coat. It's like he's waited for this moment for years, gathering dust in a work shed instead of fulfilling his purpose.

My blood burns. My eyes sting. I feel like my body will spontaneously combust.

But Padlock is calm, stoic.

Until the starting gate slides away, that is.

Until the gun fires through the magnetic air.

Until I push that magic black button and grab on to the handlebars and scream into the night.

That's when my Titan explodes beneath me like a volcano.

Dormant for too long.

Awake at last.

CHAPTER TWENTY-ONE

The ground quakes as forty-two steel horses lurch from the starting gates onto the dirt track. They run close together, a school of fish swarming in the presence of a great white. But that's not accurate. Because we *are* the shark. We are the thing with teeth and jaws and the instinct to eat everything in our path.

And what's in our path is a straightaway of possibility.

The first chance to gain a lead.

Padlock thunders beneath me, his neck jerking up and down, my left hand pushing the gas bar higher, feeling the clicks between my heels when my horse changes gears. For a moment, we are caught in the center of the storm, a swirling, tumultuous tornado of steel wrapping around our bodies.

I flirt with the gas yet again, and expect us to break ahead of the pack. It doesn't seem possible that we wouldn't pull ahead while going this fast. But the other jockeys are taking advantage of the straight stretch of dirt too. And though my Titan feels invincible, he doesn't seem to have the engine they do.

In a matter of seconds, the horses barrel past on either side. The last one's thigh grazes Padlock's front legs and sparks fly. When the jockey glances back, I realize it wasn't a mistake. Even if the jockey's eyes weren't shaded by the helmet, I know that backward look was a metaphorical middle finger waving in the wind.

My chest aches when I realize that we're in last place. It happened so quickly. The very first stretch. But what did I expect, really?

To win, I'll admit now.

Against all odds and reasoning, I expected to win because I needed it so badly.

Remembering that need now, I grit my teeth and latch on to the gas handle. The first turn is rapidly approaching, and the other Titans are already easing off the throttle for a graceful, smooth transition. But I can't do graceful. And I can't slow down. Not if I want a chance at finishing any place but last.

"Ready, Padlock?" I yell. "Ready?"

My Titan's eyes burn brighter against the dirt, and I swear his speed accelerates a fraction though I've yet to push the accelerator. When I do, though—the turn finally on us—Padlock is ready. He heaves forward as I gauge the space between the inner gate and my Titan, between the track and the leaning body of my steel horse. A fraction more, and we'll still make it through.

I nudge the bar and turn the joysticks and lean away from the turn until I feel it through my entire body. An equilibrium. Like skating on a frozen pond, wearing your mother's hand-me-down skates, and knowing without knowing exactly how far to protrude your hip and how fast to cut your blades so that you glide around that wintery arc without spilling. But skaters fall all the time, don't they?

They do.

But we don't.

My Titan's steel hooves swallow the ground as we take our turn. And then we're pulling up and away—an airliner lifting into the sky, wheels tucking neatly beneath its belly. When I glance back, I notice four Titans have fallen behind. We are far away from where we need to be, yet there are not one but *four* Titans racing to catch up with us.

If we can pass part of the competition in one turn, we can pass even more in the next.

I lean forward in the saddle with renewed determination, the sound of the crowd dying in the distance. Cyclone Track winds away from the mass of bodies and encircles the stables, but it doesn't lead into the woods. That's later in the season—the hastily built tracks with perilous jams along every furlong. That's the unknown.

But this track I do know. I've studied the turns and twists until I could draw them with my eyes closed, a stubby length of chalk in my palm.

Twelve furlongs. A mile and a half. So much time to gain ground.

But will it be enough?

Checking the stopwatch, I see only ten seconds have passed.

I utilize more gas and the gears click once again. The remaining thirty-seven Titans take advantage of the next stretch, a cloud of dust kicked up by ravenous heels. Padlock can't catch them, not without me moving past the safety zone. I eye the performance gauge and see we're already in the yellow.

Caution, caution! the orange needle cries, outraged.

But now's not the time to be cautious, is it? These other jockeys have to worry about the rest of the season, but there won't be a season for me unless I win this race. I can't afford a loss. Not one. Not ever.

I shove the gas bar with my left hand, and Padlock jerks forward as if he's relieved to have the slack.

But it's not enough.

The other Titans continue to gain a lead with their superior engines. No matter. I don't lose faith, because there's another turn ahead, and four Titans still watching Padlock's backside.

Hang on, ladies and gentlemen.

Don't look away.

Don't blink!

I touch the gas with feather fingertips and lead Padlock to the inside. There doesn't seem to be enough space for him to squeeze by the other Titans. But there is.

A slice of an inch.

"Go, Padlock, go!" I roar.

There's no way he can hear me. I can't hear myself. I can only feel my heart thrumming in my ears. My blood pounding through my veins. Sound vanishes, followed by every other sense—smell, touch, taste. Wait, no. There's one left.

Sight.

Watch the turn, Astrid. Watch the ground and the gate and the distance Padlock has to lean. Block everything else out and run the numbers.

Could I push him? Do I have room?

Yes.

I nudge the gas handle, and I swear my left knee nearly touches the dirt. I press it against Padlock's side and lean so far away from him that I have to grasp his opposite side to keep from falling. There's a woman jockey racing nearby. She looks in my direction and sneers. Her left arm swipes out to slap me away like an annoying gnat.

Before I'm taken out, I needle Padlock's joystick to the right and he slams into the woman's Titan. We lose precious seconds, but the woman is gone, fallen back amidst a glittering cloud of sparks. Soon after, I pull Padlock upright and we bolt after the remaining Titans. Once more, I glance back to inspect what damage we've done, if any.

Twelve Titans are a safe distance away, and another is a neck behind. The one that's closely trailing us begins to catch up on the straightaway, but I count it in our triumphs since I know we can take him out cleanly in the next turn.

Thirteen Titans behind.

Twenty-eight in front.

Three solid turns and two half-turns remain. I want to believe we have a chance, but then I remember that the Titans before us are there for a reason. And that each horse will be harder to pass than the last.

I check my performance gauge: halfway into the caution zone.

With one hand on the gas lever and the other on my Titan's right joystick, I lean forward.

And I push my Titan faster.

We race onward, and over the next several furlongs and three turns, we gain a lead over another ten Titans. Twenty-three behind. Eighteen in front. Only two turns and a quarter mile left to go. I erase every thought from my mind. I forget about the finish line rapidly approaching. The crowd roaring in the distance.

This is my race.

This is my time.

Pushing Padlock faster than ever before, I take the next two turns and cry out as gray steel whips by. We pass trees and rabid fans and Titans. How many Titans? I don't know. I don't know.

There's the finish line.

Padlock throws his head and I squeeze the handlebars and let him run. It's all I can do now. Hang on. Hold tight. Suck in a breath as we breeze across the finish line and a gun is fired once, twice, three times.

And once more for good measure.

CHAPTER TWENTY-TWO

Sweat runs down my face as I bring Padlock to a stop, fall forward on him and gasp to fill my lungs because all my oxygen is gone. It's been stolen by the race. By the people pressing against the gates and the photographers snapping photos of the winner.

The person who will proceed to the Titan Summer Circuit, free of charge.

His silk is blue, a color that is all wrong on him, according to Magnolia. He removes his helmet, and then a red handkerchief tied around his mouth. Anger swells inside me like a storm cloud threatening to burst open. He stole my win. The same boy who spat that I'd never sit upon a Titan. But I did, didn't I?

I raced today.

And I lost.

In all fairness, I guess I wouldn't have won anyway. Sixteen other horses finished before me in addition to Blondie Who I Want to Punch. I secured sixteenth place out of forty-two. On a better day, maybe I'd be thrilled. I rode a Titan against more experienced jockeys and I wasn't in last place. But I'm not thrilled. Because now I have to go home and hope my father finds a job and hope that the bank will hold off long enough for him to get his first paycheck and hand it over. Everything I was racing for rushes back over me. Even the anger at Blondie fades under the pressure that threatens to crush my whole family.

I slide out of the saddle and remove my helmet, ready to lead Padlock back to the stables, when the cameras turn away from the winner and start snapping photos of me and my Titan. Dirt is smeared across my face and forearms, and my entire body shakes from exertion, but the flashes don't stop. A female reporter leans across the gate, calling out, "Hey, Sullivan, what kind of horse is that? Is it the next edition? A Titan 4.0?" A second reporter elbows the woman out of the way and calls out, "Who are you? You're listed on the board but aren't in the program. Are you a late addition? Who's your manager?"

Padlock shies away from the flashes, stepping back until his rear bumps into something solid. Almost immediately, my Titan is shoved forward. I turn away from the reporters and see that a Titan 3.0 has head-butted my horse. Padlock lowers his own head, seemingly embarrassed. I jog over, but before I can console him, Padlock incurs a second hit from a different Titan.

"Hey," I yell, facing the Titan's owner.

A jockey dressed in orange merely laughs. She finished in second place, has the smug smile to prove it, and is giggling with another jockey and pointing at my Titan. I glance around and notice several other jockeys have dismounted and are gawking at Padlock, some laughing, some giving looks of disgust.

"Way to spaz out on those turns," a jockey hollers, his cheeks scarlet. "Flailing idiots. Almost got the rest of us hurt."

"We weren't flailing. We'd done turns like that—" I try to explain myself, stupidly, but now managers are joining their jockeys and scrutinizing Padlock.

"That horse shouldn't be here," a burly man accuses, his thick arm around a jockey's shoulders. "It's not a 3.0."

"If it isn't a 3.0, it should be disqualified," someone yells.

"Poseur horse," a jockey coughs under his breath, making a bystander laugh.

I turn in a circle, realizing jockeys and managers alike are taking the opportunity to turn their loss into background noise. The real spectacle is this faux Titan. And if they can peg me and him as freaks, then maybe the sponsors won't think too hard about who won and who didn't. After all, don't they see how that one Titan messed things up for everybody?

As more reporters close in, lured by the frenzy and bloodlust, I feel a slight brush on my back. When I spin around, I find Padlock trying to hide his head between my shoulder blades. He raises his muzzle for a moment, takes in the flashes and accusatory fingers and loud words, and cowers once again.

That's when I see it for the first time.

The fear and shame in his eyes.

The *emotion*.

It isn't a programmed response. The Titan is actually afraid, and sadness crinkles the corners of his heavily lashed eyelids. Fury builds in the pit of my stomach until it feels as though steam will shoot from my ears like every cartoon character I've ever seen. I spin around, my hands forming fists, and I face the first reporter I see.

"Are you seeking a sponsor?" a man in a white starched shirt calls out.

"Yes," I answer. "My Titan and I are looking into our options now."

"Are you saying you've already been approached?" another one asks.

"Several times. What I'm riding is a Titan 1.0, the first edition ever built. The *best* edition ever built. I've trained for less than a week, and this horse still beat out twenty-six others tonight. I have no doubt a better-prepared jockey would have won."

My eyes find the blond boy, and he scowls.

"So you'll be at Travesty Ball?" This question comes from a woman without a microphone.

"If I don't sign with a sponsor before then, yes."

Rags reaches me before I can dig myself in any deeper. "Get in the saddle," he hisses. "Go back to the stables and wait for Barney."

"Where's Magnolia?" I whisper beneath the shout of the reporters.

Rags gives me a look like he's going to strangle me for stalling, so I pull myself up onto a frightened Padlock. I'd like to give them one more piece of me. One more false smile and wave.

Look how confident I am! Put that *on your front page.*

But when I see Arvin Gambini, his brother, Theo, and the tall man from our church stomping toward Rags, I know it's time to skedaddle. Rags unrolls the papers still clutched in his fist like he's ready to go to war, and heads toward the brothers.

I ride past the other Titans as more bulbs flash and jockeys yell for my horse to be disqualified. Even the crowd outside the gates seems uncertain. Do they want me to stay so they can bet on me? Or should they join the mob and cast me out?

Also, who is this girl they've never seen before?

No one special, I want to tell them. *A moron who ran her mouth without thinking.*

When I get Padlock back into our unmarked stall, I dismount and watch as he cowers in the corner. "No way," I tell him, stepping close and meeting his eyes so he knows I'm serious. "Don't you dare let them make you feel bad. Did you see what we did out there? We passed more than half the Titans on that track. Titans with newer engines, being steered by jockeys much more qualified than I'll ever be. You were amazing, Padlock." I smile at him, run my eyes over his sleek exterior and steel-threaded mane. My heart clenches. "You *are* amazing."

"You're amazing too," someone says.

Magnolia stands outside the stall with a look of awe on her face. "You really did it."

I pat Padlock on the side. "Actually, I didn't. This horse could have won. But I didn't know what I was doing out there."

"Coulda fooled me."

"Me too," Barney adds, coming into view and opening the stall door. "And what you said to those reporters. Oh, man. The Gambini brothers are going to have a hard time kicking you out now. On one hand, we made Arvin look like an idiot. On the other, he needs all the publicity he can get."

"Why?" I ask.

"Expansion."

"What do you mean, *expansion*?" I ask, but before Barney can answer, Rags rushes into the stall.

"I did it," he says, his orange vest glowing beneath the buzzing stable lights. "Er, maybe you did it. Either way, they're going to let us stay."

"Stay?" My brow furrows. "What do you mean? It's over. I lost."

Rags raises his eyebrows, and I grasp what he's implying.

"You can't seriously think we should try for a sponsor," I say. "I was upset out there. I acted like a cocky brat, and no one is going to want to work with me or an old, outdated Titan."

Padlock huffs, and I rub between his eyes. "You know what I mean," I mutter to the horse.

"A cocky brat is exactly what we needed. If we're lucky, we might actually get an interview at the ball. All we need is one chance. Heck, if we could get a partial sponsorship, maybe we could come up with a way to get the rest."

"I could make you a hair accessory to end all hair accessories," Magnolia breathes.

110

I look back and forth between Barney, who is grinning, Magnolia, who is rubbing her hands together, and Rags, who looks in every way like a certified madman.

"If we don't get a sponsor at the ball, we'll look like idiots," I say.

"Complete and total idiots," Rags agrees.

I bite my upper lip. "But you think there's a chance?"

The architect shrugs. "Sometimes sponsors fight for the jockey that makes the most noise over one slated to win. Not always, but it happens."

I scratch behind Padlock's ear, and think how crazy it is that we'd even try for a sponsor. But we've come this far, and though we didn't win today, I'm not sure we really expected to either. Why not push this further? "We did make a little noise today, didn't we?" I say. My steel horse leans into my touch, and with my family's future thick in my chest, I turn so that Rags can't see my face.

"I don't even own a gown," I mumble.

"I can dig up an outfit for you," Magnolia offers. "It won't be ball-worthy, but it'll be eye-catching."

I look at Rags to measure his reaction.

"Might go along with the whole noise angle," he suggests.

I smile down at my hands, and crack my fingers one by one. Something I've seen my dad do a thousand times when he's lost in his head. "Okay," I say, "if we're vying for four idiot awards, we may as well go all out."

CHAPTER TWENTY-THREE

On Tuesday, after I've spent a morning with Zara at the park, Magnolia and I ride with Rags to training. It's wishful thinking, we know, but it feels good to break a sweat in the Detroit summer heat. Travesty Ball is tomorrow, and while the other jockeys are busy with clothes fittings and getting their teeth whitened and trimming their hair—*not too much off the top, not too much!*—my horse and I run.

No matter how we try, though, we can't find a solution to the straightaway problem. The fact is, Padlock can't compete when it comes to sheer speed. The turns are where we have our advantage. So as night falls, we give up and return to our ramshackle neighborhood. Where my house is. Where my *dad* is.

Dad doesn't seem to know about the races. Could be because I trashed the local paper before he could see it. The one that ran a quarter-page story about the winner, with a few lines about the second- and third-place jockeys. And at the very bottom, a short mention of the Sullivan girl, who ran a controversial Titan 1.0, who may or may not make an appearance at Travesty Ball.

Somehow, some way, I limboed under my dad's radar.

But that wouldn't last forever.

"I'm still amazed you didn't kill yourself during the sponsor race," Rags says, interrupting my thoughts.

I lean against his still-warm truck as Magnolia inspects her nails. "And I'm amazed the Gambini brothers didn't burn us at the stake," I tell him.

He rubs the back of his neck. "You could have gotten hurt out there racing the way you did."

"You knew how I raced," I respond. "Besides, what would you care if I injured myself?"

In true Rags fashion, the man grimaces. "I don't. Not my problem if you want to race recklessly."

Magnolia snorts, and I look down to keep from laughing. Rags talks a big game, but we know he cares more than he'll ever admit. My head falls to one side and I say, "Why do you go by that name, *Rags*? Is it short for something?"

Even in the darkness, I see the blush creep into his cheeks. "Ask Barney. He'll enjoy telling the story, I'm sure."

"I'm asking you."

He tugs on his hunting vest and mumbles, "Thought about switching from Titan architect to engineer."

"And?"

"And so maybe I made a few messes in the Hanover chop shop while I was figuring things out," he barks.

I have to swallow a breath to keep from laughing, because yeah, it would have been great to hear Barney tell this story. "Messes the engineers had to clean up with a bunch of *rags*?"

"Messes *I* had to clean up." His voice grows stern. "What does it matter? It showed I was totally vested in the Titan. Not like any of those hacks could design a single Titan part to save their lives."

I want nothing more than to tease Rags about his nickname, but he must take some element of pride in it or he wouldn't have introduced himself as such. Plus, I like it too. I can absolutely picture the guy being caught red-handed, grease smudged across his cheeks, oil dripping down the sides of a Frankenstein-type Titan. I bet those *hackers* had a good laugh when they found him in their shop. Threw their well-washed rags at him and slapped him on the back as they held their guts and crowed.

"Good night, old man," I say.

Rags grunts.

....

A few minutes later, I'm parked on Magnolia's bed, clothes strewn across her room as if her closet had an exorcism. My best friend has narrowed the choices to two outfits, and both make me cringe for different reasons.

"Classy and dangerous," Magnolia purrs, lifting black leggings, a long red V-neck blouse, and black pumps into the air, "ooor, sexy and dangerous." She plucks a pair of zebra-striped pumps from the ground and holds them next to the same leggings and blouse.

I fall back on the bed, realizing it doesn't matter what shoes I wear. I'll still be underdressed and out of place at this ball. But when I see my friend's face fall, I manage an enthusiastic grin. "The zebra shoes for sure."

"Really?" she squeaks. "I didn't think you'd make the right choice, but I see you have vision when it matters."

I cover my face with her pillow as Magnolia launches into how she can *absolutely, positively make an animal-inspired headpiece tonight to accentuate the heels,* and lift the pillow back up when I hear someone knocking.

"If that's you, Brandon, I'm going to scream."

"Mom needs whatever you have," he says through the door.

Magnolia throws an anxious look my way, so I sit up in bed, alarmed but not sure why. She opens the door a fraction for her older brother and whispers furiously. I can't make out what she says, but I hear him clear enough.

"Didn't you make anything from your stupid online store?" he says, annoyance lacing his voice. More whispers from Magnolia,

114

and then, "Come on, Mag, give me what you have. They're going down there tomorrow."

Magnolia slams the door in his face, avoids my gaze, and crosses the room. She pulls her blond hair into a pony, and then lets it fall down her back.

"Mag?" I say, in a much softer voice than her brother used.

She ignores me and reaches into a white chest of drawers that's covered in glittery Hello Kitty stickers. She withdraws an envelope and marches back to the door as Brandon pounds on it. Pulling it open, she shoves the envelope into his chest.

This time, I hear what she says. "That's everything."

She slams the door a second time, and I hear Brandon padding down the hallway. Magnolia won't meet my gaze after he's gone.

"What's going on?" I lean against her headboard, my stomach churning.

When Magnolia looks up, her eyes are red. She's not crying, and I don't expect her to, but it's clear she's upset. I swing my legs over the side of the bed and start to approach her, but she moves toward her closet, putting distance between us. "My parents are going to the bank tomorrow. See if they can keep them from foreclosing on the house."

The wind is knocked out of me, and the room starts to spin. "Do your parents have enough? Do you think they'll let you stay?"

She starts rehanging clothes, but doesn't turn around. "I don't know. Maybe enough for a month or two because of Mom's part-time gig. But if Dad doesn't find something soon, he's going to start looking elsewhere before . . ."

"Before the new school year starts," I finish for her.

Magnolia spins around. "Look, can we not talk about it? It doesn't do any good. I want to concentrate on this. On what shoes you'll wear to Travesty Ball. I don't care how petty that is. It's what I need right now, okay?"

"Okay." I stand up, my legs quaking. "I should probably get going anyway. It'll give you space to work your magic on my headpiece. It better be good."

Magnolia smiles, and it almost lights up her face. "Could anything I make be less than perfection?"

"Not a chance." I walk toward her window, and then, because everyone needs to be blindsided by a hug once in a while, I throw my arms around her. "I'll never let go, Jack. I'll never let go."

She hugs me for three full seconds before shoving me off. "Ugh. That movie is so old."

"*Titanic* is a classic." I slide her window up and say over my shoulder, "Everything will be okay, Mag. We're factory families. This happens sometimes, but it always gets better. Your dad will find something last minute just like mine will."

"Oh, I know," she says, waving off the encouragement.

But she doesn't really know if it'll get better. And neither do I. All I *do* know is that our families are both on the brink of losing their homes. And that Magnolia and I could lose each other in the process. Even if my dad ends up finding work here last minute, what are the chances that both our dads will? And what are the chances that their habits won't put us in this same position a year from now?

The pressure of this realization weighs on my spine as I make my way home. When I see my mother working in Ms. Padison's yard, darkness cloaked over her shoulders, I'm flooded with relief. There's something about seeing her doing the same things she's done for the last five years that's soothing.

She hears me approaching and her head appears from behind a butterfly bush.

"Just pruning the right side," she says, as if the bush belongs to me.

I watch her hands working lightly over the thin branches and purple flowers. There's a pile of trimmings at her feet. "Mom, did you ever have a best friend?"

She wipes the sweat from her brow, but doesn't stop working. "Sure I did. Several."

"Where are they now?"

"Oh, most are still in Texas. My family moved when I was fifteen."

She doesn't need to say any more. I'm shadowing my mother's own life. Born to a factory family, slave to job openings and union negotiations. She moved twice before meeting my dad in Milwaukee. The third time her parents moved, she stayed behind, a shiny gold band encircling her finger, a shiny new factory man on her arm.

"Are you and Magnolia okay?" she asks.

I watch her hands more closely, and a nagging sensation spiders up the back of my mind. I feel like I'm missing something. "Yeah, Mom. We're fine. I'm just worried about next year."

Her back straightens, but still her hands flutter over the bush, pale and nimble in the moonlight. "No te preocupes, my little girl. Things have a way of working out."

"You're right," I say, because it's what she wants to hear. And because I didn't catch everything she said, though half of me is made of her. I throw my mom a backward wave and head toward our house, but Mom calls out before I reach our sidewalk.

"Astrid?"

I glance back at her.

She stops pruning the butterfly bush.

"I left something for you under your bed. Don't let Dani or Zara see it. Or . . ."

Or Dad. Regardless of what it is, don't let Dad see it.

"You're my little shooting star, right, baby?"

"That's right, Mom." I'm frozen where I stand. I don't know what she's getting at, but I've been hiding a massive secret and I'm afraid the first whistle has been blown.

"Mamas worry about their baby birds." She returns her attention to the neglected bush. "But that doesn't mean we don't want them to fly."

I look one last time at her long fingers, making things beautiful as silent clouds tiptoe by overhead. Then I jog toward the house, dying to know what secret she left for me beneath my bed.

CHAPTER TWENTY-FOUR

Magnolia comes by the next afternoon when my house is cleared out; Dani with her boyfriend, Zara with my mom at the public splash park, and Dad with Magnolia's dad, probably drinking an afternoon beer and shaking their fists at early-evening commuters who don't deserve employment the way they do. Sure as the world turns, they'll have a deck of cards between them. Playing for quarters. Or nickels. Or the lint in their pockets if that's all they've got.

My friend tiptoes down the hall and then pokes her head around the corner.

I have the dress laid out on the bed.

"Oh, holy mother of Batman," she whispers. "Where did this come from?"

"My mom." I step back so she can inch closer, and remember my mother's bare hands from the night before. "I think she sold her wedding ring."

Magnolia stops and stares at me. "Things that bad?"

I shrug, because I don't want to add to her worries. And because it's not like she told me about her parents visiting the bank on her own. Her brother brought that up. "We need to pay some bills. I'm sure they'll buy it back after Dad gets a new gig. Or maybe she'll get a rock this time."

Magnolia takes the dress and holds it up to her petite frame. She could probably wrap it around herself a time and a half. "Canary yellow," Magnolia breathes. "Plunging neckline, cap sleeves—it's beautiful." Her eyes meet mine. "But it's the bottom that's going to kill."

I stroke the delicate yellow feathers that stretch from hips to floor-length hem, and my heart swells with conflicting emotions. Gratitude that my mother did this, fear that my father will soon find out, shame because I'm afraid I will fail my mom tonight and the expense will be for nothing. I think about the note she left with the gift.

Do your mama one favor. Let me give you this dress quietly. Let me love you this way.

What she meant was, *I don't want to discuss how I got this, or why I'm giving it to you.* So I honored her wish and didn't mention it, but guilt sits heavy in my chest. I don't deserve this kindness. I don't deserve her faith.

"Think she got it at Goodwill?" Magnolia licks her lips like she's imagining a Detroit boutique with a carbon copy of this dress in her size. A clothing store we'd never shop in. One with racks of dresses sparkling on well-lit floors, with mirrors that make you look like royalty.

"Probably," I say. "No way we could have bought this otherwise."

"I can't believe the stuff people give away." Magnolia shakes her head like she's furious at whoever was thoughtless enough to trade this dress for a tax credit. "Not that I'm complaining in this scenario. Astrid, you're going to blow their minds tonight! Have you tried it on?"

"Haven't had a chance. Dani just left."

Magnolia puts the dress down as if it's breakable. "I'm going to do your makeup and hair, and because you're the luckiest vixen to ever walk this here earth, the accessory I made you will still work."

"Makeover party?" I ask, remembering the celebrity magazines squashed beneath my mattress, thinking about the women with bony arms perched on narrow hips wearing dresses that cost thousands of dollars.

"We're going to need sodas. Do you have soda?"

"No."

"We're not going to need soda. But we will need to go to my house. What time did Rags say we have to be over there?"

I think back to last night. "Seven o'clock."

Magnolia folds the dress over her arm and smoothes the feathers. "I'll carry her. It'd be my honor."

My friend spends the next two hours slathering two pounds of makeup on my face, instructing me to rub her mother's Jergens lotion all over my body, and even jogging back to my house to grab my good bra—the strapless, nude, push-up number that, okay, actually belongs to Dani. But it's cool. Sisters can share bras. I mean, what's the point of siblings if they can't help in your quest for cleavage?

Magnolia also works on my hair, using a flat iron to straighten it down my back. She then takes a round brush and gathers a chunk of hair near the top of my head and brushes against the grain. I look like an eighties rock star until she flips the hair back over the ratty nest she made.

"Are you ready for your crowning glory?" she asks.

I stand and follow her to her closet, where she withdraws a shoe box wrapped in Calvin Klein advertisements. When she removes the lid, a male model winks at me before being tossed onto the bed.

"I worked on it all morning," she says, clutching the opened box to her chest.

Goose bumps rise on my skin, because I have a best friend who would work on something for my hair for hours on end. For *my* hair, not hers. A friend who apparently has an online store and could have spent the time making a piece to sell instead.

She brings out an antique floral-shaped brooch with silver stones decorating the interior. Attached to the brooch is an offshoot of black-and-white striped feathers, and the entire piece is attached to a clear headband.

"I brushed black fabric paint over white feathers and laid them out to dry last night. Couldn't find any zebra-striped ones at the craft store." Magnolia motions to a chair, and I sit. She slides the headband into place, stopping it right before the spot where my hair poofs. The brooch sits heavily to the right, and the spray of feathers shoots straight up from the side.

"It's absolutely beautiful." I stare at my reflection in the mirror, admiring Magnolia's work. "You could be a makeup artist in addition to selling your headpieces."

Magnolia sighs dramatically. "I could if these buggers didn't take up every spare second I have." She heaves the yellow dress over her arm. "It's a good thing your mom picked a neutral number. Now you can still pull off the headband and heels without clashing."

My friend helps me slip the dress over my head, and when we're done fitting it around my hips and adjusting the neckline, Magnolia's brother barges through the door. He takes one look at me from beneath his shaggy hair and skater clothes and says, "Dang, Astrid. You look like a brick house in that dress."

My cheeks flame even though the comment is coming from a guy I've known since pre–voice change.

"Oh, gross!" Magnolia shoves him backward and slams the door. After he yells something about dinner, my friend returns her attention to me. "Sorry about the troll. But, yeah, you totally do look amazing."

She hurries to pull on the outfit I'd originally intended to wear, minus the zebra pumps, and positions a large red flower in her hair. "We've got to run. As glamorous as we look, we still have to walk our rears over to Rags's place for a lift."

"Out the window?" I ask.

"Like true ladies." Magnolia slides the glass open and I wrangle myself through, wondering how often her parents find their daughter missing from her room. And why they haven't thought to get a lock on this thing. And why my friend has such an aversion to doors.

Rags lets us into his entryway when we arrive, tells us to stay there, and dashes off. A week ago, this would make me wonder what he's hiding in his house. But now I know it's just Rags being his usual bizarre self. When he returns, I take in the man's blue suit and white button-down. He's even wearing a red bow tie, though I never would have pegged him as a bow tie kind of guy.

"So you do own clothing that's not covered in grease," I say.

"So you do know how to dress like a girl," he replies. Rags wipes a hand over his freshly shaved jawline, and produces something from behind his back. "The girl jockeys wear these sometimes."

I glance down at the white rose corsage bound in a plastic tub, and my mouth pulls into a smile. "You got me this?"

"Wasn't going to get red, obviously. Just put it on. We're meeting Barney in the parking lot."

He locks the door and trudges toward his truck, shoulders slumped like the blue suit he's wearing causes him physical pain. We arrive at the Marriott at the Renaissance Center after a twenty-minute drive, and when I see the building where the ball will take place, my insides flutter. It's enormous, with blue lights snapping against a dark sky, and the Detroit River cutting a path directly behind the hotel.

Barney meets us in the parking lot wearing a brown suit, brown shirt, and brown dress shoes. Magnolia tells him he looks like a grizzly bear with a Godiva addiction, and he beams, decidedly satisfied with this description.

"Remember what I told you," Rags says as he motions toward the hotel entryway.

I remember. A twenty-minute drive isn't long, but it is when your manager is telling you what to do, and what not to do, at lightning speed the entire way. Then asking if you heard him every few seconds.

Magnolia straightens the headpiece in my hair, and then nods with such sincerity, I almost laugh. We've got two old men who lost their positions at Hanover Steel, one with an obvious chip on his shoulder, a girl whose family is facing foreclosure and smiles anyway, and me, with my own family to worry about.

But now I worry about these three as well. Because they've done so much to help me fight my way into the Titan season, each with their own reasons—revenge, perhaps, or to reminisce, or to forget. I need a sponsor to have a chance at saving my family, but it's quickly becoming more than that. I *want* a sponsor, to keep these three mismatched people by my side. Because whether I'll admit it aloud or not, these past few days have been incredible. I want to win for Magnolia because of the overwhelming support she's given me. And for Rags and Barney too, who have invested their time, knowledge, and resources, and placed their dreams gently in my hands.

I straighten my dress and stride into the Marriott.

Confidence courses through me, much more than it should, until we spill into the ballroom. Until I see the circus I'll be facing tonight. Until I spot the jockeys with their designer clothing, elegant stances, and polished smiles.

I cling to Rags's comment before we stepped out of his truck. *Just get a silver ticket, Astrid. That's all we need. Just one ticket. Just one chance.*

CHAPTER TWENTY-FIVE

Fourteen wooden boxes sit at the front of the ballroom, and I seem to be the only jockey worried about their presence. Nameplates are attached to each one, and mine is the farthest to the right.

SULLIBAN

"Did they spell your last name wrong?" Magnolia squints at the box.

Rags curses under his breath, says something about it being done on purpose, and stomps toward the Gambini brothers.

"He's going to get us kicked out if he's not careful," Barney says. "It's a miracle he was able to talk them into letting us continue at all."

"Yeah, how did he do that anyway?" Magnolia asks.

Barney lifts a glass of champagne from a waiter's serving round. "Printed some literature from their site that supports his argument that it doesn't have to be the most recent model of Titan to race. But I think it has more to do with their investor Bruce." He points his glass toward the tall man that's been Arvin Gambini's shadow this summer. "He also happens to work for the *Chicago Tribune*."

I study the man, his green pocket square and black suit. He has a long face and broad shoulders. He's maybe in his late forties, but even I see the attractiveness he's worn since childhood. Bold, brown eyes survey the room, and when they fall on a female, smiles are exchanged.

"Why is an investor from Chicago here?" I ask.

"Because Arvin Gambini is looking to franchise the tracks, and Chicago is as good a city as any. Plus, that guy from the *Tribune* has the publicity angle covered, which we all know Arvin craves. So, yeah, I think he let Rags get his way because the last thing he wants right now is a spectacle."

....

Over the next two hours, sponsors dressed in red jackets make their way around the room. Their nametags announce who they are and what companies they work for. I speak with each of them, fidgeting with the feathers on my skirt and the flowers on my wrist the entire time. There are even a couple of individual investors who stop by for appearances' sake, but neither talks with me for more than a couple of minutes.

Only one man, early thirties with a shaved head and sad eyes, chats with me in earnest. He asks me about taking those turns, and whether it's something I think I'll improve on. He also asks about my straightaways, and has my manager considered upgrading the engine to match the other Titans? Because I could be a real contender to watch if, for example, some company could pay for that upgrade. The man keeps digging in his pocket like the secrets to the universe lie in his pocket lint. He asks me one last question.

"Would you be willing to work with a new manager? Someone who had connections and could place you in a new light?"

I tell him, politely, no. I like the light I come from. And I wouldn't be here without Rags. I'm Warren County through and through, and I refuse to pretend to be something I'm not to appease these people.

The man squeezes my arm, gives a head nod that causes a bolt of hopefulness to shoot through me, and then leaves to network with a different jockey—a jockey who wears a fur shrug even though it's summer, and lifts slender fingers to allow the sponsor to kiss her hand.

"So weird," I mutter.

Magnolia trots back over, despite Rags's specific instructions to keep away, and asks me how my last meet-and-greet went.

"Not as bad as the others," I admit, watching as the man moves away from Hand Kiss Girl and inspects the room, as if he's not sure what to do with himself now. I'm about to tell Magnolia what he asked me to gauge what she thinks, when Arvin Gambini's voice rings through the room.

"Hello, everyone, I'm Arvin Gambini, as many of you may know."

Arvin's entourage chuckles, ready to touch up his hair or spritz cologne on him at a moment's notice.

"I want to thank you for coming out tonight," he adds quickly, immediately launching into business. "Matching sponsors with jockeys is a very important part of the Titan racing business, and the last step before we announce the official jockey-sponsor lineup and release the racing schedule."

Arvin waves a hand toward the boxes, and then again at a side door in the ballroom. "At this time we'll ask that the sponsors drop their silver tickets into the boxes of the jockeys they'd like to make formal offers to, and we'll ask that the jockeys exit through the side door to Ballroom B for dancing. You'll be called one at a time to enter the interview wing, and if any sponsors have dropped a silver ticket into your box, they will be there waiting for you in one of the three interview rooms."

My eyes flick to Rags, and he nods toward the side door like, *Go on. You heard the rat.*

Magnolia squeals by my side and grabs my arm. "Let's go! I want to see how many jockeys I can dance with."

"Uh, you're not supposed to flirt with the competition," I say as the two of us follow after the other jockeys and their team members.

"Don't worry, I have a plan. I'll make them fall madly in love with me, and then *bam*, I'll break their hearts and they'll lose their Titan-racing concentration and the gold medal will be ours."

"I don't think there's really a medal."

"You're missing the point."

Magnolia and I exit through the side door, and my pulse quickens along my neck. A ballroom filled with dance partners who also serve as the competition. I can only imagine how this will go down.

CHAPTER TWENTY-SIX

My friend and I spill into the smaller, more dimly lit room. A jazz band plays on a stage, and a few circular tables dot the outskirts of a parquet dance floor. A white light shines an illuminated *GB* over a jockey's shoulders as she dances with her partner.

"Does that GB stand for Goat Bagels?" Magnolia asked.

"Sounds reasonable," I say. "Or maybe Gigabytes?"

"Ghost Bashers?"

"Green Berets?"

"It stands for Gambini Brothers," someone new says.

I turn toward the sound of the voice, and groan when I see the blond dude who won the sponsor race. "Yeah, we know. We were joking around. You do know what a joke is, don't you?"

Magnolia stabs a finger into his chest. "It's you. *You're* a joke."

The boy's jaw tightens, but he manages to keep whatever insult he has between his teeth. Instead, he asks, "Would you like to dance?"

"With you?" I laugh. "You must be kidding. Don't you remember who I am? I'm the poor, jealous girl who'd never sit in a Titan saddle."

"I remember you."

"Then you'll understand why I'd rather give you the middle finger than this dance."

The jockey looks past me at something, and I follow his gaze. Two cameramen stand near the corner of the room, media badges hanging from their necks like feed bags. I know instantly who they are. Not journalists. Not real ones, anyway. They're from the *Titan Enquirer*, an online newspaper that runs petty gossip from the tracks every summer.

"You're trying to get their attention," I say.

Surprisingly, he doesn't deny it. "I won the race, and you're the girl who caused a buzz. It'd do us good to be seen together."

"Oh, yeah, why's that?" Magnolia bobs her head so hard that I almost lose the angry look I'm sporting.

"More coverage means more eyeballs. More eyeballs means more money from the sponsors."

He's talking about endorsement contracts that extend past the summer. Sometimes, rarely, jockeys who lose the Titan Derby will still make a living outside the races if enough people remember them. They turn into a reality star of sorts for a year or two before fading to black. But the money is good during that time. It's not something I want to be known for—scandal—but what are the chances of me winning the derby even if I acquire a sponsor?

Money is money. And family is family.

"You think they'll care that we're dancing?" I ask, disgusted that I'm even considering this.

"Only one way to find out." He takes my hand, and without asking permission, he tows me toward the dance floor.

"Uh, hello?" I snarl. "I didn't say okay."

"Close enough."

When I realize he's not going to release me, I look back at Magnolia. Barney is standing beside her, and she's waving her arms in my direction. Barney looks up with understanding, and starts to move his massive frame toward Overly Aggressive Guy. I almost smile—realizing this cocky jockey is about to get what's coming to him—when I spot the two cameramen slinking toward us, long black camera-snouts clicking photographs as the jockey wraps his arm around my waist.

With my mind racing, I hold up a hand to stop Barney and mouth, *It's okay*. I allow the jockey to spin me around the floor, and laugh for the camera any time my face is in their view. And when he dips me low, I allow my weight to be entirely supported by his arms without puking.

"You're from Warren County, right?" he says between the first song ending and the second beginning.

"Yeah," I say. "Guess that's more important than my name."

"I know your name, Astrid Sullivan, but you may not know mine." He releases my waist and offers me his hand. "Hart Riley II."

I laugh, because it seems unlikely that this dude, who surely has no soul, is named Hart. "Nice name. Fits your pedigree, I'm sure."

He retakes my waist and does an impressive spin for the cameras. "What is that supposed to mean?"

"Nothing. It's just that . . . why is it always the rich who can't let go of their names? It's like fathers with fat bank accounts feel entitled to make seconds and thirds of themselves instead of letting their children be their own people."

"You've got me all wrong."

I stiffen in his arms. "Tell me what county it is you live in again?"

His green eyes flash, and I know I've got him. I smirk at the sight of his downturned mouth. He may be from the esteemed Preston Park County, or maybe Highland Village, where only gentlemen are raised, but I see the rebelliousness behind his gaze.

Someone on stage announces his name, Hart Riley, and says it's time for him to report to the interview suites. Before he releases me, he leans forward and says, "You and I will never be more than competitors, no matter what happens. But if you'd open your eyes, you'd see we have a lot more in common than you think."

He leans forward, swiftly kisses me on the cheek, and pulls away before I have time to knee him between the legs. The cameramen catch his golden-boy smile and the way he clutches my hand before walking away.

I wonder if they see the way my nails dig into his skin.

CHAPTER TWENTY-SEVEN

Several more names are called before I finally hear my own. No one else has asked me to dance, but Magnolia upholds her vow to break every heart in the room. In reality, I think she's enjoying herself, and the male jockeys certainly relish having a pretty girl in their arms who isn't competing with them for sponsorship.

I hear *Sulliban* announced over the speakers, and Rags makes his way to my side. "Are you ready?"

After ensuring that Magnolia is still smiling, and that Barney hasn't gotten kicked out from stuffing mini quiches into his pockets, I nod.

The two of us pass through a side door and into a brightly lit hallway. It takes a moment for my eyes to adjust, and for my mind to switch from soothing music and jovial faces to white, sterile linoleum and office space.

Rags walks ahead of me by one pace, and I'm not sure I mind. I don't want to be the first to see that all three rooms are empty. He steps up to an open doorway and cranes his neck. Then he looks at me and gives his head a little shake. Once again, we're on the move, and I'm learning just how quickly Rags and his long legs *can* move. It makes me think of those gas station scratch-off cards. How some people scratch them real slow-like, savoring the thought that they might win. And other people scratch as if their life depends on it, like if they take too long any possible win will slip off their lotto card and find residence elsewhere.

Rags would definitely be in the latter category.

When he gives me a second grimace after finding the next room empty, I cringe. Only one room remains, and there's only one man I figure could possibly be in it. I hold my breath, hoping Rags will smile and shake hands with a guy who has a shaved head and sad eyes that'll make me very happy.

But Rags doesn't shake hands with anyone. In fact, when he looks inside the last room, he freezes in place and his face loses what little color it normally holds. He shakes his head like a defiant child and mutters, "Nuh-uh. No way."

"Rusty, just hear me out," a woman's voice says.

"Nope," Rags says before grabbing my arm and turning tail.

We're halfway down the hall, me yelling about too much manhandling in one night, when the woman steps out of the room.

"I have the money for her entrance fee and anything else she needs."

"Don't care," Rags says.

I rip my arm away from him and stop my forward hurtle. Has he forgotten why we're here? "W-wait," I stutter. "You want to sponsor me?"

The woman responds to me, but her eyes don't leave Rags. "I do."

Rags throws his arms up and takes two steps in the woman's direction. "Why're you doing this, Lottie? You trying to hurt me? Because I'll tell you right now that won't happen. I can't be hurt by someone who means nuthin'."

The woman, Lottie, clutches a brown bag decorated with gold LVs. I know that particular purse brand, Louis something-or-other, but only because Magnolia has schooled me in All Fashionable Items We Can Never Afford But Should Be Worshipped Anyway.

The lady has long, dark hair worn loose over her shoulders, and one of the largest mouths I've ever seen. She's curvy in the way that turns men's heads, and is dressed in a tailored hot-pink suit. Her makeup is flawless, no doubt bought at department stores with shiny counters and saleswomen in black blazers, versus the drugstore, where Mom picks up Maybelline mascara twice a year. From her polished heels to her gaudy earrings, this woman screams Grosse Pointe. But that part of Detroit is reserved for old-money types. And something about the way Lottie fidgets as she looks at Rags tells me her Louis Something purse hasn't always been so heavy.

I glance back and forth between Rags and Lottie, and think about the name she used for my manager.

"You two know each other, I take it?" I say, interrupting their stare-off.

"I don't know this woman." Rags's hands form tight fists. "Never have."

"Yeaaah, that seems unlikely. Look, why don't we all go into that room and sit down for a few. If you didn't notice, *Rusty*, we don't have any other interested parties. And may I remind you we were fairly confident there wouldn't even be *one* to speak of."

Rags points at Lottie. "I won't be in cahoots with the likes of you. I'd rather give up now."

I put my hands on his old man chest and shove lightly. "Okay, that's great. But here in the real world, I need a sponsor. So if you don't like this person for whatever reason, then take a walk and let me speak with her."

Rags finally looks at me. "You'll botch the negotiations."

"Negotiations?" I laugh once and lower my voice. "Rags, there's *no one else*. I'm going to take what I can get."

The woman chances moving a few steps closer. "It's *his* money I'll be spending, Rusty. And I won't be shy about using it."

Rags glares at the woman for several more beats, and then turns and marches away. Right before he disappears, he turns back and yells, "I don't like this. I don't!" Then he glances around like he just realized how ridiculous that sounded, and lets himself out through the doorway.

Lottie waves an arm toward the room, and I head inside and take a seat, my hands beginning to sweat. As strange as this feels, I can't help growing excited. Is there really a chance I'll race again? Does this woman really have the fifty thousand we need?

And if so, what will she expect in return?

CHAPTER TWENTY-EIGHT

Lottie folds her skirt beneath her and sits across from me in the interview room. "You're probably wondering how I know Rusty."

"Rags?"

She smiles. It's a nice smile. Makes me want to touch her mouth, which I realize isn't healthy. "That's right. He got that nickname from the engineers, didn't he? Rusty was quite ambitious when it came to the Titans. He wanted to know everything and do everything." Lottie's smile dims. "He sacrificed a lot in order to spend so much time with those horses."

I study Lottie's face. Her eyes seem sad like the bald-headed man's, but for a different reason. It's obvious Lottie and Rags have history. The question is what kind, and what happened in the end. Out of curiosity, I glance at her left hand. No ring.

Lottie produces a stack of papers. "I met Rusty at Hanover Steel seven years ago. I thought he was brilliant then, and I still do. And I saw the way you raced on Sunday night. You're a natural. A little reckless, perhaps, but a true jockey."

My chest expands. If she's trying to bait me with praise, she's doing a solid job.

"Here's what I'm offering, Astrid. I'll pay the entrance fee and any expenses you may incur along the way, including riding equipment and maintenance for the horse. In exchange, you'll attend any and all practices your manager sets, and you'll follow my lead when it comes to your public persona."

I squint at her. "What do you mean, *my public persona*?"

Lottie folds her hands. "I want you to accurately represent the county you live in. So, no pretending you're something you're

138

not, or wearing designer clothing to jockey social events. That sort of thing."

I grin. "So I can keep my jeans and tennis shoes?"

"Not exactly. I want you to be relatable to the working class in the greater Detroit area, but I also want you to be someone they aspire to emulate. A role model. Not a pipe dream."

Once again, I think about the magazines squashed between my mattress and bedsprings. My dirty little secret. She doesn't want me to be like the models inside. She wants me to be real, but better. An improved version of Astrid Sullivan that Warren County citizens and others like them can look up to. I like the idea. I wish I'd had that when I was younger. I wish Zara had it now. But how can I be that person?

"What if I can't be what you want me to be?" I mumble.

Lottie takes a ballpoint pen from her purse and slides it across the table. The pen cap has been chewed to bits, making it less intimidating somehow. "All I'm asking is that you try. Follow my lead off the track, and Rags's lead *on* the track, and together we might have a shot."

I take the mangled pen. "What about Barney? He's been helping us. And my friend, Magnolia? I want them to stay involved."

Lottie laughs lightly. "That's fine. What else?"

I swallow and lean back in the chair, avoiding her gaze. "How much will I get if we win? If you're paying for the sponsorship fee, then you'll want a cut of the winnings. How much will be left to me and my team?"

"I'll take back whatever we need to cover the fees and expenses, let's say seventy thousand, and then an additional two hundred thousand to cover the risks of putting my money on the line. That's two hundred and seventy thousand to me, an almost three hundred percent return. More than enough." Lottie nods to the paperwork. "The remainder would be split between you and Rusty. If my expense estimates are accurate, that'd leave you with eight hundred and sixty-five thousand dollars each."

It's more money than I've ever dreamed of holding in my hands. That kind of cash would pay off our house, and Magnolia's family's house too. Maybe I could even invest a portion into Magnolia's secret online store. She deserves that, and so much more.

"What about after the races end?" I ask, thinking back to the photos Hart and I supplied to the *Titan Enquirer* cameramen. "Will I be free to sign an endorsement deal if a company wanted me after the summer is over?"

Lottie opens her palms. "What happens after the summer isn't my business. I only want to be a part of you winning."

I chance a smile. "I want to be a part of that too." Studying Lottie under the fluorescent lighting, I know she wants more than what she lets on; most likely something to do with Rags. But she already changed the subject once when I asked. My concern is continuing the Titan season, and this woman is offering me a way to do that. So I read the paperwork quickly, breezing over parts because she's watching as I read and I'm afraid she'll change her mind if I take too long.

Then I take the pen and sign my name at the bottom of each page. After she does the same, she offers me her hand. We shake and grin at each other like two love-struck morons.

"I'll meet you at Barney's place this Friday after the race schedule is announced."

"You know where he lives?" I ask, fishing for information.

She shrugs her purse onto her shoulder. "I'm familiar."

Rags is waiting for me outside the interview hallway. He sees the papers in my hand, and looks at me expectantly. I nod to tell him what he wants to know. My manager curses loudly, but I don't miss the excitement flash across his face.

"We've got ourselves a sponsor," I say. "No cost to us. And no company to report to."

He presses his lips together. "It'll cost me."

I want to know what he means, but I'm too astounded that this is really happening, and I don't want to ruin the moment. So instead, I find my best friend and we dance for hours, celebrating, before Rags and Barney insist it's time to leave.

I fight the twosome initially, but after grabbing another two truffles, I relent, my mouth full of chocolate. After taking a few steps toward the exit, I overhear Theo Gambini listening to his younger brother talking passionately about salt mines, of all things. Theo stops listening and looks at me, tilting his head to one side as if he's studying an alien species. Maybe it's the buzz from securing a sponsor, but I find the courage to lift my hand and wave.

Theo hesitates. Then he raises a single finger in acknowledgment and the hint of a smile touches his mouth. It's gone the moment his younger brother sees who he's looking at. Arvin's brow furrows and he runs his tongue across his teeth like he's imagining the taste of my overcooked, ill-flavored flesh.

Arvin glares at me long enough for my stomach to turn. I didn't think anything could rupture the mountain of hopefulness I'd constructed in my mind. But I know what Arvin is thinking when he looks at me that way—*trash*. Unworthy trash that could reflect poorly on his precious, prestigious circuit. He may promote his races to the working class, but I can't overlook the gate that separates his expensive track and gleaming horses and privileged riders from those who are less than.

When Magnolia pulls me away, I have a healthy supply of dread coursing through my body.

The feeling is nothing compared to what awaits me at home.

CHAPTER TWENTY-NINE

Rags is gracious enough to drop me off out front. It's a first for him; not making me walk from his house. I thank him for that, and for the flowers. I don't expect him to say more than what he does, which is a gruff, "Be at my house at eight in the morning. No excuses."

I roll my eyes and smile as he pulls away, but when I face my house, my smile falters. The light in my room is on. Maybe Dani finally came home to, I don't know, gather her strength before leaving again to be with Jason. But if I know my sister, she'd be asleep already. It's eleven o'clock, and though Dani likes herself a good party, if she is at home, she's hibernating in bed. Always.

Raw nerves bloom in my stomach as I gather my feathered skirt and head toward the front door. I stop outside and peer through the window to the left to ensure my dad isn't up. He's nowhere to be seen. Probably off making a microwave function with only the use of a fork and a box of toothpicks.

Even though Dad's MIA, I'll still have to deal with Dani seeing my dress. My mom asked me to keep it from my sisters, and now I'm going to start a household riot.

I swish through the door and close it gently, then tiptoe down the hallway. My parents' bedroom door is shut tight, and so is Zara's. So I form a plan. I'll peek around the corner, and if Dani *is* back, I'll hop in the shower for a few minutes and return wearing a towel. The dress can spend the night in the hamper.

Though I'm not sure why, I find myself holding my breath

when I slyly glance around the corner, a criminal in the making. But it's not Dani I see sitting on her bed.

It's my father.

His hands are on his knees, and his head is lowered as if in prayer. But I know that's not right. I pull back lightning-fast, but that breath I'd been holding rushes out. Before I can make a break for it, my dad catches sight of me.

"Dani?" His voice is misleadingly soft. I stop, hoping he'll say my own name instead of my sister's using that same exact voice. If he did, I'd go in there. I might even sit next to him and lay my head on his shoulder. Tell him everything about my night and pray he understood my reasons for doing this. Pray I understand *his* reasons for putting us in this situation.

He doesn't say my name, though, and I know I'm avoiding the inevitable by standing in the hall. Am I really going to hide from my dad? Is he really that big of a monster? Guilt leads me to step into view.

As soon as he sees it's me, and I mean the *moment* his eyes wash over my face, he rises to his feet. Gone is the softness he fooled me with. Gone is the aging man sitting on his oldest daughter's bed, wishing she'd return.

Now there is only anger.

"Where have you been?" His voice is dangerously low. It takes five years off my age, and all of a sudden I'm twelve instead of seventeen.

My tongue attempts to answer him truthfully, but my brain won't have it. Call it survival instincts. "I went to a dance with Magnolia. At the Knights of Columbus hall."

"And you're just now getting home?" he says. "Did you think to tell your mother or me where you were going?"

I'm stunned silent, because my dad rarely asks when I will be home or where I'm going. He says he trusts his kids and doesn't need to hover over them, but in actuality, I don't think he wants the headache of constantly questioning us.

Before I can form another lie, he leans his head back and his eyes narrow. "That's a nice dress, Astrid. Where'd you get it?"

Ooh, that one is too easy. "Borrowed it from Magnolia."

I'm proud of myself for that answer. Look at me, one step ahead of the grizzly man!

My dad crosses the room in an instant and takes hold of my elbow. "I'd like you to look me in the eyes and answer all the same questions I just asked. Let's start with *Where have you been?*"

My body turns inside out: firing nerves and throbbing brain and pounding heart are now open for public viewing, free admission. I can't think with my dad this close to me, can't breathe when he's gripping my elbow this tight. My father has never laid a hand on me or anyone in my family, but right now, his fingers feel like they're made of iron. Like they'll cut right through muscles and tendons, and from here on out, I'll live with half an arm.

"I . . . I went to . . ." I can't finish the sentence, because I can see it in his flared nostrils. I can see it in the way his head shakes ever so slightly, like I've upset him in the worst of ways.

He knows.

"Say it," he growls.

I swallow a lump in my throat and whisper, "I went to Travesty Ball."

"Why?"

"To secure a sponsor."

"Why?"

"So I can race in the Titan season."

"WHY?!" His voice fills the room. It's so loud my brain rattles inside my skull. Tears sting behind my eyes and my bottom lip trembles.

"To try and win. So we can keep our house and be a family again."

"And you thought gambling was the way to do that? Did Grandpa teach you nothing? It was his debts that made us lose the last house. It was his debts that led to us living out of a car. And do you remember how that ended, Astrid?"

"I remember he was a better gambler than you, Dad!" The words leave my mouth before I realize what I'm saying. My grandfather's addiction was a loud one. He didn't care who knew so long as someone would lend him a ten spot. My dad, on the other hand, has the decency to be ashamed. I'm not even sure he knew that *we* knew. And now I've put it out there that I do.

"Anyway, I'm not gambling," I whisper, afraid I said too much. I try to pull my elbow away, but his grip is vise-like. "A man who used to work for Hanover Steel is lending me a first-edition Titan, and tonight . . . tonight I got a sponsor. Someone who's going to pay for everything so I can race." I raise my chin in a final attempt to maintain an adult conversation, instead of one between child and father. Even still, my voice quakes. "It's because I'm good." And then, a bit louder, "I ran in the sponsor race, and I finished in the top half. You should have seen it. You should have seen how this horse—"

He throws my arm away like a rotten piece of fruit. "You think I have any interest in seeing you make a fool of yourself? The only thing you're going to do is get yourself hurt."

I press my lips together to keep them from trembling. "I won't get hurt. You'll see if you come watch."

His nose scrunches like he's smelled something bad. "No. No, if I go up there then they'll all know you're my daughter. And that's a shame far worse than losing my job. My kid pretending to be one of them? Involving herself in the same gambling circuit that robbed us of every dime I'd saved over the last five years? You do what you want, but just know I want nothing to do with you as long as you're a part of that." He shakes his head and motions toward my dress. It burns against my skin, and suddenly I see myself in his eyes. Dressing like them. Pretending to be something I'm not.

Reminding him of every bad decision he ever made.

Like father, like daughter.

"You disappoint me," he says dejectedly, like he's given up on a great task. "I can't even look at you."

He walks by me, and that's when I lose it. That's when I stop pretending his lack of affection doesn't tear me to pieces. That this last bit of rejection doesn't burn those pieces to dust. My voice isn't my own when I speak.

"Daddy, please."

He stops in the doorway, but doesn't turn around.

Tears flow down my cheeks and slip salty-sweet onto my lips. "I wanted to help. I *needed* to help after what happened with Grandpa."

When I left Grandpa at the house when you told me to stay home, is what I mean. When I told Mom, and Dani, and even Zara that I'd be back soon, and what to do if anything happened to Grandpa while I was out. When my disobedience killed my family member and the trust I had in my family.

Every muscle in my body tenses awaiting my dad's reaction. He has to turn around. He must. If he doesn't, my heart will shatter into a million parts.

My mother's voice comes from the hallway, asking what he's yelling about, telling him to come to bed after he grumbles a response. My dad listens to her. For the first time in as long as I can remember, my dad listens to someone other than himself.

It's too bad that when he does so, it involves leaving me alone in my room.

Hours after he's gone, when I'm lying in bed wishing Dani would come home from Jason's, I'm still cycling through our conversation and what I should do to repair things. If I quit racing, we'll go back to normal. He'll spoon baked beans onto my plate and hand it over without a word. He won't complain when I bring a book into the room and sit as close as I can to a man I wish I knew—but never *too* close.

He won't be disappointed in me anymore.

But is that enough? No. I know what I have to do. I have to show my father I won't quit. I have to show him that mistakes can be forgotten, and he doesn't need to carry our weight alone, because that's what family does.

I have to win the Titan Derby. I won't settle for the way things are.

Not when I know they could be so much better.

PART III
THE SEASON

CHAPTER THIRTY

The next morning, before the sun has risen, I make my way to Rags's place. He opens the door in jeans and a white shirt, stained yellow near the belly button region. His white hair sticks up like it's trying to escape his head, and he rubs the heel of his hand into his eye.

"What is it, kid?"

"Let me take your truck."

"What?" He drops his hand. "No."

"I have a driver's license," I lie.

"Well. That's more than I've got." Rags studies my face, zoning in on the circles beneath my bloodshot eyes. "I know you didn't drink that much champagne."

I don't respond.

"All right, out with it. What's wrong with you?"

Again, I plead the fifth.

He scratches his armpit and squints at something over my shoulder. "Let me get my vest, at least."

Then he slams the door, leaving me on the porch, in the dark, until he returns ten minutes later. Once we've loaded into the truck and stopped by Magnolia's house, where she tells me through her cracked window that *No, she's not getting up this early, and why the heck am I waking her up?*, we make our way down a route I've memorized over the last two weeks.

The sun slumbers on when Rags pulls up outside Barney's house. He kills the engine. "What's this all about? You that eager to start training?"

I lower my head and mumble, "I needed some space. Mind if I hang in the barn for a while?"

Rags wipes invisible dust off his dashboard. "Yeah, all right. I'll go inside and wake up that good-for-nothing senior citizen. See if I can't make breakfast. It'll be a miracle if that man has anything more than stale bread and half a stick of margarine."

I peel myself off the worn vinyl seat and head toward the barn. Inside, I find the gray mare leaning her head out of the stall. I spot another horse too, a black stallion with one white ear, but he's not all that interested in what I'm doing there so early, and soon disappears into his feed trough. The mare, however, whinnies for attention, and so I rub her soft nose while keeping my eyes on the back of the barn.

Why hasn't Padlock poked his head out yet? As a Titan, his hearing is heightened above flesh-and-blood horses. I give the mare one last scratch and then make my way to Padlock's stall. When I see him huddled in the corner—a black tarp thrown across his back, his head buried in a mound of straw—frustration boils through my limbs. His eyes are unseeing, his body unmoving.

He's turned off.

I throw open the stall door and search the wall until I find his key. Then I slip it into his ignition and turn, ensuring the autopilot switch isn't engaged. Almost immediately, heat warms his cold steel body, and in another couple of seconds, the Titan draws up his weary head. It's a much different reaction than the one he had the day we first woke him. He seems off-kilter now, as if he didn't expect to have fallen asleep, and is now disoriented.

"Padlock?" I say, kneeling beside him. "Are you okay?"

His steel ears turn in my direction like mini satellites, and he moves his head so that it lies across my lap. I drop down into the straw—the morning light now slipping through the barn slats—and run my hand tentatively across Padlock's smooth neck.

"I don't know why they turned you off, but I won't let it happen again." I think about Lottie, and how she agreed to pay for any expenses we incur. Well, one of them is going to be enough diesel fuel so that Padlock doesn't ever have to be disengaged. If he's to help us win this thing, he deserves to be cognizant at all times. "Guess what, horse. We got a sponsor. She's going to pay our entrance fee so we can race in the circuit."

Padlock flicks his tail, which I take as a sign of enthusiasm.

I glance at the stall door and listen to hear if anyone is coming. All is still, so I lift Padlock's head and lie down in the straw beside him. Maybe he's not groggy at all. Maybe it's just this place, this certain time of day. When all is quiet and colors are muted and you can think clearly about what lies ahead. Or what happened in the past.

My thoughts fall instantly to my father.

You disappoint me.

"Padlock, I want to tell you something." My voice is barely a whisper, and already my throat is thick with lingering emotion. "I'd never be disappointed in you. No matter what happens this season, I'm proud to call you my Titan."

And then I lose it. Because right now, I need someone. It can't be Magnolia, because she has her own problems. And it can't be Rags, because he's so much like the man I let down when I went in search of my colored chalks. But this here—this hunk of metal that's burrowing his nose into my neck and looking at me with large, thoughtful eyes—this is perfect.

I lie next to Padlock and ugly cry for several minutes, and not once does the Titan pull away. He only keeps his head close and nuzzles my side, and my belly, and sniffs at my hair. Only when I've exhausted myself does the horse climb to his feet. Leaning down, he nudges me to do the same. I shake my head because I don't trust myself to stand on my own. But that's okay, because Padlock is there, offering his strong neck for me to wrap my arms around.

When we're both upright, I wipe my face and snort real lady-like. Padlock stares at me dead on, almost as if asking whether I'm okay, and I grow ashamed. It's ridiculous how much I'm letting my father affect me. And it's ridiculous that I care whether a machine sees me crying. Rubbing away the rest of my tears, I say to Padlock, "This never happened."

Padlock snorts louder than I did.

"I'm serious, horse. Tell anyone and I'll spill the secret about your raging crush on Miss Gray down the aisle."

Padlock glances down the way as if looking for the mare, and then ducks his head.

"Oh, boy. You know, you gotta do more than sniff at her if you want a chance over that white-eared stallion."

I allow my imagination to run wild and envision Padlock a year from now, long-legged gray colts fumbling after their father—half-flesh, half-steel. How awesome would that be? Pretty sure it's entirely impossible too. But then again, I wouldn't have thought architects and engineers could create a horse with human-like emotions, and yet Padlock surprises me more every day.

When the sun has appeared enough so that I can see the stable in all its run-down glory, Rags makes his way outside. He has two paper plates in his hands, and frustration masked across his face. When he sees me, he lifts one in offering. "I was right. Barney's kitchen is useless. But I got a couple of eggs from the coop, and found a ripe tomato in his garden that somehow survived his neglect."

I leave Padlock's stall and stride toward him.

He clears his throat. "You, uh . . . you get done whatever it is you needed to get done out here?"

I take the plate and dig the fork into the scrambled eggs, kicking my leg back onto the stall behind me. "Yeah. Thanks for this, Rags."

My manager leans back and shovels food into his mouth.

"I don't want Padlock being turned off anymore," I say between bites.

The old man studies me for a moment, and then looks at Padlock's outstretched head. "He's programmed to experience fatigue after enough physical exertion, so resting shouldn't be a problem."

"So he can stay on?"

Rags finishes off the rest of his eggs. "Yeah, fine." After tossing our plates into the aluminum trash can, he says, "You ready to train, kid?"

"I've been ready all morning."

"That's good," he replies. "Because we're going to try something new today."

CHAPTER THIRTY-ONE

For the next two days following Travesty Ball, I train with Rags. Magnolia comes along on Friday, so she's there when I attempt— for the hundredth time—to race Padlock off-track. The lesson is simple: learn to trust my Titan enough to use autopilot. But I can't get the image of that first day out of my head; the one where Padlock ran like a feral animal. He seemed faster then, sure, but he also seemed volatile, and I'm not sure I could have reined him in the way Rags did.

So I tell my manager, when Padlock and I dive into the mouth of the forest, that I engage the autopilot for a few seconds longer each time. He drives to the other side of the dense crop of trees and waits with a stopwatch while Magnolia cheers me on. But I never get faster. Not that I'm slow. Far from it, Rags says. But of course the constant turns Padlock and I make to avoid tree trunks and thick, claustrophobic foliage work to our advantage. Still, according to Rags we should be gaining speed with each run, at least a fraction. Padlock is programmed to learn patterns and anticipate almost any challenge when operating on his own.

"Plus," Rags says, pulling on his stubbled chin, "the horse should want to improve. It should want to win."

Yeah, sure, maybe computers can want things, I think to myself. *But not the way I do.*

"Maybe it's because it lacks competition," Magnolia suggests. "When Astrid switches him to autopilot, maybe he's not running at his fullest potential because there aren't other Titans around."

Barney quirks an eyebrow. "Not a bad theory."

Rags considers this. "Astrid, you *sure* you're using autopilot?"

"Yep."

Nope.

"And you're keeping it on longer each time?"

"Yep."

Nope.

He shoves his hands into his hunting vest. "Maybe we should have you start on autopilot and see what happens."

Tension forms a tight ball between my shoulder blades, and I'm afraid I'm going to have to actually attempt this autopilot business. Rags glances at me sideways, as if he's had me figured out this whole time and is just now calling me out on my lying.

Barney is mumbling his agreement that this is a good idea when I hear the sound of a vehicle approaching. I turn in Padlock's saddle and spot a pearl-pink luxury sedan cruising down Barney's drive. The Jaguar emblem on the front has been replaced with a shiny *L* set with giant rhinestones.

Rags curses under his breath as the Jag pulls off the gravel drive and heads straight toward us, slicing a path through the tall grass. I see Lottie smiling through the windshield as bright as that sparkling *L* announcing her arrival. She's still grinning when she steps out of the car.

"I don't know who you are," Magnolia breathes as my sponsor climbs out of the car. "But I know I like you."

Lottie laughs easily. "You must be Astrid's friend. I'm glad I'm met with approval."

"With a car like that, you're met with my deepest respect and servitude."

"Would you like to drive it?"

Magnolia's eyeballs nearly burst from her head. "I don't . . . I don't have a license. I got my permit, but I never took the test."

"How'd you find this place, Lottie?" Rags asks, interrupting their conversation.

"I've been here before, remember?" Lottie glances back at Magnolia. "You can drive it around Barney's property, if he doesn't mind. Just don't take it on the main roads."

Magnolia looks at Barney, and Barney looks at the Jaguar.

"I ain't gonna be seen driving a pink car," Barney says gruffly, but he's already walking toward the vehicle, running his fingers lightly over the hood and licking his lips.

Lottie tosses Magnolia the keys, and just like that I'm abandoned by my best friend. Barney slips in the passenger seat, pointing to the gauges excitedly, his mouth moving silently behind the windshield.

The woman chuckles. "How are you, Astrid?"

Deciding I'm being rude, I dismount and come to stand beside Rags. "I'm good. Thanks."

For the first time, I see Lottie is holding a large envelope in her left hand. When she sees I've noticed it, she brings it to her chest as if she's afraid I'll steal it away. "I brought the season schedule," she says, her eyes running over Rags's face. "They'll announce it tonight along with the jockey-sponsor lineup, but I wanted to show it to you as soon as possible."

This time, Rags can't hide his enthusiasm. He rushes toward Lottie and snatches the envelope. Lottie steps in closer as he studies the schedule, stopping occasionally to look at her as if she were giving off a manure-esque smell.

"There was a separate packet that included information on the Circuit Gala, and interview opportunities. The Gambinis are really putting on the works this year."

Rags hands me the schedule.

CYCLONE TRACK SCHEDULE

PRELIMINARIES

RACE DATE	DISTANCE	SURFACE
June 11	Medium	Cyclone Track
June 25	Long	Cyclone Track

*Circuit Jockeys Announced—July 2

CIRCUIT

RACE DATE	DISTANCE	SURFACE
July 9	Short	Fire Walker
July 16	Long	River Runner
July 23	Medium	Shooting Stars

*Titan Derby Jockeys Announced—July 30

TITAN DERBY

RACE DATE	DISTANCE	SURFACE
August 6	Undisclosed	Darkness Falls

*Titan Champion Announced—August 6

"I guess the preliminary races will be harder than the sponsor race, huh?" I ask.

"Bet your bottom they will be. A lot of those jockeys don't put in much effort during the sponsor race because they've already aligned with someone beforehand. Don't want to push their horse too hard before they have to." My manager shrugs. "Doesn't matter. You've proven you can run with the best of them."

"Why is that?" Lottie asks sincerely.

Rags glances at her like he's seriously considering feeding her to an alligator, if only he could locate a handy swamp. "The kid's got a gift. What are you trying to say?"

"Oh, I didn't mean anything—" Lottie begins, but I cut her off.

"It's fine. Honestly, I think we were all surprised my Titan did as well as it did last Sunday. I like the turns because I can calculate how to lean into them, I suppose. But really, it's the horse. It was well-designed and well-built."

Rags's face brightens from my compliment. "Baloney. The kid races well because she has more to lose, and more to gain. Simple as that."

"So she's a fighter," Lottie chances. "She's fighting for what she wants."

Oh, man. That look. Rags glares at Lottie, his jaw working back and forth. Whatever she said struck a serious nerve. After an uncomfortable moment, he takes the schedule back. "First prelim is next week. We need to start training harder, and get you prepped for the circuit races at the same time."

"Those are the ones with the jams, right?" I ask.

Rags meets my gaze. "Don't be afraid of those."

"I'm not." I square my shoulders, and Padlock nudges me from behind, reminding me he's there, and that he's also unafraid. Or so I like to believe.

"You've got a lot of training to do," Lottie agrees. "But don't forget I need her from time to time."

"What the heck for?" Rags challenges.

"For publicity training," she responds. "And to learn about her competition. She can't effectively outrace the other jockeys until she understands them."

Rags looks at me like I had a hand in what this woman's proposing, but actually, what she's saying makes sense. So I shrug and utter, "It's in the contract."

My manager grumbles about the "blasted contract" and something about a "devil woman," and eventually waves his fingers at Lottie's face, excusing her from our space. Then he all but shoves me into the saddle and instructs me to run the same path, and that he'll meet me on the other side.

He leaves Lottie standing alone in the tall grass as he beelines for his truck, and I shrug an apology, not sure what to say. Padlock prances beneath me, showing off for our new company.

I check my Titan's gauges and reposition my feet in the stir-rups, readying myself to shoot through the forest. I even allow my finger to linger over the autopilot switch in case Rags is watching.

"Faster this time," Rags roars out the driver's side window. "Eight days until the first prelim!"

CHAPTER THIRTY-TWO

On Sunday afternoon, two days after she first arrived, Lottie demands her first hour-long block.

Magnolia is beside herself with excitement.

Barney has cleared a room in his colossal, albeit crumbling, farmhouse, and says we can use it to do our "girl stuff."

"How was church this morning?" Magnolia asks.

"Awkwardness at its finest," I respond. I'm not sure my family said more than ten words to one another.

"Good times." Magnolia cringes as we climb the burping stairs, eyeing the dusty black-and-white photographs of people we've never met, places we've never been. "Do you think Barney inherited this place?" she asks, changing the subject.

"Without a doubt," I respond. "He got his hands on this house because his daddy left it to him, and he does nothing to keep it maintained. But that's Barney for you. He'd be just as happy living in the barn, and that's why you can't hate him for lucking into a place like this."

Magnolia runs her hand over damask wallpaper that peels at the corner. "It could be beautiful."

When Lottie hears us coming, she pokes her head out of the small room and grins. Her dark hair is pulled into a French braid, and she no longer wears the makeup she did at Travesty Ball. I can see her more clearly this way, though her features are less defined.

"Magnolia, I'm thrilled you've decided to join us."

"Uh, I wouldn't miss this for the world. Any woman who drives a pink Jaguar is someone I'd like to learn from."

Magnolia drops down in a chair, crosses her legs, and folds her hands on her knees. "Annnd . . . begin."

Lottie laughs and glances in my direction. "I take it you aren't quite as enthusiastic."

"I need all the time I can get on Padlock," I admit. "But you're my sponsor, and we made a deal."

Lottie crosses the room to where oversized sheets of paper are pinned to the wall. She picks up a red Sharpie from a cleared table and writes these words:

Etiquette
Grace
Aspirations
Loyalty
Strength

She sets the pen down. "We're going to learn about these five words every day, for an hour a day, except Sundays."

Magnolia raises her hand.

"Yes, Magnolia?"

"Today is Sunday."

"Today is an exception."

Magnolia nods like this is the most obvious thing in the world.

Lottie sets her gaze on me. "The first thing we'll go into detail on is etiquette. But because your first public race is in six days, we'll briefly touch on the others as we go along. Do you understand?"

"Yeah," I say. "Got it."

Lottie smiles. "Sit up, dear. And from here on out, you'll call me ma'am. This falls under the umbrella of etiquette, which are societal rules set by the upper class."

"But I'm not upper class."

"No, you're not. And don't you ever be ashamed of that. But proper etiquette is a language in which you should be fluent. That way you can communicate with anyone, on any level, and gain their respect. You don't always have to use this language, but you'll have it in case you need it."

"Cool," I say.

Lottie stares at me until I modify my response.

"Uh, that's cool, *ma'am*."

Magnolia rubs her hands over her thighs. "I'm going to like this. I can tell." She opens her arms. "I am but a piece of clay, madam. Make me into something more."

"Shut it, Mag," I mutter.

She sticks her tongue out. "Bite me."

Lottie returns to the board. She draws five lines from the word *etiquette* and attaches those lines to new words—meals, gifts, invitations, attire, language. "For the next hour, we'll go into detail on how to eat a proper meal, and the utensils you should be familiar with. We'll discuss what gifts are appropriate to give, at what times, to what people, and what amount is proper to spend. We'll talk about invitations, and how it's important to extend them to people of influence even if we don't prefer those people, and how to respond to invitations we are granted.

"Using me as an example, we'll also go over proper attire for different occasions, and how to put an outfit together that is both timeless and enviable by those of all ages and social statures."

Magnolia especially enjoys this last part, asking for a pen and paper to jot down ideas. When I glance at her, she mouths, *I got you*, as if she knows I'll never remember Lottie's points when it comes to dressing myself.

"Language," Lottie says, "is something I'll teach you over time. It's a delicate balance, speech. You want to use proper grammar and address people with respect, but you also don't want to lose your roots. Try too hard when you're speaking into a camera, and you'll come off as pompous. Don't try at all, and you'll come off as ignorant. You need to find a balance of educated and approachable." She picks up a small booklet and hands it to me. "These are presidential addresses, both major and minor. I want you to read through the more recent ones, in the back. Notice how the president uses words that are confident and precise, but never words that the common man wouldn't have in his vocabulary."

Magnolia nearly falls out of her chair to get a look at the little yellow book.

I clutch it between my hands with an eagerness that causes my cheeks to warm.

CHAPTER THIRTY-THREE

During the last half-hour of class, Lottie disappears down the stairs. When she returns, she's bearing a tray of food. My mouth waters, taking in the smells. After carefully setting the meal upon the table, she motions for Magnolia and me to pull our chairs close.

We don't need further encouragement.

Lottie motions to two small plates next to our larger ones, and then at a basket of rolls and dish of butter near the center of the table. "Please, take a roll and eat it."

Magnolia and I hesitate, as if we know we'll do something wrong. In the end, I shrug and make a grab for one. The smack on my hand comes when I split my bread in half and attempt to butter the entire thing at once.

"No," Lottie says gently. "Proper etiquette calls for you to place a small portion of butter onto your bread plate. Then, using your own knife, tear a bite-sized piece of bread away from the rest and butter only that part before eating it."

"Can I do a lot of little pieces at once?" Magnolia asks.

Lottie frowns. "One at a time. And as you eat that piece, be sure and place your butter knife down. In fact, you should almost never be chewing or swallowing anything with utensils in your hand."

Eating our bread takes an eternity, and Lottie explains that this is the point. It gives us time to chat with our dinner partners, and the smaller bites prevent us from having to speak with our mouths full.

Next, she gives us each a bowl of tomato-basil soup. The rules are fairly easy to remember on this one. Spoon away from our bodies, and then to our mouths, making a half circle each time. It's much different from the rapid-motion, loud-slurping bowl-to-mouth method we Sullivans adhere to. But I'll admit, when I lower my spoon to the bowl's lip while swallowing, I'm better able to taste the soup. And I notice things like what Magnolia is saying across the table, and I'm able to comment on what Barney is doing outside the window between tastes.

Lottie teaches us other things too, like how a salad is actually supposed to be eaten by slipping our forks beneath the lettuce and bringing it to our mouths, as opposed to piercing it. "In America, this tradition is fading," she explains. "So watch your dinner partners for cues. If they pierce the lettuce, you may as well. But, again, always place your fork down between bites while chewing."

Magnolia and I then share a breast of lukewarm chicken. I know Lottie must have brought this from home, and probably had to reheat it in Barney's microwave. Still, it's flavored with lemon-pepper sauce, and is juicy when we cut off a bite—*one bite at a time*—and slide our fork beneath the meat and bring it to our mouths. "Just like the salad, you may pierce the meat if others at the table are. But check first in case they're the old-money type."

Lottie holds up a paper towel. "Imagine this is your white cloth napkin. If you must leave the table, put the napkin in your chair. When you are done eating, place it to the left of your plate." She places it next to my plate as an example. "Also, when you're done with your utensils, place them diagonally across the plate, top left to bottom right."

Magnolia and I practice doing these things with fascination, learning this code we never knew existed, as Lottie checks her watch. She must decide we're out of time, because she says, "You are not of age to drink, but when you are, never order a stronger drink than your host, or outpace them in rounds. And if faced with a menu, ask your host what they plan to eat, then use that item as a benchmark for what to order yourself. If they are paying and are ordering a forty-dollar dish, for example, be sure your own dish costs that much or less."

"Forty bucks for a meal?" Magnolia exclaims. "What are they ordering, a golden goose?"

Lottie touches her shoulder. "I assure you there are many meals at many restaurants that are twice that amount. And if you learn to compose yourself as a lady, and keep ambition in your back pocket, you will eat at such places long after the Titan season concludes."

"Pfft. Yeah, right," Magnolia scoffs. "How do you know so much about this stuff anyway?"

"I didn't always," Lottie admits. "I was raised by a single mom, and helped raise other people's children before I knew restaurants with cloth napkins existed. But I got married about three years ago, and everything changed."

"Ooh, you got yourself a sugar daddy," Magnolia says, wide-eyed.

Lottie chuckles lightly. "I'll admit he had money, but he was a man of false promises, and so I used his money to become the woman I always wanted to be. I wasn't in it for the money . . . until I realized that's all there was."

I run my eyes over Lottie: her beautiful smile, hypnotic hips, and thick, black hair, subtly streaked with gray. When I look at her, I see two people. The girl she once was, and the woman she's become. I decide she didn't need this man's money to have class. Maybe just the confidence it gave her to become what she already was.

"Are you two still together?" I ask gently.

Lottie shakes her head. "No. The man I married wanted his work more than he wanted me. And I wanted the man I lost long before I met my ex-husband."

Rags appears in the doorway, breaking the sullen moment. He scowls at her before ordering my rear out onto the track. I jump up and make for the door, but then turn back and do three things: I place my napkin to the left of my plate, lay my fork and knife diagonal across the porcelain, and bow like a humble servant before her queen.

"Thanks for the lesson," I say with a mischievous smile.

"You may be joking, but you did everything correctly save for that bow," Lottie notes appraisingly. "Oh, and be sure to announce that you are leaving. Don't just bolt upright like a savage."

"This is what you're teaching them?" Rags snorts. "What a waste."

Though I teased Lottie myself, I grimace. "Why is it a waste? I could be like one of those rich track kids if I'd had someone to teach me."

Rags shoots me a look like he's disappointed. "You don't want to be like them, Astrid. Be a girl who likes a little dirt under her nails. Be a girl who isn't afraid to eat with her hands or speak her mind."

I think on what he's telling me. Then I say, "Why can't I be both?"

Lottie beams like I've handed her a silver moon.

Rags glares at her. "To the devil with you, woman."

Lottie ignores him and hands me an envelope that I'm to take in addition to my presidential addresses. "We'll cover these more in detail when we reach *Strength*, but until then, study these when you have time."

I give her a soldier's salute before racing down the stairs and into the sunshine. Padlock gallops toward the house when he sees me, and though I fight the grin that works its way onto my mouth, it's no use. I pat him on the shoulder and he noses my neck.

"If Lottie has her way, I'll become a lady before the summer is out," I say to my Titan. "But I'll always ride you like a savage."

CHAPTER THIRTY-FOUR

On Saturday, June 11, I wake with a nervous racket in my stomach. The feeling never leaves me. Not as I do six practice runs with Padlock (two apiece, stretching eight, ten, and twelve furlongs). Not as I wash my Titan inside the dimly lit barn. Not as Magnolia braids my hair, weaving in a yellow ribbon she embroidered with *Strength*, one of Lottie's magic words. And not as I sit in my room, waiting for the moment it's time to leave.

Tonight, I will run in the first preliminary race.

And though I have a team that's thick as thieves, I feel alone.

My father won't look me in the face, hasn't since the night of our argument. I think about what he said; that he could stop me from racing if he wanted. But he hasn't, and sometimes I wonder if it's truly because he doesn't want to call attention to our being related. Or more accurately, call attention to the fact that his daughter is involved in the same thing that shamed him the year before.

I haven't seen Dani for more than fifteen minutes in the last week, and my mother is already elbow-deep in Mr. Lakely's vegetable garden, though the sun still burns low in the distance.

After knocking on Zara's door, I poke my head in. She's in bed, her light off, her drapes shut. "Zara, I'm going now."

There's a rustle, and I see in the hallway light that she's turned over to face the ceiling. "Can I come with you?"

"No, Zara. It isn't safe outside the gates."

Zara has learned about my racing a Titan. I don't know how she found out, but one day she simply looked at me and said, *I know about the horse. I'm not so stupid.*

Zara rolls toward her wall again, and I watch as her back rises and falls.

"I can take you to the park tomorrow morning if you want," I say. "Like last week."

"Don't bother."

"Zara—"

"Leave me alone," she says, louder. And because I'm afraid my father will hear her and decide he'll lock me in this house after all, I softly close her door. She needs me, I know that. But what she needs more is stability, and we can't have that if I don't race to win. My mother's ring bought us time, but how much?

Not enough.

....

An hour later, Magnolia, Rags, Barney, Lottie, and me are unloading at Cyclone Track. The moon hangs heavy overhead, watchful, as we push the iron plank into place—diagonal from the ground to the lip of Rags's truck bed. True to word, neither Rags nor Barney has turned off Padlock since I asked them not to. So when the plank is secured in place, the horse simply rises out of his casket and walks downward of his own accord.

It isn't a glamorous entrance. Not when compared to the other Titans appearing from trailers that are sleek and black, or wrapped in sponsorship logos bearing the jockey's last name.

"Those big companies work quickly," Lottie says. When she sees I'm biting my bottom lip, she leans toward my ear. "Remember, Astrid, they're always watching. Show them a brave face."

She motions toward the cameramen stationed around the track, one hovering just overhead on a two-story platform. I react immediately, hold my head up higher, pat my Titan and smile as

170

if I'm hiding a deadly secret. I pray they don't catch the way my knees weaken with each step.

Padlock doesn't fidget as much as he did last Sunday, but his silver hooves still dance below his body.

"Let's get you in the stall," I say before reining him and placing a bit between his teeth. He walks after me without complaint, and I'm relieved to have a task to focus on as the cameramen snap pictures, and bet makers scream names and odds, and race-goers wave wads of cash. They are a good fifty feet away, behind the short chain-link fence, but it's as if they are inside my head.

Once we're in the stall—same booth, this time with my name hastily scribbled outside the door—I pull on my silks and attempt to drown out the shouts from jockeys up and down the corridor. Barney and Rags leave to fetch the saddle, and Magnolia escorts Lottie outside to see about securing me an interview after the race.

I'm alone with Padlock when I spot Arvin Gambini walking down the aisle. He stops at each stall and speaks briefly with the jockeys' managers. When he grows close to our stall, Padlock stomps his front left hoof into the dirt. Over and over. *Thump-thump-thump.*

Arvin smiles at me, and my skin crawls. "If it isn't the underdog, or shall I say, the underhorse."

I open my mouth to tell him what I think of his humor, but he shakes his head and cuts me off.

"I'm kidding. You two have added an element of excitement to this year's circuit, and I'm glad for it."

I find myself speechless, knowing I shouldn't trust him, but wanting badly to believe him. "You . . . you don't mind that I'm here?"

He shrugs a shoulder and leans over the stall gate as if spill-ing gossip. "I may have been hesitant at first, but it gets tiresome watching these Titan replicas race year after year. I always wanted to see a Titan 1.0 operate on the track. But then Rags—your manager, I believe?—left the company, and no one could quite finish or duplicate what he'd done."

"Oh" is all I say, because I thought Rags was fired. And Barney too.

Arvin slaps his hand against the stall door and straightens. "Where is that manager of yours? Gotta fill him in on some details regarding today's race."

"He went to get my saddle. Want to tell me and I'll relay the information?"

"Nah, I'll catch him." He studies me for a moment longer as Padlock *thump, thumps* his hoof. "You know, you remind me of myself. A fighter who doesn't mind bending the rules."

The back of my neck burns as I work out whether to accept this as a compliment. For years, Arvin Gambini has been labeled a slick-talking, money-hoarding businessman, preying on others' gambling habits. But as I look at him now, I wonder if he wasn't just a man with little money of his own. A man who had to prove to his grandmother, and himself, that he was worthy of running an underground empire.

"I'm glad you're okay with my being here," I say. "I've been a fan of the horses since I was twelve. Since before the first season."

"Because you were a dreamer," he tells me. And then he grins—shiny, bright—and I back up. Because I see it then, the crocodile grin he's giving me. He must see the crack in my cer-tainty, because he gives a quick wave and tromps away from my stall and out of the multi-million-dollar stable.

By the time my crew has returned, the Titans are already lining up, the lady with the clipboard checking off the parts to ensure no one is racing with an advantage. Rags and Barney secure my saddle, and I pull myself up.

"Did you talk to Arvin?" I ask Rags.

His entire face scrunches. "God, no. Why would I do that?"

"He came by. Said he was going to tell you something about today's race."

Uncertainty washes over Rags's features, but then he shakes his head. "Whatever he would have told me would've been mind games, nothing more. You know how to run this horse, and you know the course will be ten to fourteen furlongs, at best guess. So just do what we've trained for, and remember to check the cutoff time."

The cutoff time.

That's one of two qualifying elements to move on to the second preliminary race. First, I have to complete the race in a certain amount of time, which will flash on the board alongside the track length sixty seconds before the starting gates open.

Second, I have to place well enough to continue. Forty-two horses ran in the sponsor race, but only thirty-five will run tonight. That's mostly because of the *one horse, one jockey, one season* rule. The jockeys who didn't secure sponsors figured it was because they weren't prepared enough to compete this season, and probably opted to try again next year. Or maybe it's because they couldn't afford the entrance fee. In any case, I'll be racing against those thirty-four remaining.

And after tonight, there will be only twenty.

"I'll do my best," I say, my eyes focused on the line of Titans. "I have to go."

Rags pats my leg awkwardly, and Barney tells me he'll keep an eye on Magnolia. I hardly hear them talking, though, because now I'm remembering Lottie's lecture this week, and the envelope she gave me that first day we spoke about etiquette. I narrow my gaze on my competition, and in the folds of my mind, I run through what I've learned.

CHAPTER THIRTY-FIVE

Batter. That's the name of the jockey who's built more like a doughnut than an éclair. Where the rest of the jockeys are lean, aware of how extra pounds could slow their Titans, Batter is round with a swollen belly folding over his saddle horn. *They call him Batter* is what Lottie said. *As in, cake batter.*

His parents apparently own two high-end toy stores in Detroit, places that sell one-of-a-kind keepsakes. Have an old sweater from Penn State? Batter's family's toy stores can use the fabric to create a soft, dough-faced elephant for your new, bouncing baby girl. The family isn't rich, but they have one child who's never been told *no.*

Batter is a boy who is used to getting what he wants. He has blind confidence, something Lottie says I shouldn't ignore.

My eyes sweep over three more jockeys. Jockeys Lottie singled out on paper as being the front-runners this summer. The first is a girl no taller than five feet with a bright streak of blue running through her hair. Her parents christened her Roxanne, but she goes by Skeet on the track. Lottie writes that she's a scrapper. *Gets into fights on and off the track. A foul-mouthed twenty-something who wouldn't know proper mannerisms if they slapped her across her heavily rouged cheek.* Lottie's words, not mine.

Skeet got the money for her Titan from an uncle who died weaving his Porsche 911 through traffic on 8 Mile Road. When he passed away, he left behind a will bequeathing 2.4 million dollars to Skeet, and a winning strategy for racing a Titan. Today, it's Skeet you have to watch coming up your side, weaving her way through tight spaces, passing you by when you were certain there was no passing by to be had.

Skeet spits into her palms as I rub Padlock on his neck. I'm behind the tiny girl now as the Titans make their way to the starting gate.

I won't underestimate your stealth, I think at her before eye-balling another female jock. This one, Penelope, is closer to forty; a soccer mom who tired of watching her kids from the sidelines. She made her own money selling charms that hang from the corners of sunglasses. Everyone cheering for uniform-clad sons or daughters now wears Sun Charms on their eyewear, sterling silver wolves and red, glittery high heels and #1 MOM.

If you wanted to be friends with Penelope, you bought Sun Charms. If you wanted to have dinner with Penelope, and post pics arm-in-arm with her on social media sites that embarrassed your children, you became an ambassador, selling Sun Charms to your friends. And if you wanted to vacation at Penelope's step-father's Malibu home, you worked on her Sun Charms, Inc., empire until your French manicure chipped and your hair stylist called to say you were two weeks late getting your roots touched up.

Twenty bucks says those same drunken heathens outside the Titan gates have bought Sun Charms for their wives and girlfriends alike, Lottie wrote.

So Penelope created her own success. I won't let her teased blond hair, fake tan, and porcelain veneers fool me. She spent a decade building Sun Charms, Inc. into a multimillion-dollar business. And then she withdrew exactly two hundred and fifty thousand of those dollars and bought a Titan. Her first and only grand expenditure since her company took off. If Lottie is right, it's the Titan that she always wanted, not the business.

And those stay-at-home, bored-to-the-bone moms—with tiny trinkets dangling in their peripheral vision—were only a means to an end.

Penelope sees me watching and raises her head.

I'll hold your gaze all day long, her eyes say. *Try me.*

I look away, expecting her to smile complacently from the corner of my vision. But she doesn't. She only studies me as a robot might. Like her brain isn't tacky gray matter, but hard drives and cleanly written computer code.

Finally, finally, I glance at Hart Riley II. The jockey who told me I'd never touch a Titan. The jockey who thinks we have more in common than I think.

I think he's a pretentious, cocky, one-dimensional human being, that's what I think.

Even Lottie didn't have much to write about him. *I didn't find anything on the family name, Riley, and I don't know where he got his Titan from. But he finished first in the sponsor race, and I know he refused a partnership with Exxon-Mobil. Rags says his racing style isn't strategic. So I wouldn't expect him to do well consistently. Still, keep him in your sights.*

Hart's dark eyes flick across the track, taking in every grain of dirt, every pothole kicked up by Titan heels. When his gaze falls on me, I freeze. I'm not afraid of running against Hart Riley, but I don't like the way he looks at me—like an opportunity. Like a silly girl he can use and discard. His mouth twitches at the corner, and I have no doubt why. That smug jerk thinks he'll beat me again. He thinks I'm recognizing him as worrisome competition, and is grinning to drive the fact home.

And so as Padlock enters the starting gate stall, and the door closes behind us, I respond most appropriately. The way Rags would have me do. The way Lottie would shudder at.

I salute Hart Riley with my middle finger raised, and throw him an old-fashioned Astrid Sullivan wink.

Then I turn toward the digital display board.

The lights flash on, and the race length is announced.

Behind the gates, where I once stood on hot summer nights, the crowd erupts.

CHAPTER THIRTY-SIX

The race is of medium length. Two miles, slightly longer than the sponsor race. Long enough for me to gain an advantage. Sixteen furlongs. Thirty-five horses in total. The first of two preliminary races. And only three minutes to cross that finish line.

Digging my heels into the stirrups, I lean against my Titan's neck. I breathe in the smell of diesel oil, and listen as the chain-link gates rattle under the weight of frenzied onlookers. I don't glance away from my horse again. Not to study my competition, and not to seek out my trainer or best friend.

My eyes are on Padlock now.

I reach forward until I'm as close to his ear as I can manage. "We can do this. We have a longer run this time. And no one can take corners like we can."

I close my eyes. "I believe in you."

Padlock's ear rotates toward the sound of my voice. I hear it squeak as it turns on tiny gears in need of hinge oil.

I sit upright and run my hands over the control panel. Red splashes like a blood-soaked omen in our prison cell when I push the small black button. *It's the same track*, I tell myself. *The finish line will simply be farther away.* I repeat this in my mind, but my back prickles with goose bumps and my scalp tingles and it feels like someone is breathing down my neck.

But there's only me. And Padlock. And an iron gate standing stubbornly between me and my slippery sanity.

Oh, never mind.

The gate is gone.

I push that magnificent turbo button and Padlock jolts to a start. It takes him a moment to process the request. To realize it's go time. The other horses have already launched forward. But remember the slow and steady tortoise. Remember the early bird is actually annoying with his self-righteous eagerness.

An extra second.

Maybe three.

And then my Titan is off and I'm screaming my battle cry and Padlock is barreling down the track like a bullet that held its breath.

Thirty-five Titans race ahead of us.

But not for long.

Leading the pack is Hart Riley, the infuriating boy with his ridiculous red handkerchief covering his nose and mouth. How did he get out of the gate so quickly? He did the same thing at the sponsor race.

I brace myself in my polished leather saddle, the wind whipping past my cheeks as we dive into the black mouth of the forest, tree trunks molar-white against the darkness. My body rattles when we hit a dirt path, my eyes adjusting to the twinkling lining the temporary track like runway lights. I push the gas bar in concentrated bursts, eyeing how the small lights disappear in the distance into a turn. A heartbeat later, maybe two, we're leaning together—two lovers performing a sacred dance to the beat of rolling hooves. Padlock is down, he's down . . .

And then he's up, up, and away!

Already, we've passed three Titans. It's been twenty seconds according to my stopwatch. One hundred and sixty remain before we're disqualified. But no worries, because here comes another turn to save the day. To save the night.

Lean, lean, lean . . . fingers brushing the soil cast in red.

Straighten.

Repeat.

Seven Titans chasing Padlock's twitching tail now. Up ahead, I spot the four jockeys Lottie warned me about. Skeet is in the lead, then Penelope, Hart, and Batter. Batter is galloping with one hand waving over his head like he's riding a roller coaster, unsure on whether to let go with his other hand. *What if the ride bar isn't secure? What if the next downward dip is steeper than it appears?*

I'm close enough to make out the blue stripe in Skeet's hair.

One glance at the performance gauge tells me we're already flirting with the *warning* area.

You feelin' lucky?

Maybe.

Padlock and I brush past another Titan in the next turn, and again I tap the gas bar as we bend with the tide. Numbers form before my eyes.

100-degree arc.

Make that 108.

Counter-lean to the right at sixty-five degrees.

Keep Padlock steady.

Feel our weight as gravity sharpens its teeth. Adjust. Another five degrees.

There.

My fingers find Padlock's mane. I gather the silver threads in my palm and smile into the night. My heart pitter-pats watching my horse run. Wild, free, eyes rolling in his head. He may be on manual, but Padlock is present. He's here, anticipating what I need from him the same instant I input instructions. Maybe Rags is right about one thing.

Maybe Padlock really could perform as well on autopilot.

I push the thought from my mind, because I need this sense of control. If there's a cavity in each of us, unbearably empty in our bellies, this is what fills mine.

Twenty-six horses race behind us now. Eight are ahead. Four jockeys I know, the others I don't. I concentrate on the unknowns and charge toward them. Up ahead is another turn. If I time it well enough, we may be able to bypass another three horses. Padlock seems to sense my anticipation, and his steel hooves dig deeper into the soil. I glance down, marveling at his speed as my pulse shotguns through my veins.

It's then that I see it—

A red line.

We cross over it so swiftly I almost don't register its existence. When I glance back I see the mirage of it beneath a syrupy moon. Already, it slips away, too far back. I gaze forward, refocusing my attention on the next outside turn, this one to our right. Using the joysticks, I veer Padlock toward it, but my mind is still on that red line. On why it was there. On what it means.

My suspicion deepens when I spot those Titans ahead of us. They pull to the left as if they're afraid of this next turn. For one stolen moment, I consider doing the same. But what they're giving me is an opportunity I won't regain—a chance to take a tight turn while they lose ground. I could easily bypass the four jockeys I singled out. Maybe even one or two of the big dogs while I'm at it.

I lean forward, my braid lifting from the back of my neck. We close in on the turn and Padlock takes it like he's done it a thousand times. We're halfway through it when I realize the other Titans have slowed. Not simply veered away from the turn, but slowed.

I sit up, eyes widening—

And the ground falls away beneath my Titan's feet.

A trench, four feet deep, opens beneath us. The gate tumbles into the cavern, and in its place springs a line of spear-like objects.

Padlock falls.

Padlock falls and I fall with him.

CHAPTER THIRTY-SEVEN

At the last moment, I pull my right leg from the stirrup and whip it over the saddle. No sooner than my thigh is out of harm's way does Padlock crash to the bottom of the pit. I glance up and watch as six Titans leap over our heads with expert precision. Soon after, five more do the same. And then more, and more. We're in last place again. All because of a jam I should have seen coming. But jams are generally reserved for the circuit races, and this is just a prelim.

Padlock lies still, but after I push on the brake bar and twirl the joysticks, he's back on his feet. Grinding my teeth, I navigate my Titan upward. Padlock climbs the steep incline to the opposite side, and I lead him backward. Then we face the jump again. The other Titans are racing away in the distance. Though it's felt like an eternity since we fell, it's only been eight seconds. Enough time that we can still finish the race in under three minutes. But will we be able to catch up to the other horses?

I press down into the saddle and slam the gas bar. Padlock gallops ahead, and before I can think about what I'm doing, I press the purple hurdle button. My Titan leaps over the spears as I hang on to the handlebars. If Padlock hits the jagged fence below, it'll do little to slow him down. But for me . . .

My eyes snag on the arrowheads pointing straight up from beneath my Titan. They seem to stretch away from the poles they're attached to, aching for a taste of my flesh. But Padlock clears them easily enough, and soon we collide with the ground on the other side. Now we're off Cyclone Track, tearing down a narrow path that cuts between the trees. My hands return to the control panel, and I release a breath I'd been holding since we thundered past the red line.

We're more than halfway through the race, and I have no idea how many turns this new route will hold, but I steer Padlock faster, knowing that if I finish in the bottom fifteen it's over for me. And for Rags and Barney and Magnolia and Lottie too.

And for Padlock.

I glance at the performance gauge and see we're halfway through the warning area. Not too far from the red. But still, there's some wiggle room. And if I ever needed wiggle room, now's the time.

I drive Padlock onward.

His legs pump harder, as if he likes skirting this close to danger.

There, coming up in a few yards, is a turn around a crop of trees. Four Titans trail behind the others, and I set my sights on them. Clenching my thigh muscles, I hang on as my Titan attempts to make up for lost time. The dirt-and-stone track twists through the forest as the sound of the crowd dies away. Now there is the sound of hooves. The sound of jockeys straining against the repetitive impact. The turn is on top of us in an instant. Right before we take it, I think to myself, *What if this is a second jam?*

But no, the other Titans aren't shying away, and as they angle their bodies, nothing happens. And so Padlock and I join their ranks, my Titan and I hugging the turn like we're dear friends that time and distance have separated.

When we hit the sweet spot, I touch the gas bar. The smallest brush of my fingers sends Padlock driving faster right as the other jockeys are schmoozing with their brake bars. It buys us the critical seconds we lost, and when we straighten from our turn, we're able to blast away like never before.

There's a straight stretch, and in the distance is a line in the dirt, a man with a gun at the ready. It's the finish line, but I still need to beat out eleven horses between here and there.

The sound of the crowd resurfaces, growing in volume as the Titans rumble past. The noise of hooves stampeding toward the end is deafening, but it can't drown out the screams of the spectators, their hands shaking the chain-link fence, eyes widening like stars that ventured too close to the earth.

I see the white tickets in their grasps.

I smell their sweat and hope and desperation.

Did any of them bet on me, the girl from Warren County?

Time seems to slow this close to the end. I pass another Titan. Then another. As we increase our speed, we fall into a cluster of horses. How many do I still need to pass? Too many. Way too many this close to the finish line. There's nothing to do now. I can only hang on and watch, slack-jawed, as Padlock pummels the ground.

I breathe in.

I breathe out.

And we blaze across the finish line.

But we didn't make it. Not really. We only passed seven horses at best guess, and we needed fifteen.

The crowd cheers and curses and throws their beer bottles to their feet in excitement or frustration, depending. When the scoreboard lights up, my throat tightens. Magnolia is running out onto the track and the cameramen on the sidelines snap pictures of her as she flies toward me. They have no idea who she is, I'm certain, but there's a wild banshee girl appearing out of nowhere and no way are they missing that.

Magnolia yanks on my leg until I slide off the saddle. She smiles and yells something I can't hear. The crowd is too loud and my head is pounding.

"What?" I ask.

"You did it!" Magnolia turns me toward the scoreboard, and that's when I see my name, along with my time: 0:02:53.

"But I didn't place well enough," I say, dejected. "I only beat out seven horses."

Magnolia laughs. "No, dork face. You beat out seven*teen*. Were you paying attention on that last turn? It was amazing!"

A grin parts my mouth and Magnolia takes my hands and it isn't long before we're dancing in a circle. We yell things over each other like we do when we're excited, and I don't even see the other jockey coming until he's almost on top of me.

Hart Riley II jerks me away from Magnolia. At first I think he's going to hit me. It's what I'd like to do to him, no reason necessary. But then he takes my face in his hands and the look on his own can't be mistaken for anything other than concern. He runs his eyes over my body like he's checking for wounds, and then hugs me close. I'm too shocked to do anything other than sputter when he nabs the handkerchief from his pocket and wipes my brow.

I find my voice at last. "What are you doing, freak?"

"My darling, are you okay? I saw you fall!" He leans forward so his lips touch my ear. "Smile for the cameras."

He positions our bodies so the flashes engulf us, and the concerned look on his face deepens. Only I can see the falseness beneath his mask. Using my elbow, I jab him in the ribs. He grunts and backs away, letting Magnolia reclaim her rightful place as my person.

"What a tool," Mag says before smiling. "But seriously hot."

Before I do anything else, I turn and throw my arms around my Titan. My imagination may be taking liberties, but it feels as though Padlock's stone-solid chest swells with pride beneath my touch.

CHAPTER THIRTY-EIGHT

As trainers and sponsors flood the track, I glance back at the scoreboard. First place went to Skeet, second to Batter, third to Hart, and fourth to a name I don't recognize.

As I'm studying the board, Rags grabs me by the shoulders and jostles me like we're two dirtied, victorious guys on the rugby field. "You're okay, Astrid. You're okay."

"Yeah, I know."

"Him, on the other hand . . ." Rags's face suddenly twists with anger, and when I follow his gaze, I see who his frustration is directed toward.

Arvin stands between the tall man who works at the *Chicago Tribune* and his older brother. He's staring at me with a grin that sweeps from California to Delaware. It hits me then, why he's smiling that way.

Where is that manager of yours? Gotta fill him in on some details regarding today's race.

Those *details* were about the unexpected jam. Details that would conveniently impact me more than anyone else if I didn't know about them. If, for example, the person with those details never relayed them to my manager.

Rags must have made the connection before I did. That must be why he's marching away from me like he's about to put Arvin on his back. In the corner of my vision, I see Lottie running onto the track, yelling for Rags to stop.

Magnolia takes off after Lottie, I take off after Magnolia, Padlock takes off after me, and the cameramen take off after the four of us. If we all joined forces—cameramen included—I still don't think we'd be able to stop Rags from pummeling Arvin Gambini.

Rags collides into his prey and the two of them fly into the lush green grass growing inside the track, fists landing on shoulders, boots kicking shins. Now my manager is dragging Arvin to his feet, shaking him by his pressed white shirt, calling him a soul-sucking money-hungry scumbag.

Theo dives to separate them, but I can't help thinking his reaction is delayed when he wedges himself between Rags and his younger brother.

"You knew that jam would affect my jockey!" Rags bellows.

Arvin points at Rags from behind his brother's back. "You're out of here, you waste of space. You're *gone!*"

"You'd like that, wouldn't you?" Rags growls. "Toss me out like you did when I wouldn't give you the credit for the EvoBox. Hey, Arvin, have you been able to replicate what I built? Have you found my replacement as easily as you said you would?"

Arvin notices Lottie pulling on Rags's sleeve, and the smile returns to his mouth. "Hey, Lottie. There's a gal who found a replacement for you." Arvin opens his arms wide. "I like my women a little older, polished, and refined, with enough sense to realize when they're wasting their time with a penniless android-of-a-human-being."

Lottie's hand lands cold across Arvin's cheek. "You took advantage of me when I was hurting."

"I took advantage of *you?*" Arvin covers the place where she struck him. "It's good to see you're spending your settlement money wisely. Six months of marriage bought you entrance into *my* race, which I can respect, but with *that?*"

He points to me, and damn him—*damn him*—I suddenly feel like I'm the one who's been punched. Maybe it's the look of disgust on his face, or the sympathy on Theo's, but shame colors my cheeks. Padlock noses the underside of my arm like he's trying to reassure me that what Arvin implies isn't true.

Rags makes another lunge for his target, but Theo keeps him from advancing while simultaneously pushing Arvin back. The cameras don't miss a thing. They're faceless, those cameras, blinding flashes hungrily soaking up every last millisecond of my humiliation.

"You'll always be a has-been, Rusty," Arvin barks as he strides away from the scene.

"And you'll always be a scoundrel." Rags motions toward the journalist, and then at Arvin. "Don't trust him. He'll use you like he would a Kleenex, and with as much consideration."

"Let's go." Lottie grabs on to Rags's arm. When his gaze lands on her, his eyes swim with pain. As much as I adore Lottie, her betrayal cuts through me too. Lottie was married to *Arvin*? And she left Rags to be with him? It doesn't make sense, but then, I can't imagine many women would survive a romantic relationship with Rags. He's probably not the best with public displays of affection. Or private ones either.

Magnolia places her arm around my shoulders as the warmth seeps out of my cheeks. "Come on."

I stride toward the track, unsure what I'm expecting. Sympathy, perhaps? But that's not what I see in the jockeys' faces. They seem sickened by me, as if it's my fault their race day was dampened by drama.

"This is what happens when you bring trash onto the track," someone utters.

A couple of jockeys laugh.

"Did you have a nice trip back there?" Batter asks, grinning broadly.

More laughter.

Padlock is by my side in an instant. My nervous fingers swim through his mane.

Another jockey, one I don't recognize, speaks up. And when she does, it's like she's rehearsed these words since she first laid eyes on me. "Why are you here? We have one place left in Detroit where we can keep things normal. Without your kind shoving their way in, complaining about discrimination and handouts and special scholarships set aside just for *you*. These races are for those who can afford them!"

"That's right," Penelope says, nodding. "Those who earned it."

"Whose families worked for it."

Tears sting my eyes, because I can't believe this is happening. The cameramen are busy chasing Arvin and Theo in their retreat. Little do they know they're missing prime-time action.

Batter takes a step forward. Red blotches paint his cheeks. Like he's oh-so-cheerful. Like he's freaking Santa Claus. "You from Warren County?"

I don't respond.

"Yeah, I know you are. Do your parents work at all?"

"You shut your mouth," Magnolia says quietly, appearing when I need her.

Batter shakes his head, red curls bouncing. "You think we're being cruel. But we're only calling attention to the obvious. There was a day when the privileged were allotted, ya know, privileges. Now everyone thinks they're owed a piece of everything."

"You shouldn't be out here," someone else states.

I'm shaking with shame, but with anger too. Are they for real? This is like a part in a movie where I think to myself, *That'd never happen. People aren't really that ridiculous.* But this *is* happening, and I see my own hurt in Magnolia's eyes. She blinks it away, but the damage is done.

I storm toward their group, fury blazing behind me like a villainous cape—my father's rejection, our eviction notice, my grandfather's death, my mother's denial, my older sister's abandonment, my younger sister's anger. This cape of fury will protect me from the look in their eyes, because I have no more room in my heart for hurt.

"You think you're better than me? Because you have money and I don't? Because you have this sport that allows you to loom over those you deem less worthy?" I spit at their feet. Lottie would have my hide if she saw. "Let me tell you something, people like me keep this track in business. It's people like me who stand outside those gates and pay for bet cards. It's people like me who put their hopes and dreams on you and your horses. So I guess in a sense you're right. During these races, we look up to you. I know I did as a kid. I imagined you were brave and strong and resilient—everything I aspired to be. Everything every one of those men wishes to be when they return to their crap houses and crap jobs and crap lives."

I tilt my head like I'm seeing the jockeys for the first time. "I was wrong about you, and so are they. You're just a bunch of judgmental elitists, thanking the gods for that chain-link fence that separates you from the pigs. Am I right?"

Batter glances at Skeet before looking back at me. "Uh, yeah, that's about the gist of it."

The warmth returns to my face. I suppose I thought my speech would instill some guilt in them, but that doesn't appear to be the case.

"Are we supposed to be changed now?" Batter laughs. "Don't think for one second we're ashamed that we're rich and you're poor. That we're sad that we're here"—he digs his heels into the dirt—"and they're there." He points toward the men who are watching us speak without hearing.

Padlock pushes closer to my side, and I push closer to his.

I don't have anything left inside me. These jockeys stole any fire I had left to burn tonight. So I do the only thing left I can do, I tell my best friend that we should go home, and I lead her and my Titan away from the wolves.

I can't help looking back once. I'm not sure why I do it. Maybe I like the pain. Maybe it's better than being numb. When I do, I meet Hart's gaze. He's grinding his teeth, and I know in that moment he's not on their side. He hates Batter and Penelope and Skeet and the other jockeys who prodded me. But he isn't going to stop their harassment, either.

And just like that, my anger returns.

CHAPTER THIRTY-NINE

On the way home, after we drop off Barney and Padlock, and then Magnolia, I find the courage to ask Rags about what happened between him and Arvin.

"He's a dirtbag," he says. "Not much else to say."

I clear my throat. "But what did he do to you, exactly?"

Rags drives the distance between Magnolia's house and mine at a snail's pace. "Short version? Arvin worked temporarily for Hanover as a consultant, and promised the designers a hefty bonus if we could create an emotional hub for the Titan 1.0. And after I successfully did it, he tried to skirt his way out of paying when I said I wouldn't give him credit for the EvoBox." Rags grinds his teeth. "Back then Hanover Steel was a start-up company, so they had every excuse to pay us pathetic wages and get away with it. I needed that bonus, and I deserved it."

"Did you fight for it?"

"Bet your rear I did. Arvin's lawyers found some emails he sent promising the bonus and told him it was grounds for me taking him to court as long as I was employed there. But bonuses aren't a promise of payment, and if you're gone from the company, they're not necessarily owed to you. That's the beauty of a bonus."

"So he got you canned."

Rags shrugs. "Yep, you can do that when you hold that much stock. He told me on the way out that since he was quitting his temp position anyway, he didn't have to pay me a thing. Good thing we built Padlock at Barney's place. Those lawyers would have confiscated our project if they could have found him hidden beneath Barney's stable."

My blood boils for Rags. "What happened to Barney?"

"He quit when he found out. I told him it was pointless, but he wouldn't listen." Rags laughs. "Barney slashed the tires on Arvin's beemer that night."

"What would you have done with the cash?"

Rags stops laughing and sadness creeps into the corners of his eyes. "Do you want to know why I showed you the Titan Barney and I built?"

I overlook that he sidestepped my question, because this one is much more interesting. "Why?"

He glances over. "Because you have two things that make a winner: stubbornness and heart."

"How do you know I have heart?" The stubbornness goes without saying.

"Because you helped an old man on a hot day."

"You're not old," I say.

He raises that bushy eyebrow.

"You're *ancient*."

Rags chuckles, and some of the hollowness in my chest is quenched.

Since I've got him laughing, I chance a dangerous question. "Why do you hate Lottie so much? Because she left you for Arvin?"

Rags sighs. "It's not like she cheated on me. We weren't together when she started seeing him."

"So . . . ?"

"So don't hate her just because I do."

"I don't hate her," I say softly.

Rags remains quiet for a long time. And then, "Neither do I."

We're parked outside when I say, "Thank you."

"For what, kid?"

"For giving me a chance to do something big."

"It was either you or me. I'd rather you be the one who chances breaking a leg."

I bark a laugh.

Rags stares past me at my house. "Everything okay at home?"

I follow his gaze. "Why do you ask?"

"Because it's tough living in Warren County. And because you're awfully young for no one to wonder why an *ancient* man is dropping off their daughter at this hour."

"It's fine." It's not fine. We're teetering on the edge of a cliff, about to nosedive into homelessness.

"If you say so." I close Rags's truck door and pat the outside twice, signaling that he can leave. But before he does, he squints at something in the distance and says through the open window, "Look at that woman. It's almost two o'clock in the morning, and she's pruning her bushes."

I smile before heading toward my house, because that bush is actually a holly shrub. And that woman is my mom.

CHAPTER FORTY

The next preliminary race goes better than the first. It's longer, which allows Padlock and me to gain a better lead, and this time there are no jams to trip us up. The memory of the jockeys' taunting rested neatly in my mind as I ran that day, and in the end Padlock and I finished eleventh place out of the twenty Titans who remained.

Rags tells me I performed brilliantly, that the second prelim race is cutthroat because of jockeys wanting to keep their sponsors. It looks bad to bettors and the media when a jockey loses a sponsor, and with it free upkeep, fuel, and incidentals incurred by racing. *It doesn't take long for a jockey to lose their confidence on-track if the sponsor, media, and bettors turn their backs on them*, Rags told me.

Lottie swore she'd stand by me no matter what, so I didn't worry about that too much. What I did worry about was my placement. Even though I secured a better rank than I had in the sponsor race or first prelim, I still was only two horses away from failing before the circuit races even began.

Today is July 2, the day the local news channel announces which thirteen jockeys will proceed to the three Titan Circuit races, the ones the track engineers create. Rags informs me that these tracks will include jams at every turn, and it's time to get serious about training. I inform him that I've been serious since the beginning.

Tonight I have another session with Lottie, but today belongs to me. Well, sort of. Rags dropped Padlock and me at a pond at the east end of Warren County. The pond's still water breeds the plumpest mosquitos, and the abandoned factory on the edge grows spongy green mold up its walls. Small white blooms sprout around the perimeter of the pond, weeds that my mother would call wildflowers, and there's a span of crunchy grass to the left that stretches into the early-morning horizon.

Rags's instructions were detailed as always: *Spend time with your horse.*

That's all he said before shutting his tailgate and driving away. After two prelim races, he knows I'm not utilizing the autopilot switch. Says when I fell into the trench that should have been my first move until we were back on solid ground. Adds that if I don't learn to trust Padlock, he'll pull me from the season.

He'll never actually do that, though. Rags was sweating bullets after his argument with Arvin, afraid we'd really be kicked out. But word is the man from Chicago has an interest in seeing me continue.

Maybe he wants to see me nosedive in the circuit races. It'd be a lot more interesting than my being kicked out.

Padlock ventures to the edge of the pond and dips his head toward the water. For a moment, I think he'll touch his muzzle to the algae-coated surface and pull in a lukewarm drink. But he only turns his head toward me, the squeaking hinges in his neck reminding me he's a machine, not a real horse.

"We're supposed to bond."

Padlock snorts.

"That's what *I* said, but the old man's stubborn."

Padlock takes a couple of shuffling steps in my direction and stops.

"I mean, what if there are vagrants living in that factory? We could be mugged!"

I imagine Padlock having an eyebrow. I imagine him raising it.

Groaning, I fall back on the grass, watch as a grasshopper leaps to safety. The sky is having an identity crisis overhead, blue sky and white clouds on one side, darkness and doom on the other.

"It's going to rain, I think."

Padlock swallows the remaining space between us and kneels down in the grass. I turn my head, expecting him to look back at me, but he only gazes at the water. Unsure what I'm supposed to do with my Titan, I stare at the water too, watch as dragonflies dance above the surface. After a long silence, something splashes. A catfish, or maybe a man-eating alligator. One thing's for sure, there's one less dragonfly than there was before.

I flick my eyes toward Padlock. My chest tightens ever so slightly. "It's not like I don't trust *you*," I say quietly. "I just don't trust anyone."

Padlock's ear twists around. It's a sure sign he's listening. But that doesn't mean he understands what I'm saying. Even if he can experience human emotions, he's not actually human. So if I said things to him right now it's not like it would matter.

"I only trust myself now. It's easier that way."

I sit up, hug my knees to my chest.

Padlock lies still, front legs folded beneath his chest, his back ones kicked out to the side.

"I used to trust people. Like my grandfather . . ." I lick my lips, feel my heart clench. "But he lost our home because he couldn't pay for it anymore. Because he gambled too much. So we had to leave Wisconsin."

A small lump forms in my throat. "We had to live in our car for a while. It wasn't even that long. No big deal. But it put pressure on my grandpa, who had a bad heart. He took, like, eight pills a day."

I chew my bottom lip, consider biting my tongue off so I'll stop talking to a mechanical horse.

"We had just gotten an apartment in Detroit when my grandpa started gambling again, and he and my dad had an argument. My dad was pissed, so he left to cool off, but before he did he told me to keep an eye on my grandpa. Because even when my dad hated his father, he loved him."

My eyes burn. "But I remembered I left my chalks in the park. So I left to get them, but before I did, I asked my mom to watch Grandpa. And I tossed Grandpa's pills to Dani and told her he was having a bad day. And just in case, I told Zara to stay off the phone."

I get to my feet and angrily swipe tears from my cheeks. "It's not like I expected anything to actually happen. But it did. Grandpa had a heart attack and I wasn't there. And neither was Zara, who snuck outside to call her friend. And neither was Mom, who was busy looking for Zara. And even though Dani was there, she swears she doesn't remember me tossing Grandpa's pills onto her bed. So when he fell, she looked in the kitchen. And the bathroom. And in Mom and Dad's room. But the pills weren't there.

"By the time I got back, it was too late."

I glance at Padlock. The horse is certainly looking at me now. Big, dark eyes taking me in, both ears pointed in my direction. How long did I last before I told this hunk of metal my deepest regret—twenty minutes? Jeez, I need a therapist.

I shuffle toward the pond, stop at the edge. "I thought you should know why I can't trust you to save my family. This time, I have to do it myself."

I stand like that, my lungs pulling in jerking breaths, the tears continuing to flow, though I'm feeling lighter. Like releasing the story into the thick summer air somehow helped. Eventually, I feel a nudge on my back. Spinning around, I find a looming Padlock.

"Hey," I say, avoiding eye contact, feeling embarrassed about what I revealed, even though that's nuts.

Padlock nudges me again and I smile, relieved to have the tension broken. When he lowers his head again, I wrap my arms around his neck, bury my face in his steel-threaded mane. We stay like that for some time, the loons wailing to one another, my shoulders aching from how tightly I'm holding Padlock. My heart opens to this horse that lay dormant and dusty in Rags's basement, but has done so much for me since. What will happen to him after the races end? Somehow, already, I can't imagine him not being around.

My Titan takes a step closer, and I smile at how comforting this steel horse is behaving. It's almost as if he's a real, live animal with . . .

Padlock takes another step and I stumble backward.

"Hey, be careful. You're going to accidentally—"

Padlock dips his head lower until his nose nuzzles my belly button. Then he tosses his head upward and my arms flail. At the last minute, I grab on to his neck. But now Padlock is walking toward me with gusto, and I have no choice but to fumble backward or fall under his hooves.

"What are you doing?" My shoes splash into the pond as I attempt to stay upright. Now the water is up to my ankles. "Padlock, stop. *Stop!*"

Padlock pauses and looks at me with what can only be described as a robotic grin.

"You think this is funny?"

Padlock head-butts me.

I fly backward and land on my rear in the pond. The water soaks through my jeans and shirt and dampens the ends of my hair. My mouth gapes open. I tell my horse my worst nightmare, and this is his response? I consider turning him off. I consider marching miles to the closest town, calling Rags, and screaming through the phone. Instead, here's what I do—

I splash my Titan in the face.

His head jerks up and he blinks long lashes to clear the water from his eyes.

"How's it feel?" I ask.

Padlock blows hard through his nostrils, and a fine mist sprays across my face.

"Oh, dude. Gross!"

Those are the last words I utter before my Titan backs up and then barrels toward me. My eyes nearly explode out of my skull watching him advance so quickly. I cover my head and scream, terrified he's about to pummel me. At the last second, I uncover my face and watch, mystified, as Padlock soars over my body. The underside of his black, shiny belly reflects my awe as he arches toward the water.

There's a loud splash, and a second later a wave curls over my head and slams down on my shoulders. Water no human on earth should touch rushes into my mouth and ears and nose. I spin around, my rear still stuck firmly in mud, and prepare to give my Titan a tongue-lashing.

But when I glimpse him swimming in circles, head bobbing above the surface, I can't help but laugh. Because he looks absolutely absurd. And though this pond is filthier than Dani's boyfriend, the cool water is invigorating.

Since I'm already drenched, and infected by whatever water-borne bacteria calls this pond home, I stand up, take three powerful steps, and leap toward my Titan. When my head breaks the surface, I swim toward Padlock, splashing him and laughing when he snorts more water.

I reach my horse at last and climb onto his back. He remains still as I curl my legs around his sides and grab on to his mane. Then we're off, wading through lily pads and cattails.

Padlock eventually tires of swimming and arises from the water like a mythological creature. I ride bareback as he trots through swarms of grasshoppers and startled robins. Though it's useless at this point, I wipe my hand over Padlock's control panel, hoping his dashboard is water resistant. After cleaning it off as best I can, I find myself wondering about this mechanical horse, and how exactly he does what he does.

"How'd you jump over me without being commanded to, Padlock?" I ask softly. "How do you do anything without my working your panel?"

Padlock swivels his head partway, and one glittering eye stares back. Then he picks up his pace, his trot morphing into a gallop. My heart reacts, but this time it's not for the grandfather I lost. It's for the horse that's reassuringly solid. No matter how far he travels, I don't grow anxious. No matter how fast he runs, I'm not afraid. And when the sun washes over our backs, I gaze up and let the warmth spill across my face. It seems the sky has finally made up its mind.

It's going to be a good day.

CHAPTER FORTY-ONE

Lottie's lessons are beginning to sink in, and that's good, because the woman tells me she's set up my first large-scale interview to take place after the first circuit race. Rags is irritated, of course, because he'd prefer that I focus on the track. But I'm starting to enjoy learning Lottie's secret language. I love my parents, but they haven't been exposed to the things Lottie has.

She teaches Magnolia and me about grace, about holding your tongue when you'd rather bash in someone's face. She shows us how to walk like a lady, reminds us to cross our legs while sitting, and tells us we must always have sympathy for those experiencing hardships, regardless of who they are.

She also talks about aspirations. How a lady worth knowing is one who pursues her desires. *Rub your goals into a stone*, she says. *Keep the stone close, and each morning when you put it in your pocket, and each night when you remove it, repeat them to yourself. Look in a mirror. Tell yourself you are all the things needed to accomplish this goal.* Lottie actually had us spend ten minutes alone in Barney's bathroom, staring into the mirror. For the first eight, I purposely ignored my reflection. That or I made faces, curling my lips back and opening my mouth as wide as I could. When Lottie knocked on the door and announced that I had a few seconds left, I glanced back at the mirror and said, in a rush, in a whisper—

"I am brave. And strong. And intelligent. And anything else that'll help me with the Titan Derby." I grimaced. "But not graceful. Never graceful unless Lottie's watching."

Lottie yelled through the door then. Guess I'd said the last part too loudly.

Now, as I swing Padlock's saddle onto his back, I remember Lottie's words, feel the smooth stone heavy in my new breeches. I run my hands over my new boots and silks, the ones Lottie bought. My colors are the same—yellow and black—but whereas my old silk had simple stripes, this one has an alpha symbol.

Padlock was the beginning is all she said.

Lottie bought a secondhand trailer too, had it painted black, and put that same symbol on its side. I look like one of them now, can walk and talk like them. But I am not them. I'm me. I'm a girl from Warren County who's here to save my family.

"You're going to do great." Magnolia makes me sit down and hold still while she braids a piece of my hair across my head and twists the rest into a bun, securing it with a yellow shimmering net. "About what you said before. About your racing being the same as what our dads do."

I hold my breath.

"It's not," she says firmly. "Our dads gamble for the rush. They hold cards in their hands and toss money on the table, but that's it. They're not *working* for anything when it comes to those bets. They're not putting in the effort." Magnolia tucks a stray piece of hair behind my ear. "It's one thing to gamble away money you don't have. It's another to bet on yourself."

My chest tightens with gratitude as I mumble an inadequate "Thank you, Magnolia." And then, because I know she needs to hear it, I say, "I'll be fine out there."

She shrugs. "We've seen a lot of jams over the years. How many new tricks could they come up with?"

Her voice is small when she says this, though, because over the last five years we've never seen a jam repeated twice. Magnolia continues fussing with my hair, and I know why.

"Mag, I won't take any unnecessary risks."

Lie.

"You promise?"

"Swear."

Fingers crossed behind my back.

I hug my friend close, for everything she's done for me over the last five years. She sees the best in me, and having her around makes me a better person.

"What was that for?" she asks.

"Because you're fan-freaking-tastic."

She bobs her head. "You speak the truth."

Rags and Barney come in a moment later, and while Barney checks my saddle, Rags gives me a pep talk. It goes something like this: "Do good. Don't get hurt or we won't make it to the next race."

Then he does something extraordinary: Rags pats me on the back. Three pats, quick succession. I grin as he clears his throat and avoids eye contact.

He may not know this, but his touch means everything. He's nervous I'll get injured, and for good reason. But he also believes in me the same way Magnolia does.

"Thank you, Rags," I say.

Rags coughs. "You already thanked me before. Now you're just being irritating."

I laugh and pull myself up into the saddle. "Away with you, old man. I've got a race to win."

This time, a smile graces his face, and when he meets my gaze, he nods. My manager leads Barney and Magnolia outside the stables, and I lean down onto Padlock's neck.

"There are thirteen horses left, Padlock. All we have to do is finish in tenth place or better." I swallow, and my heart picks up. "This race won't be like the others. It'll go off-course, and we'll need to be ready for anything." I sit up and stroke my Titan's mane, nervous energy coursing through me.

There's no time left to worry, because the woman with the clipboard is checking off our names and inspecting our horses for illegal parts. And soon we're corralled into the starting gate. I don't miss the way the jockeys glare as I lead Padlock into our stall, but I block it out. They don't exist anymore. Nothing does except this race.

The crowd is thinner tonight, but not for lack of attendance. The men weave through the forest, past Cyclone Track and into the trees beyond. The circuit tracks are lined by temporary fences, illuminated by miniature glowing lights. The first race of three will be a short one, and the crowd will get an intimate look at every moment, cheering from the sidelines or throwing beer bottles and cigarette butts and cursing the horses that run against their own.

If the first three races were chaotic, the next three will be sheer insanity.

I set my gaze ahead and try to see where the track ventures. What jams lie ahead. But there's nothing. I only have one piece of information. The name of the race: *Fire Walker.*

I do as Rags instructed. Envision myself finishing in the top ten. Envision attending the Circuit Gala in three days' time with my head held high. Magnolia will be my radiant date, and my team will be proud to call me their jockey.

Yellow.

Yellow.

Padlock throws himself against the starting gate, a wild, manic thing who matches my mood like he can feel it. It seems we both remember our first preliminary race. The one where the other jockeys told us in no uncertain terms where we stood in their pecking order.

Yellow.

Tonight, we have something to prove.

Tonight, I must remember why I'm racing.

And just like that, I find myself searching the crowd for my father. I'm not sure why it's his face I want to see. And I have no idea why I believe for one second that I'll spot him. But I look anyway, and my heart breaks all the same.

Thank goodness for distractions.

Thank goodness for the starting gate pulling away.

Green.

CHAPTER FORTY-TWO

The Titans rumble from their chutes, and once again Hart is the first to appear, with everyone else a heartbeat behind. One five-minute mile lies against us, and the horses drink up the distance. This time, when I cross over a red line painted faintly in the dirt, I'm ready.

Funny how I never spotted the lines as a kid.

That's what's on my mind as the fence arching around the first turn falls away. Just as it did two races ago, the ground collapses and the fence vanishes. This time though, no spears appear. Instead, something much more dangerous does.

Fire roars from the pit, licking upward, huffing smoke into the air.

The first jockey to reach it, Skeet, navigates her Titan up and over without missing a beat. It's almost enough to make me wonder whether Arvin filled the others in on the jams this time too. But I know better. He may have tried to get me disqualified, but he also wants a fair race among the leading jockeys since the journalist is watching.

Another two Titans blast toward the fire. The first one soars over it with ease, but the second one stumbles when it reaches the other side. The horse seems dazed, and the jockey running it quickly punches orders into the control panel. The fire must have overheated the Titan's engine. The horse recovers quickly, but I make a mental note to treat this jam with caution as Padlock and I near its border.

Hart leads his Titan to the outer edge of the fire and hits the hurdle button. The flames burn lower on the perimeter of the jam, and he's able to clear them with ease. As the other jockeys continue to take their Titans straight over the top, I follow Hart's lead and line Padlock up near the left side. I punch the gas bar and my horse rages forward. I wait until we're close. Then I wait even longer. Only when I feel the heat of the flames tingle against my skin do I slam the hurdle button.

Padlock flies over like he's Neil Armstrong, his hooves hitting the dirt the first steps on a terrestrial moon. I eye our competitors and set my gaze on the Titan whose engine has overheated. Though the horse still runs, it's slower than before. As trees whip by, and men cheer from behind temporary gates, I drive Padlock faster. There's a turn ahead, and I have to use it to bypass the others. With the race only a mile long, there's no telling how many turns there will be.

I press down into the saddle, and when I navigate Padlock toward the turn side, he charges toward it as if in agreement.

Way ahead of you!

Batter and Penelope reach the turn first, and when they do, a brightness flashes through the fog. I touch the brake bar, and as we grow closer, I understand what slows the horses.

Flaming arrows shoot across the track, stemming from the same turn I need to hug. While the other horses don't display anxiety, my own Titan raises up on his back legs. I'm nearly thrown from the saddle, and I have to yell words of comfort to encourage Padlock to keep galloping.

We're five yards from the turn when I spot a second injured Titan, a steel spear protruding from its glowing red eye. The horse bucks wildly, its computer system sending errors throughout the Titan's body. The man driving the machine gets it under control, and soon they're off again, but much slower than before, and with whirls of black smoke curling from the Titan's eye.

I slow Padlock and watch as the remaining Titans race past the flaming arrows. Numbers fill my head as they always do. This time, it's the number of seconds between each arrow.

One, two, three, four—*shoot*.

One, two, three, four—*shoot*.

After the next arrow releases, I ease off the brake bar and slam on the gas instead. Padlock races past the place where the danger lies, and we're off again.

After a powerful dash, two horses fall behind, both injured from jams. Ahead lies a second turn, and after Padlock and I take it, we pass another Titan. Electric energy courses through my veins, believing I've tackled another race. After all, we can't be that far from the finish line, and already I've passed three Titans.

I scan the track as the crowd roars from either side, and try and make out who's in the lead. It's Skeet, her blue-streaked hair whipping behind her head. No sooner do I have her in my sights than her Titan is thrown onto its side. I don't understand what's happened until I spot cannonballs of fire dropping from the sky. I look up once, try to decipher the source of the jam, but my eyes are no match against the low-hanging clouds.

Skeet's Titan struggles to its feet while the rest of us charge our Titans past. This time, there's no pattern to the jam. The cannonballs land in different places, and there isn't a set time between the moment one hits and when the next will fall. I grit my teeth and shove my fear deep into my belly, remember that both my family and Magnolia's family is at stake. But mostly, I push the fear down because it threatens to overwhelm me. Treacherous thoughts slip into my mind as we blaze past the cannonballs.

Is saving my family's home worth risking my life?

And another thought too—

What about Padlock, my partner? Is it worth risking him?

My hands shake as I steer Padlock through the use of the joysticks. Sweat coats my face from the heat of the flames, and from the panic rising up my spine. I realize I'm failing at controlling my emotions, that I'm losing my grip and my place in this race. My mind reels and my arms quake and Padlock veers recklessly, confused by the mixed signals I'm sending through the control panel.

Run faster. Faster!

No, slow down or we'll die!

A voice rings out louder than the others. I'm not sure where it stems from, my left or right, but it's sure and strong and it calls out my name.

"Let's go, Sullivan! Go, go, go!"

Just as soon as it's there, it's gone. Already a distant sound. But I heard it. Someone at this race was calling my name. Someone has placed a bet on me. Renewed confidence blazes through my veins. My name is Astrid Sullivan, and I am the same as the people outside those gates. If one person believes I can win, then maybe another one does too. There's no telling how many fans hold my name in their hand, how many hold Padlock's name too.

I lean forward and push Padlock past the remaining cannonballs. Checking my performance gauge and ensuring we're safe, I set my attention on the last remaining jam. There's no way more than one stands between here and the finish line. There's too little time remaining.

Narrowing my eyes, I make out more fire, flickering orange and red against the darkness. A narrow wedge cuts a path between the flames, more like a bridge than anything. Three horses race behind me, and nine lie ahead. If I can pass two more between here and the end, I'll finish in fifth, my best place yet. It's not good enough for the final Titan Derby, but it's good enough for a circuit race.

I set my sights on the closest jockey, Penelope. She's fallen from her first-place spot into ninth, and though Lottie believes she has a chance at winning this whole thing, tonight I want her watching Padlock's tail.

The problem is, I don't know how to pass her.

The bridge is coming up faster than I'd anticipated, and already I see Titans clashing against each other to get onto the bridge before their competition. This is the moment Rags would have me use Padlock's autopilot. But how could a machine utilize this jam better than a human brain? It couldn't. And so I toggle between two ideas to pass Penelope.

One, thrust farther into the performance gauge and cut her off at the last moment. Two, use the hurdle button to leap over her Titan and land on the bridge.

My brain buzzes between the two options until I have no time left to contemplate my next move. Releasing a scream, I push the hurdle button. The problem is, I also slam the gas bar and turn the joysticks as if I'm going to bypass Penelope. I had two options, and in my panic, I tried to do both.

Padlock takes two more accelerated steps, veering to the left, and then soars into the air. I hold my breath as my Titan arches up and over the jockey. Midair, I glance down and see the whites of Penelope's widened eyes. I'd smile at her if I wasn't worried about our landing.

Padlock lands hard in front of Penelope, his back legs kicking her Titan in the muzzle. Because we took off at an angle, my horse fumbles to regain solid footing, the momentum we built threatening to send us over the side. I shouldn't have pulled to the left. I'm an idiot and now we're both going to burn.

Heat travels up my leg and flares close to my breeches. We're terrifyingly close to spilling over the edge, one footstep away from being engulfed. The jams all have an off switch in case jockeys' lives became endangered. But would the engineers be quick enough this time? Would the medics be close enough to help if I fall?

They aren't always.

At last, Padlock finds his balance, and with Penelope firmly behind us, my Titan races forward. I ease off the gas bar as we gallop across the bridge, giving my horse a chance to recover. Then as we reach the other side, it's full steam ahead.

Padlock's eyes cut through the fog as we chase the remaining eight horses. The cries of the crowd grow louder, telling me the finish line is close. I can't see it, though, which can only mean one thing . . .

A single steel Titan races just ahead of us, and one beautiful turn lies between us and the end. Numbers flash through my head as the jockey guides his horse toward the curve. He's close enough to use the bend to his advantage, to shave precious seconds off his time, but there's still space for Padlock and me if I'm right.

I nudge the gas bar, check our stopwatch, and steer the joysticks to the right. Then I lean with my Titan and bite down. Sparks fly as we sail past our rival. No one I know well, but they must know me, because I hear them curse my name as Padlock and I zip toward the finish line. A gun fires, and I ease off the gas, say hello to my old pal the brake bar.

Eighth place, our best yet. And at 0:03:27, we're well within the allotted time.

Outside the gates, people shout my name with glee. Only a few of them, but it's enough. I raise my arm and wave to my supporters, and when Magnolia, Rags, Barney, and Lottie meet me on the track, my heart swells with pride. It isn't until I slide down from my saddle, and throw my arms around Padlock, that I can breathe again.

"You did well," I tell my Titan.

I don't miss the way Rags grins, as if he's calling me on the fact that I've fallen for this piece of metal he calls a horse.

Suppose it's true.

Suppose I have.

CHAPTER FORTY-THREE

The Circuit Gala is everything Magnolia and I could have hoped for, with a side of mini raspberry tortes. To our amusement, we find that no matter how many times we swipe food from the servers' trays, they return with more. It almost seems as if they're happy to have two girls enthusiastic about their food.

When it comes time to sit down at round tables covered with white cloths and orange overlays, Magnolia and I use every trick Lottie taught us. The four other guests seated at our table aren't pleased to be there, but when we take tiny bites, and make polite conversation, and place our utensils down at all the right moments, the tension leaves their shoulders.

Lottie sits at a nearby table with Rags, and though she checks on us often, she has her hands full trying to get my manager to behave. The invites were for jockeys, sponsors, managers, and one guest, but I have no doubt that Rags will sneak Barney in once the dancing begins.

"I read the interview you gave after the first circuit race," an older woman says between tastes of her steak tartare. "You made some rather intuitive remarks about the upcoming races."

. . . for a girl from Warren County is what she doesn't add.

I swallow a fingerling potato, wipe my mouth, and place my fork down. "Thank you. I'm doing my best to represent my county." I note that she's the mother of a jockey who's seated across the room with her manager. It's like they're trying to intentionally create gossip fodder for the *Titan Enquirer* by separating us. I rack my brain, and recall her daughter's name. "You're Janelle's mother, right? You must be very proud. She interviewed with several publications after the race as well, all far more esteemed than *Warren County Morning*."

The woman smiles, pleased that I've acknowledged her daughter and my societal place beneath her. "She did well," she agrees. "But you held your own."

The last part is difficult for her to admit, but Lottie swears it's true. She says race-goers are starting to think of me as their representative. If I can ride a Titan in the circuit, acquire a sponsor, and have a chance at winning two million dollars, why can't they?

If I can follow my dream, why not them?

You're relatable, she says. *And yet you give them something to aspire to.*

If they only knew I spent every waking moment terrified that I'll fail my family, afraid I have no chance of winning, they wouldn't think so highly of me. Of course, we're probably only talking about a dozen or so people.

"They really made this place beautiful." Magnolia admires what the Gambini brothers did to the community center. Ribbons of gold and orange dangle from the ceiling, and the walls are splashed in similar colors with the help of party lights. A parquet dance floor is assembled in the center of the room, and a string quartet plays softly on a stage. The Titan Derby logo glows on the dance floor, and horse ice sculptures decorate the room. When I find one that looks like Padlock, I make Lottie take a picture of Magnolia and me standing before it.

Padlock is outside with the rest of the Titans, proudly displayed for the gala attendees. Two boys dressed in black washed and polished our horses when we arrived, and gave them as many oil sticks as they desired, a treat Rags introduced to me.

"What's that waiter giving the jockeys?" Magnolia asks.

I follow her gaze and see what she's referring to. A coiffed man dressed in a tux is walking up to each table hosting a jockey and lowering a silver serving tray. One by one, the jockeys pluck a cream-colored envelope. They tear into them with eagerness, but I can't see what the letters say from here.

I shake my head, telling Magnolia I'm not sure. Penelope saunters by, and I can tell by the look in her eyes that she wants to tell me about the envelope in her hand. She lingers close by, taunting me, until I can't stand it a second longer.

"What is that?" I ask, my face warming.

"This?" She slaps the envelope against her open palm. "An invite to the after-party. You going?"

Magnolia searches the table, and then answers for me. "There's an after-party?"

Penelope's eyebrows rise. "Yep. From what I hear, the real fun starts tonight. This is just a formality. A pretty tiresome one at that, don't you think?"

Penelope is pretending to be friendly, but I know what she's doing. Magnolia was having the time of her life before this jockey told her she shouldn't be. That this is nothing to get excited about.

Seeing the interest in Magnolia's eyes, and noting how the waiter is returning to the kitchen empty-handed, I say to my best friend, "I'll talk to the waiter. He probably forgot to come by."

A grin sweeps across Magnolia's face, and my chest tightens. Has she forgotten how the jockeys teased us? I'm betting she hasn't, but she's pushed it from her mind. That's one thing, among many, that I love about my friend—her ability to concentrate on the positive, and dismiss the negative.

"Oh, yeah, I'm sure he has your tickets," Penelope says. "They're addressed to all the jockeys with Titan 3.0s."

Magnolia's face falls. Now she gets it.

"Go away, Penelope," I say.

Her nose wrinkles like she's shocked by my curtness, but she does leave, her business here complete.

Only because I know my friend wants to attend the party do I contemplate how to get those tickets. If I ask the empty-handed waiter, he'll surely direct me to Arvin Gambini, and that'll cause a scene. This is another obvious measure to put Padlock and me in our place. My eyes scan the room, taking in the jockeys and their excitement over this newest development.

My gaze falls on Hart Riley II. He plucks the invite from the table, says something to someone across from him, and then flicks the envelope away like he could care less. Well, if he doesn't want those tickets . . .

I look at my friend. "Magnolia, do you really want to go to that party?"

She shrugs. "I *did*. Kind of. But I don't want to go anywhere we're not welcome."

"We should be welcome at anything that's centered around the races, because I am a jockey, and Padlock is my Titan. And you"—I bump her shoulder—"are my fabulously dressed friend who will turn into a pumpkin if she returns home before midnight."

Magnolia beams. "Maybe we could crash for a minute or two. See what the big deal is. Because you're right, this mermaid dress has waited for this night its entire chiffon-inspired life. Amen."

I laugh and admire the dress Lottie bought Magnolia, which she most certainly wasn't required to do as my sponsor. The dress is a greenish-blue that lives up to its mermaid style. With that silk ribbon the color of sea foam tied around her waist, it looks like Magnolia strolled out from the waves, blond hair wet on her shoulders—and in a magical moment—her fins became legs. My friend is right. That dress needs more than a few hours of glory. It needs all night.

I rise from the table, excuse myself, and beeline for Hart. "Hey," I say when I reach him. "You going to the party?"

Hart barely registers my existence, what with the lack of cameramen present.

I raise my voice loud enough to embarrass him to his table-mates. "I'm talking to you, pretty boy."

He glances up lazily. "Nah, I ain't going."

"Then you won't mind if I take these." I reach for his envelope and pull an invitation and two tickets from within. *Perfect*.

Hart snatches them from my hand. "Just because I'm not going doesn't mean I'll give my tickets to you." He studies me, his eyes lingering on the skin color my mother gave me set against the white sequined dress. Specifically, the sweetheart neckline region. His voice softens a touch. "Why do you wanna go anyway? You know what they're doing."

"My friend wants to go," I reply.

His gaze darts past me. "The hot one?"

"My smart, funny, talented friend, yes."

"The hot one."

I roll my eyes. "Just give me the tickets. Please?"

He shakes his head. "I'm not in the habit of doing people favors. What's in it for me?"

Frustrated, I search my brain. What do I have that Hart Riley does not?

Jack squat, that's what.

Glancing over my shoulder, I spot Magnolia. She's using her fork and knife to make a point to the woman at our table. It seems the knife is a Titan, and the fork is . . . me? I think about her parents at the bank, begging for an extension, and my friend giving up every dime she's earned on her own to help keep their house. I want to give her this, and anything else that'll put a smile on her face.

The answer comes to me simply.

"I'll race you for them. A two-minute race, outside through the woods, winner gets the tickets."

Hart Riley II takes a long pull on his iced tea, sets down his glass, and grins.

"You're on."

CHAPTER FORTY-FOUR

Ten minutes later, Magnolia, Hart, and I are outside. Before I left, I noticed Rags and Lottie on the dance floor. They were one of the first couples to grace it, and though Rags looked put out to be there, I noticed he held Lottie close as they shuffled across the open space.

"Two minutes, you said?" Hart confirms, already leading his horse away from the community center.

"Would you like your saddle, sir?" one of the cleaning boys asks.

When Hart doesn't respond, nerves tingle in my feet. Have I thought this through?

"I want to ride too," Magnolia says.

"What? No," I respond, guiding Padlock after Hart's Titan.

"Why not?" Hart asks. "You want two tickets, right? The girl should ride for her spot at the party."

Magnolia points at him as if he's making her point better than she ever could.

I shake my head. "No way, it's too dangerous."

Magnolia grabs my hand, stopping me. She lowers her voice. "Come on, Astrid. Between a party and a chance to ride Padlock, you know which I'd choose."

I purse my lips, hating the position she's putting me in. If I were her, I'd hate being on the sidelines, never in the saddle. So I want to say yes. But even though I've told her otherwise, riding a Titan is dangerous, and I don't want to risk her safety.

"If you're not considerate enough to give her a ride, I will."

Hart winks at Magnolia and pats his Titan. "Want to give Ace a shot?"

I grind my teeth. "Don't even think about it."

"So you'll take me?" Magnolia asks.

I groan, returning to the cleaning boys to retrieve my saddle. Magnolia cheers triumphantly. There's no chance I'm winning now, but giving Mag a chance to ride has been a long time coming.

I align myself behind Magnolia in the saddle in case she falls, and instruct her to hang on to the horn with everything she has. Hart guides us across the street, far away from the community center's lights, and references the shadows born by trees.

"Two minutes, head to head. Whoever is farther into the forest when our stopwatches call it, wins."

"Easy enough." I slam my hand on Padlock's turbo button and we're off.

"Cheater!" Hart cries, but I hear the delight in his voice.

Magnolia screams happily as we charge through the woods. The seconds tick off as trees roll past in a blur, and though we're going faster than I'm comfortable with while Magnolia's in the saddle, it isn't nearly fast enough to beat Hart. But that's okay. Magnolia's laughter is sufficient.

Even so, when I notice Hart is a fraction behind, competitiveness twinges in my belly. If I only played with the gas bar a little . . .

"Magnolia, nudge this bar," I tell her, though I'm perfectly able to do it myself.

She does as I instruct, and when Padlock thrusts forward, she squeals. Magnolia goes to push it again and I slap her hand.

Padlock and Hart's Titan, Ace, are neck and neck as we barrel through the darkness, the bloated moon our only source of light. Though Padlock is doing the same thing he always has, and my hands are working the joysticks with familiarity, this run is different. There is no sound outside of the occasional whoop from Magnolia, or an antagonizing word or two from Hart as he charges ahead.

I can hear leaves crunching underfoot, twigs breaking off as we whip past. I hear the sound of my lungs working, and if I concentrate, I can feel Magnolia's heartbeat through her back. Padlock grunts as he runs, but even he seems happier, as if he'll always remember this run above all others.

I glance at the stopwatch and note there's only a minute remaining.

"Let's go faster," Magnolia yells over her shoulder. "We've got to beat him."

She doesn't mention the tickets. It's not about that anymore. She wants to experience a win. To have the exhilaration of being *first* rush beneath her skin. And truthfully, so do I. But not at Magnolia's expense.

"Is this the autopilot thing?" Magnolia asks a second before her hand comes down on the control panel. A second before she flips up that clear casing and engages the silver switch.

Padlock's heels dig into the ground, and we are nearly thrown forward from the abrupt stop. Hart charges into the distance, leaving us behind as he races toward his win.

"No, you're not supposed to push—" I'm a hair away from clicking the switch to the *off* position when Padlock's head jerks up. I stop talking, jostled in the saddle as he tears his muzzle from side to side. Fear shoots through my body, sizzles in my fingertips.

It takes only a second, maybe two, for Padlock to realize he's on autopilot.

He lifts his head. Snorts once.

And he's flying.

My hands find Magnolia's and I cover them with my own. Now we're both hanging on to the horn, our knuckles white as Padlock charges forward like a volcano throwing ashes to the wind. He's been released, and there's no stopping him now. If I remove my hands from Magnolia, I may fall. And if I fall, Magnolia may do the same. My only option is to hang on as Padlock runs faster, and faster, the performance gauge moving rapidly from green to yellow to that precarious place between caution and danger.

His hooves tear up the ground as our dresses are caught by the wind, streaming out behind us. A fallen tree lies ahead. I close my eyes and grit my teeth, but Padlock lunges over it with perfect precision. Before long, he's almost caught up to Ace. My horse tosses his head with agitation and storms forward. He closes the distance between them until I could reach over and shake Mr. Riley's hand.

How do you do?

Now that Padlock is in such close proximity to another Titan, it's as if a primal instinct kicks in. My horse gains speed, and the orange needle meets angry red space. My stomach twists when I realize we've entered the slay zone. Frantic, my hand releases the saddle horn. I'm about to flip the autopilot off when Magnolia begins to slip from the saddle. She cries out and her arms flail.

I grab on to her as Padlock races with expert accuracy, arching around tree trunks, diving over limbs and large rocks. His body is a work of art, his footfalls a thing of beauty. It isn't until

I spot a large crevice that I release my hold on my friend. The trench must be fifteen feet across, and there's no telling how deep it delves. At this speed, there's no going around the gap. Padlock is going to attempt leaping across in order to outpace the other horse, and there's no way Magnolia and I can both stay in this saddle if he does. There's hardly enough room to properly stay seated as it is.

Reaching across my friend, and feeling her slip a second time in the process, I fumble for the autopilot switch. My hands shake from the impact of Padlock's hooves pounding the uneven surface, and my heart shotguns in my chest. I find purchase on the switch at last, and flip it downward. Then I grab the brake bar and pull as hard as I can. Padlock skids through the dirt as I cling to Magnolia, attempting to keep us both from falling.

We're treacherously close to the ledge when Padlock jolts to a stop. Four beats later, Hart flies across the open space, man and steel horse soaring across the divide.

It's a bird. It's a plane.

It's Hart Riley and his trusty Titan extraordinaire!

The twosome lands safely on the other side. Hart turns his horse toward me. He smiles his thousand-watt smile and says, "Time. I win."

CHAPTER FORTY-FIVE

The fire crackles and pops, throwing shadows across Magnolia's face.

And Hart's face. He's here too.

Magnolia drills Hart across the open flame as he drags on a cigarette. Turns out he's a moderately skilled poker player himself. He won his Titan in a lucky hand, he admits. Though he only has it on loan.

"So you have to give the horse back when the race is over?" Magnolia prods, the after-party forgotten now that Hart's here providing Grade A entertainment.

Hart nods and flicks ashes onto the dry, highly flammable grass.

"It's kind of like you have a sponsor," my friend continues.

Hart's eyes harden. "No, I'm working alone. The Titan's on loan, that's all."

Magnolia scrunches up her nose, thinking about this. "You don't come from money, do you?"

"Magnolia!" I scold. But I watch Hart's face, awaiting his answer.

Hart shrugs. "I'm an opportunist. My mom died when I was young, and my dad always loved Percocet. Not a lot of opportunity in my family name. But this race . . ." He waves his cigarette around his head. "It's a fresh start." He sobers, and his voice lowers. "I won't end up like my father."

Another puff on his cigarette.

Magnolia and I quiet. It's obvious Hart isn't going to

elaborate, but I can't help looking at him differently. He's here for a similar reason I am; I'm trying to maintain my life, and he's trying to change his. I wonder what will happen if he loses. What kind of life awaits him?

I dismiss the thought, remind myself that I need to focus on my own family, not my competition.

"You say you won the use of your Titan in a card game, eh?" Magnolia smirks.

Hart leans his head back. "What of it?"

"Care for a wager?"

Hart glances at her with interest, a smile playing on his lips as he eyes her lean legs. "What'd ya have in mind, buttercup?"

"Eww, gross," Magnolia says, but I don't miss the way she returns his smile. Magnolia withdraws the playing cards from her pocket. "If I win, you tell us how it is you get out of the gate so quickly."

My eyes dart to Magnolia. So she'd noticed it too.

"And if I win?" he asks.

"I'll pretend to be your girlfriend for the cameras." The answer flies from my mouth before I have time to think, because I don't want him asking anything of my friend.

Hart considers this, trying to determine whether I'll stand by my promise. He sighs as if his playing cards is doing us a solid. "Fine, but don't say I didn't warn you."

....

Magnolia beats him.

Hart demands another game.

She beats him again.

"Really," she says through a yawn. "It's like you're not even trying."

228

But Hart is trying. In fact, I think he might be sweating. And when Magnolia beats him for the third time—*best two hands out of three!*—I can actually see the perspiration accumulating at his temples.

"Spill," Magnolia demands, a triumphant smile on her face.

I can't help mirroring that smile, and watching Hart for a reaction. Will he really tell me his strategy? Does he even have a strategy, or is it simply luck?

Hart leans back on his hands, his eyebrows knitting together. "There's a hissing sound before the starting gate opens. I push the accelerator button then instead of waiting."

I think back to the four races I've run. "I don't remember hearing anything."

"Then you haven't been listening."

"Wouldn't your horse hit the starting gate if you accelerated before it pulled away?" Magnolia asks.

His jaw muscle jumps, irritated that he's revealing his trick. "No, it's perfect timing."

I think about what he's saying, and whether it would be cheating if I replicated his tactic.

"I don't know why you need my help," Hart says, acting aloof. "You do all right on that rusted hunk of metal."

"Whoa." I glare at him. "You can talk about me, but don't talk about my Titan."

Padlock snorts in agreement. It's the first time he's acknowledged our conversation. He's been too distracted by Hart's horse, Ace, and why it won't interact with him the way the gray mare does.

"What I mean is . . ." Hart hesitates, and I can tell he's struggling to get the words out. "You're not half bad when you stop trying so hard."

"Excuse me?" Magnolia says this on my behalf, bless her.

"You think too much," Hart continues. "You need to relax and let your horse do some of the racing. Like you did in the woods there at the end. Whatever you did those last few seconds wasn't quite as tragic as your usual racing style."

"Is that supposed to be a compliment?"

He waves his hand, dismissing me. "Forget it."

He's right, though. I felt Padlock come alive when Magnolia switched him to autopilot, and though I couldn't risk him staying that way with Magnolia riding alongside me, I can't help wondering how I'd fare in the next circuit race if I were to give him control.

I get up and brush off my backside. Then I go to Padlock, run my hands over his back and chuckle when he nuzzles the top of my head. This horse is my ticket to saving my family's home, and keeping my friend close. But he's much more than that now. He's my partner, my comrade. And I'd be lying if I said he hasn't stolen a piece of my heart. Padlock lowers his head, pressing his forehead against my own. As Magnolia and Hart discuss her mad poker skills, I breathe in the smell of my horse—steel and iron and gasoline, and yeah, a little rust.

I allow myself to wonder what will happen to my horse when this race ends, and my insides clench imagining him being turned off and left to gather dust in Rags's shed.

"I won't let that happen," I whisper to Padlock, in case he can sense what I'm thinking.

"You always look this sexy sitting in the dirt?"

Hart's voice, and Magnolia's responsive giggle, nabs my attention.

I turn away from Padlock and shoot daggers at Hart Riley. "Say one more thing to her. I dare you."

Hart looks pointedly at Magnolia. "One more thing."

I tackle him and press the side of his face into the ground. His laugh echoes through the dense, muggy forest.

My best friend laughs too.

PART IV
THE DERBY

CHAPTER FORTY-SIX

It's been a long time since I spent a morning at home, so the day after the gala, I do just that. The problem is no one is there to spend time *with*. There's a note on the counter from Mom to Zara saying she's running to the store, and telling her to clean up her room. I frown at the note, unhappy that my mom is leaving my ten-year-old sister at home alone. Our phone got cut off six weeks ago. What would Zara do if there was an emergency?

When I see that my dad and Dani are also gone, I head to Zara's room. She's asleep in her twin-sized bed, a hand-me-down blanket covered in smiling lions pulled to her chin.

"Zara," I whisper. But she doesn't respond.

Rags wants me at the track by noon, no exceptions, and I really wish I could hang with Zara before I leave. But I also don't want to wake her, so I head to my room and crawl in bed too. My chest is hollow as I stare at my older sister's cold pillow. How much has she been here the last few weeks? And what about my dad? What's happened to the man whose pride hangs on his ability to provide for his family?

I remember a time when our house was full. When me, Dani, and Zara finger-painted on clean sheets of paper in Grandpa's living room, and then proceeded to paint his bald head at his request. He was a paying customer, after all. Dad had Mom on his lap, and said he'd only let her get up if she made cookies. With chocolate chips. And M&Ms.

We were the Sullivans, and where there was one, there were five more on their way.

I attempt to fall back asleep, trying to recover from my late night with Magnolia and Hart. But I miss my family. I miss my broken, warped, split-down-the-middle family, and I wish we could sit on the couch and eat fried eggs and bicker about the necessity of cable.

I'd argue right now simply to hear their voices. To hear my mom's quiet opinions and Dani's passive-aggressive ones. To watch my dad's face pinch with impatience, and Zara roll her eyes and sigh with exaggerated annoyance. I want all of that. I want to be sandwiched between it even if it's the best we've got at this point.

I just want it in this house.

And I wanted a little piece of it this morning.

As if by some divine miracle, the bedroom window slides open. My heart leaps and I bolt upright. I don't care how ridiculous the smile is on my face. I can't hide how happy I am that Dani chose this exact moment to sneak in for a change of clothes or a shower or whatever it is she needs.

She's sliding her tanned legs through the window—good, solid Sullivan legs—when her dress snags on the frame. She curses under her breath, and I glance away as her yellow summer dress hitches to her waist. But not before I see it.

A green-and-yellow bruise circles her left hip, as glorious as it is grotesque. It's almost a perfect circle with swirls of deep color, like I'm looking at planet Earth from outer space. If I concentrate hard enough, maybe I can spot our brown clapboard house from my rocket ship.

I lunge to my feet and pull her through the rest of the way. She gasps with surprise that I'm actually home. But it's me who's shocked. I hold on to her arm, and even when she shakes it and calls me a slug and tells me to get off her, I don't let go. Because

I see them now. Small, round bruises dotting her wrists—the meteors in her galaxy of pain.

"Who did this?" I ask.

She pulls away at last. "What are you blubbering about?"

"You have bruises all over you, Dani. Who did this?" The realization hits me hard, square between the eyes. "Was it Jason?"

For a moment, it looks as if she'll deny it. Say she fell a hundred different ways, and my, oh my, isn't she clumsy? But she doesn't. She only purses her lips and turns toward the ceiling and says something so clichéd it actually hurts my freaking *teeth*. "He didn't know what he was doing. We went out with his friends and had too much to drink."

"So he's allowed to hurt you because he was drunk?" I can't believe what I'm hearing.

Dani strides away, goes to her closet and rifles for a suddenly important piece of clothing. "Chill with the melodrama, okay? I yelled at him when it should have waited until morning, and we both did and said things we shouldn't have." Dani's voice lowers. "He already apologized like a thousand times."

I cringe. "Do you know how you sound? You sound like Mom, making excuses for a man who should know better. But Dad would never do this. He would never hurt Mom."

Dani spins around. "Dad hurts Mom every single day, Astrid. Every day he snaps at her. Every day he makes her feel uncomfortable in her own home. Every day he pushes her, and us, further away. He didn't keep Grandpa safe, and he won't keep us safe, either. He's the one screwing everything up! Jason can keep *me* safe, though. He messed up once, but every other day he treats me like royalty. And when we lose this house, and you know we will, Jason will put a roof over my head and food in my stomach and he'll love me out loud. And he won't gamble that away either." Dani turns away. There's the ghost of red lip-stick smudged across her mouth. "He thinks I can get my GED and go to college. Says he'll help me pay for it. I can't lose that."

I listen to her speech and dismiss it at once. "You've got to tell someone what happened. We've got to tell Dad."

That does it. Tears fill Dani's eyes, crest over mascara-laden lashes. "If you tell him, or anyone, I'll leave with Jason. I'll leave and you'll never see me again."

Now I'm crying too, because I know she isn't bluffing. And because for the first time, I see I'm not the only one who's lived in fear of losing my small sense of stability. I don't want to lose my sister too.

"Why are you guys being so loud?" a new voice asks.

When I see Zara standing in the doorway, the morning sun granting her an ethereal glow, I wipe the tears from my face. Plaster on a winning, reassuring smile. "Hey, there you are, sleepyhead."

Dani turns her back to Zara—more camouflage, more denial that anything bad has happened under the Sullivan roof.

Zara steps farther into the room. "I heard you guys fighting."

"We argue because we share a room," I lie. "It happens. You want pancakes? I'll make them with applesauce like you like."

"I'm not stupid." Zara's cheeks redden. "I know what's going on."

"Be quiet, Zara," Dani says.

"Don't tell me that!" Zara's yelling at Dani now, her small hands balled into fists. "I know you basically live with your boy-friend, because you're never here when I wake up. I know Mom and Dad fight, because I hear them." She looks at me now. "And I know you're more interested in flirting with Hart Riley than being here." When my face contorts, she says, "Yeah, I know about your stupid boyfriend. Mom gets the *Titan Enquirer* and I see the pictures of you." I want to correct her, but she plunges onward. "You two both have a place to run away to, but I'm stuck here. I hear every time Mom and Dad argue about the house, and about where we'll go if we lose it. I hear when Mom leaves in the middle of the night, and when Dad snores from the living room couch. Were either of you two here when the guy came to take our car last night? No, just me. You were probably both—"

"Wait, what? Who came to get the car, Zara?"

"They took Mom and Dad's car," she repeats. "They're using it to pay for the house or something."

The room spins, and I hardly hear whatever else Zara says, though I want to listen so badly. Right now, she needs me to be her sister, but my mind clicks to survival mode the same way Padlock switched to autopilot last night. If we don't have a car, and we don't have a house—where will we go? At least last time we had the backseat to curl up in on hard nights. We had air conditioning and a little heat if we could afford the fuel. What will we do without our vehicle to fall back on?

Zara must see the change in my face, because she starts to cry in earnest. "See? That's what happens when you go away."

A lump forms in my throat. "I didn't go away. I'm right here."

But when I reach for her, she jerks backward. "You're *never* here anymore. You don't care about us at all. All you care about is your stupid horse."

"That's not true. I love you, Zara. And Mom and Dad. And Dani too." I glance at my older sister, who's chewing her thumbnail. She doesn't meet my gaze. "Everything I'm doing at the track is to try and save this family. If I win, we can stay here. You

237

can keep going to your school and stay with your friends. Mom and Dad won't fight anymore, and Dani can come home."

This time when I look at Dani, she stares at me intently.

"I have to worry about saving our house right now, but after this summer is over, you'll see me every day." I bend down so Zara and I are eye to eye. "You understand?"

Zara glowers at the ground, but I don't miss the way her lower lip trembles. She mumbles something under her breath I don't catch. When I ask her to repeat it, she fills her lungs and yells, "You're just like Dad! All you care about is gambling and money!"

I straighten, stunned by her words. Hurt rains over my body, slips into my cracks, makes a home for itself in my heart. I don't know how to feel about what she said. Do I defend myself and argue that my father and I are nothing alike? Or apologize and admit that maybe we are? That maybe the man I believed emotionally abandoned us is simply doing the same thing I am.

Trying to save our home.

Trying to piece our family back together.

Trying to shoulder the burden himself so the rest of us can sleep at night.

That kind of stress could make even the most cheerful person irritable. It could make them distant in their constant quest to solve a difficult problem. It could make a man like the one my mother married into one she escapes at night in favor of other people's gardens. Because him she can't change. Him she can't get to open up and return to her and thrive, but hydrangeas and delphiniums and coralbells—those she can.

I think about this, but I also recall what Magnolia said to me at the track. That I'm putting in effort, whereas my father simply sits and *hopes* with his gambling. We may seem alike, and perhaps in a way we are. But I'd never put Zara in the position she's in now. Almost homeless. Almost destitute.

"Zara, listen to me—"

But she interrupts me the same way I did her. "Are you going to practice today with that man?"

I know what I should say. I should tell her absolutely not. That I won't leave her when she's this upset. But how much more upset will she be if she doesn't have her bed to sleep in? If she loses her place by the window where she reads the magazines I keep beneath my mattress? If she loses her friend Derrick, who walks with her to school and will probably become her first crush?

I can't look at her when I respond. "For a little while, yes. Because I have to. For you. For all of us."

Zara wipes her face and crosses her arms over her chest. In this moment, she looks a lot like a little girl pretending to be a grown woman. "Sorry. I miss you. That's all."

I reach for her again, but she turns and pads toward her room. She's trying to forgive me for not being around. She understands what I'm trying to do. But she's still a ten-year-old who's tired of living invisibly within a family of five.

Dani pulls her sundress toward her knees and chews the inside of her cheek. Finally, she stands and returns to the closet. She rifles in the back and finds what she's looking for. She walks over and pushes her hand out in a silent offering.

I glance down and see a pair of black Oakley sunglasses. When I don't immediately take them, she shoves them into my stomach.

"Don't be too proud," she says. "You can use them when you practice or whatever."

I take the sunglasses, but continue staring at my feet. I feel suddenly childlike standing before my older sister, tears pooling at the corners of my eyes. Dani and I have always shared a room, and it was her bed I sought when thunderstorms rolled in, or when I'd spy on the horror movies Mom and Dad rented. She never complained when I crawled beneath her covers. In fact, I think she may have enjoyed it. Looking back, I can't remember how that ended: if she said I was too old for such things, or if I stopped on my own.

"You don't need them?" I mumble.

Dani waves away the question. "Jason gave them to me."

Recalling the bruises, I raise my head to insist we talk to Mom and Dad. Or to someone. But the look in her eyes stops me cold.

"Remember what I said before, okay? I mean it." Dani passes by on her way to the bathroom. Or maybe to leave through the front door. That'd be a first. When I turn to object, she's staring at me. "That race thing . . . I knew about it, you know."

I don't respond, because I wasn't certain she did. When Dani is with Jason, it's like the rest of the world doesn't exist.

"You think you can win?" she asks.

The hope in her voice is nearly my undoing.

"I'll win," I say.

I wait for Dani to respond. To say something profound. Or to reassure me it doesn't matter either way. But she doesn't. She just nods, and then turns to go.

A few seconds later, I hear the sound of the shower running.

CHAPTER FORTY-SEVEN

Padlock and I are positioned inside the starting gate. If I have one chance before the Titan Derby to prove myself capable of winning, this is the race to do it. A long race. Thirty-two furlongs. Four miles of track stretching deep into the forest, looping through the trees, and returning. I can spot the finish line from my place inside the gate, but it's what lies between here and there that has me worried.

My confrontation with Dani and Zara zips through my head over and over, like a circuit board, lighting up different areas of my brain: frustration, sadness, understanding. But most of all—determination. I've never wanted a win so badly, after seeing Zara's sense of abandonment, Dani's desperate need for stability. Our family car is gone. We don't know anyone who can afford to take us in. And my father still hasn't found work.

I am our last hope of staying off the streets.

I must win.

But before I do that, I have to prove myself capable.

The light flashes outside the gate, turning from the safety of red to stomach-churning yellow. I trigger Padlock's racing capability and his eyes illuminate our small space. It's like he senses my resolve, quieting beneath me instead of thrashing about like our competitors.

Outside, the crowd rumbles. I imagine I hear Magnolia's voice among the others, reminding me there's one more thing I'm racing for. I imagine Rags and Barney too, and how they deserve this win. It's no longer enough for me to finish better than I have before.

Tonight, I must be the best.

The yellow lights continue to flash, teasing us, throwing our Titans into a state of chaos. All except for one.

Before the gate slides away, I listen for the sound Hart told me about. And right before the light changes to red, when my heart feels as though it will burst inside my chest, I hear it—a slight hissing sound.

My hand twitches over the turbo button. But I don't push it. I don't. Instead, I wait until the gate rattles open and the light screams green.

When I win, I don't want any doubts as to how I took first.

Hart barrels ahead of us all, and Padlock and I take our place in the back. This time, the gate surrounding Cyclone Track doesn't fall away. A piece of it is already open, giving way to a smooth pebbled track, providing a false sense of security. But I don't buy it for a second. This second circuit race—*River Runner*—has me on high alert.

My instincts prove correct when I hear the first of the jockeys scream. A Titan in the distance falls, disappearing beneath the ground. I think I must be seeing things until Padlock and I grow closer. Squinting, I notice patches of the track that appear slightly different. They're darker, though they seem to be made of the same pebbled material. It isn't until another Titan crosses a shadowy patch and splashes downward that I realize what it is.

The track engineers have dug holes into the ground, lined them, and filled them with water. Floating on the surface is a substance that looks identical to the orange-and-white pebbles we race upon. Already, the Titans have slowed as their jockeys navigate around the dark places.

My eyes scan the area, and I count. Try to find a pattern to the madness. There's always a pattern. Whether it's intentional or not, people thrive on order, and nothing is as ordered as a numerical system. Excitement rushes through me when I notice the holes are three feet apart, laid in two tracks so that each one is diagonal to the next. The tracks are four feet apart, and there's a deviation to the system of maybe three to four inches. If I run Padlock on the outside, and then zigzag through the holes at a swift canter, we should be able to keep moving at all times.

I lead Padlock to the right, pull back on the gas bar, and push up on the brake bar. When we reach the far edge, I bite down and jerk the joysticks to the left. Padlock dodges the first water hole before I navigate him, hard, to the right. We repeat that over and over—left, right, left, right—until we've passed all the dark places, and two Titans in the process.

Hart is still in the lead, having hurdled over the holes, stopping only twice to find the next safe landing spot. Batter and Penelope are ahead of me as well, as is Skeet, her Titan's eye repaired after the last race.

The crowd cheers as we race forward, our first jam completed. Even the two horses that fell have climbed out of their watery graves to resume their flight to the finish line. Padlock and I wind through the forest, taking tight turns when we can to gain an advantage, and running as fast as I can push him without compromising his engine during the straightaways.

The second jam arrives after what feels like a mile and a half.

A ditch has been dug into the ground, and churning water whirls beneath the surface. I don't know how deep the water is, but it's obvious there are two options: One, cross the ditch by wading through the water, or two, take one of two narrow bridges that arch over the crevice. The obvious choice seems to be the bridges, but there are risers every few feet, and you'd have to jump your Titan over them, slowing you down.

There's little time to choose as we barrel forward. Over or under? Over or under?

Hart takes the bridge. He performs two perfect jumps and then his horse stumbles and nearly slips over the edge. It's only when I've gotten closer that I see the bridge is coated in a thick, black tar-like substance. The risers force the horses to jump, and the tar is there to ensure they fall.

There's a Titan on each bridge, and because I don't want to get stuck behind anyone, I release a guttural cry and charge forward. Right before we hit the water, I push the hurdle button. The two of us fly through the air and splash into the small churning river. Several other Titans have chosen the same option, and we all seem to realize our obstacle at once. The bridge threatens to spill your Titan over the side, but the river has sticky mud at the bottom, trapping our horses' hooves.

Padlock whines, and though I try everything to get him to move faster, nothing works. We trudge through the water, every leg lift an eternity. I'm halfway to the other side when a sharp crack sounds over my head. I glance up, and a chill rushes down my back. A Titan has slipped. It struggles to regain its balance, but it's no use.

The horse and jockey fall.

I throw my body over Padlock as if he's the one who needs protecting. As if when this eight-hundred-pound machine and its owner crash into us, it's *his* fragile bones that will break. As the twosome plummets downward, I recall in detail the four jockeys who lost their lives racing in the Titan Circuits.

Water explodes to my right, and every muscle in my body twitches. They've missed me by inches, but the horse's legs kick into Padlock's neck.

"Padlock!" I scream, frantically feeling along his side for

damage. But my horse only pushes onward, either ignorant to what happened or too manic to care. When I clear my eyes, I spot a jockey thrashing in the bubbling, swirling water. I slow Padlock and reach an arm out to the fallen jockey.

"Grab my hand!" I yell. The jockey is an older man, sturdy, with long limbs and a broad chest. Even still, I can't leave him in the water when I'm not sure he can swim. I grab ahold of his wrist and yank him toward Padlock as the other Titans charge ahead.

"Get off me," he roars, ripping his wrist away.

I watch, jaw agape, as his Titan surfaces and stills while the jockey remounts. The horse seems dazed, and I wonder if being submerged in the water damaged the Titan's control panel. Padlock never did lower his head beneath the water when we were at the pond.

Gritting my teeth, I push Padlock through the muck, using as much gas as I think he can tolerate without damaging his interior. After what feels like an eternity, we're out of the water and racing again. We tear down the track, chasing Titans, watching as a fine mist of water balloons behind them. The race-goers love it, and I even spot a grown man holding a boy on his shoulders, his small face getting sprayed. There are now three horses behind me, six ahead. If I finish in the top seven, I'll move on to the final circuit race. But that isn't enough. I refuse to just scrape by.

After a tight turn around a cluster of photographers, I gain a lead on yet another Titan. I need to pass five more horses for the win, and there's almost half the race left to go. As a rush of adrenaline courses through my veins, I realize I have a shot.

Hart, Batter, Skeet, and two others blaze down the track, while Penelope has fallen back. Taking tight turns may not be enough to win the *River Runner* race. I'll need a jam I can excel at in order to pass the others. And as it so happens, another one is coming right up.

A blue light shines down from above, accentuating a thin curtain of rain. The water crosses the entire track, but every few seconds, it lets up. Then it falls again, splashing the ground. I notice clear plastic barriers protect the crowd from coming in contact with the water, which must mean it's dangerous.

My mind works through the possibilities. I can't go around it. I can't go over or under it. That means I have to go through the curtain of water. This could be good. I can calculate how often the curtain falls and see if there's a pattern.

I'm thinking this through—already counting the beats between when the rain starts and stops—when Hart rushes through the water. He isn't trying to find a system. He hasn't solved a riddle or figured out a way to navigate through it unharmed.

He simply doesn't care.

The sound of him screaming reaches my ears, and I remember at once the words he spoke while sitting aside the campfire.

I won't end up like my father.

Hart screams, and the sound is deep and nerve-rattling. But here's what I notice: It doesn't last long. In a matter of seconds, his screams fall away and I glimpse his Titan resuming its quick pace. Batter does the same thing I do—stops to create a plan. No way is he chancing harming himself. My concern is for Padlock, though, because if the waterfall damages me in some way, surely it'll have consequences for him as well.

I do some quick calculations, and find the sequence. The time between the curtain falling doubles three times—two seconds, four seconds, eight seconds—then the last time is the average of the last two numbers—six seconds.

The ticker goes back to two seconds. And so after the water pauses, I count four beats and then charge through. Batter's tactic is a simpler one—he goes when I do.

Once on the other side, I nudge Padlock's gas bar, almost relishing the fact that I'm racing next to Batter, neither of us leading the other. Batter glances at me and sneers, flashing way too much gum beneath thin lips. I return my attention to the track before being slammed from the side, sparks flying between our two Titans. The crowd cheers and boos and waves their white tickets.

Because I'm taken by surprise, Padlock careens wildly to the right, and it takes maneuvering on my part to keep us from slamming into the temporary gates. Batter charges on, but I'm right on his tail.

I've almost caught up to him, almost secured my third-place position, when I hear a sharp yell and a splash of water. Batter and I look away from each other and gaze ahead, our heads snapping up, spines at attention.

I make out a single dark spot in the track, and while Skeet neatly dodges it, another jockey wasn't so lucky. It was an easy mistake to make. Who'd expect another jam so soon after the curtain of burning water? Who'd expect the track engineers to repeat one, single water hole along a seemingly safe stretch of track?

We wouldn't, which is why they did it.

It takes me a few moments to wrap my head around who it was that fell—two seconds, four, eight.

And then I know.

CHAPTER FORTY-EIGHT

Hart Riley II crawls out of the watery ditch screaming and clutching his arm. His Titan, Ace, bobs beside him, useless without his jockey inputting commands. I pull back on my gas bar, slam on my brake, and dismount. Batter rushes past, but I don't care. Hart is moaning and rolling onto his side, blond hair matted against his head.

"Hart!" I yell. "Is it your arm? Did you break it?"

Hart's eyes pop open and he seems utterly confused to find me crouched beside him. "What are you doing, you idiot? Get back on your Titan!"

"Like hell. I'm not leaving you here."

Hart bites down, groaning through his teeth. His head falls back, but he manages to maintain eye contact. "The medics will come. Get back in the race!"

As if to emphasize his point, Penelope gallops past, throwing us a smiling salute. The look on her face is almost enough to make me follow Hart's instructions, but I don't see the medics anywhere, and Hart's beginning to lose consciousness. What if it's not just an injured arm? What if he hit his head too?

I drag him a few inches from the water in case he passes out and rolls back in. Hart's eyes slip closed and he sucks in a labored breath. Then his lids blink open and he grabs my jersey in one hand.

"Don't let those pricks win, Sullivan. Get on your Titan. There's no way in hell I would have stopped if you'd fallen."

I hesitate, but not for long. Not long enough for another horse to pass me by.

"Go!" Hart screams. "Go now!"

And because I finally spot the medics trotting toward Hart, and because I'll fail my entire family if I don't make it to the final circuit race, I remount Padlock and slam the turbo button and gas bar.

It doesn't matter that three horses race behind me—never mind, make that two—what matters is I only have two minutes left to finish this race, and I have no idea what jams lie ahead. Dismissing the autopilot button, I race Padlock faster. I skirt the line between yellow and red on the performance gauge, and knowing I have few seconds to spare, I race with an exactness I can feel down to my core. It's like taking a test and knowing you aced it before it's even graded.

I fly through two more jams with ease, and when I cross the finish line, it takes a long time before I'm myself again. Astrid Sullivan, the girl who overthinks things. The girl who trusts no one but herself. Hart Riley is being taken on a stretcher toward a waiting ambulance. Right before the doors close, I see Hart waving his good arm, making some sort of demand. A medic jogs over to me with a look of frustration smeared across his face.

"The jockey wants to see you," the medic says.

I'm surprised to hear it, but I follow the medic as we race toward the ambulance. Hart pulls at the straps securing him to the stretcher and sits up. He waves me over like he's having trouble speaking loud enough to be heard. With more concern than I care to admit, I approach his side.

He utters something quietly. So quietly I can't make out what he's said.

I press against him, lower my face to his. "What did you say?"

"Smile for the cameras, sugarplum," he says clearly. Then he kisses me hard on the mouth, wrapping his arm around my waist.

Hart Riley tastes like grape juice. Grape juice and mud and aggravation.

He falls back on the stretcher and grips my hand.

He moans loudly.

The cameramen capture every moment.

CHAPTER FORTY-NINE

The Wednesday after the *River Runner* race, Barney calls a team dinner at his house. He makes a roast in his Crock-Pot, the only piece of kitchen equipment the man knows how to use, according to Rags.

We sit at a rustic wooden table and eat off blue plates and drink from mason jars. Lottie doesn't correct our table manners, and even Rags wears an unshakable grin.

"It's a shame about that boy," Barney says.

Lottie shakes her head. "You don't care about that kid and you know it."

Barney waggles his eyebrows and raises his wineglass. "Nope. I suppose I don't."

"He broke his arm, you know." I shove a bite of roast into my mouth and chase it with root beer. I leave the softened carrots and peas on my plate where they belong.

"You going soft on me, kid?" Rags asks. "Living up to all those romantic rumors the *Enquirer* spreads?"

"There's only one person in this house involved in romantic scandals." Magnolia grins at Rags and Lottie, who sit close to each other. "Or, make that two people."

"I don't know what you're talking about," Rags barks. "Why are you even here?"

Magnolia laughs, accustomed to Rags's standby put-down for her. She's right, though. Ever since the Circuit Gala, Rags and Lottie have done more gentle whispering than arguing. Even now, I notice Lottie's hand sits remarkably close to Rags's. Barney grins knowingly and reaches for more wine. His glassy eyes shine, and his cheeks are rosy. He looks like a man who won't make it another hour before seeking his bed.

"Whatever," Magnolia continues. "We all know Astrid isn't really involved with Hart."

"How can we be sure?" Lottie says, prodding me for a response.

"She's *not*," Magnolia says. This time, we stop and stare at her. Her tone has given her away. Or maybe it's the smile she's fighting to hide. The one that says she has a secret she's dying to reveal.

I lean back in my chair. "Oh, gross, Magnolia. Tell me you're not talking to him."

"He called my house. What should I have done? Hung up on him?"

"Oh, man." I groan like my life is ending. But my best friend just slides back and forth in her seat, working her shoulders in a funny dance.

"Don't be jelly," she says. "You'll find love in your own time."

"Don't you dare use that word at my table," Barney says, slurring. "Not you. Not with that boy."

Lottie throws a dinner roll at Barney, breaking every etiquette rule she's ever taught us. "You know as well as I do that no boy would be good enough for your little Magnolia."

Barney grunts. "She gets tied up with some boy, who's gonna make me pastries?"

My trainer places his napkin in his lap and grows serious, even for Rags. "You've got one race left before the Titan Derby, Astrid. Think you're ready?"

My skin tingles. There are only seven Titans left going into the final circuit race—me being number seven—and only four will move on to the derby. Hart was disqualified for finishing in the bottom three, and though Rags didn't say anything about it, I know he's disappointed that I dismounted to help him. I was racing well before that happened, and he and I both wish we knew how I would have placed if I'd stayed in the saddle.

I don't regret the decision, though. I want to help my family, yes, but I won't become less of a human to do it.

"I'll do my best," I respond.

....

After Magnolia and I help clean up, Lottie shuffles the two of us upstairs for our last lesson.

"You've done well putting my teaching into action, Astrid," Lottie begins. "In fact, both of you had impeccable manners at the Circuit Gala."

Magnolia beams.

"And you've certainly learned grace. Don't think I didn't notice when that Penelope woman approached your table. I'll admit I was waiting to break up a fight when I saw the smug look on her face. Whatever she had to say to the two of you wasn't polite, and yet you responded with patience and kept your temper in check."

I notice when Lottie says the word *temper*, she looks only at me. If she knew my spitfire best friend better, she'd reserve one of those sharp, judgmental eyes for her.

"Astrid, you also displayed wonderful grace during your interview, casting off your performance in the races as a product of good management, support from your friend, and the community inside Warren County. The people of Warren County have done little for you besides place an occasional bet on your horse, yet you credited them anyway because you knew they'd be reading your interview. That was graceful."

"It was also calculative," Magnolia interrupts. "Cause my girl's smart like whoa."

Lottie digs her hands into the pockets of her lilac-print dress. "Maybe a little. But it made Astrid come across as classy and humble." Lottie points to the third word on the board. "Aspirations. Astrid, you told the interviewer that you might consider college after you finish high school. Is that the truth?"

My face flushes, and I can't look Lottie in the eye. No one in my family has ever attended college. But Lottie said we should set big goals. That to do so makes a person respected. So I thought about what I would like to do with my life, outside of marrying a factory worker and raising two-point-five kids in a home I'm terrified I'll lose. I thought and I thought. And in the end, I decided I'm not sure what I want to do with my life yet. But I figure the answer might be found in classrooms much like the one Lottie made for Magnolia and me.

"Yeah, I want to go to college," I say to Lottie. "And I want Magnolia to come too."

Magnolia sits up straighter. "I would if I could afford it, but I don't know that I need to go. I was born a stone-cold business-woman. Once I finish high school and have more free time, I'm going to really ramp up my hair accessories line."

"College could teach you ways to do that well." Lottie taps Magnolia's makeshift desk. "They even have classes tailored to starting your own business in the fashion industry."

"Say it's true," Magnolia breathes.

"It's true."

Magnolia glances in my direction. "If you win this race and go to college, you could sneak me into these classes."

"I'll do you one better," Lottie says. "I'll bring you information on how to apply for financial aid and scholarships. You do the research on what school you'd like to attend, and I'll help you as best I can."

Magnolia gazes out the window and squints as if trying to spot something in the distance. But I know my friend, and what she's really doing is hiding how much this means to her. I do my own version of this by staring at the ground.

"I don't think I need to reiterate the importance of loyalty again," Lottie says softly. "You two have learned it through each other. Just remember what I said; there will always be opportunities to get ahead in life by stepping over someone who's helped you. You may get ahead by leaving people you care about behind, but your heart will always be heavy. That's no way to live. And there's no faster way to lose respect than by being disloyal.

"The last thing I'd like to touch on is strength." Lottie returns to the board, taps her fingers on the word, smudging the letters. "I want the two of you to understand proper etiquette, and to behave gracefully in the presence of others. I want you to have aspirations you can be proud of, and be loyal to those who are loyal to you in return." Lottie pauses, smiles slyly with that wide mouth. "But I also want you to be strong."

Before now, Lottie has rarely touched on strength. It didn't seem like a word that belonged with the others. It's the outlier, and the one that captured my interest the most. I fold my hands on the desk and lean forward.

Lottie walks over to my table, raps her knuckles against the surface, looks in my eyes with steel-gray irises. "Just because you are loyal to those who deserve it doesn't mean you can't put shameful people in their place. You can be a lady people admire, one with dreams worth having, and then slip on your silks, wear a warrior mask, and be ruthless in your pursuit of victory."

My blood catches fire, pours magma through my body.

"Strength is forgetting everything I've taught you and becoming a machine. It's reaching inside yourself and finding you are not someone to be toyed with. It's taking every doubt you have and crushing it beneath your heel.

"You, Astrid Sullivan, are an oleander—beautiful, graceful, intoxicating.

"May God have mercy on the person who touches you, and brings their fingers to their lips."

CHAPTER FIFTY

The night before the final circuit race, I stand in Barney's stable, running a brush through Padlock's threaded mane. Every few minutes, he nips my back and I playfully push him.

He doesn't move an inch.

If Padlock is afraid of the upcoming race, or even understands what's coming, you can't tell from his body language. He stomps the ground and nibbles my hair, then takes the brush between his teeth and tosses his head. The brush flies across the stable and hits the wall.

I put my hands on my hips. "What am I going to do with such a poorly behaved horse?"

Padlock neighs and sticks his head out the stable door, searching for his gray mare. When I put my own head out, my Titan takes a clump of my hair and begins chewing.

"Dude, that's disgusting." I rip my hair out of his mouth, thankful it's only a touch of oil that dampens my locks, and not real horse drool.

Padlock's eyes sparkle with amusement, and I spot the hint of crimson lying dormant behind his dark irises. Just twice. That's how many times his eyes will glow inside Cyclone Track before he retires.

My horse lowers his head so that his heavy muzzle lies on my shoulder. I close my eyes and run my fingers through his mane. The steady, false breaths leaving his nostrils warm my back, and the smell of diesel fuel touches my nose.

Padlock is a happier horse when he's allowed to stay on at all hours, and it was me who made that call. But I'm the one who's benefited the most from our relationship. I reach up and run my fingers over his control panel, pretend I'm dusting it off when really I'm fingering a single button.

Autopilot.

Rags says we'd run better with the two of us performing at our full potential, but what does that mean? If I were to use this feature in the final two races, when would I do it?

And what if it backfired?

I have too much riding on this to gamble.

"You ready to go, kid?"

I startle at the sound of Rags's voice. After giving Padlock one last hug, and purposely leaving his door open so he can visit his friend three stalls down, I trudge toward Rags's truck. My trainer locks the barn doors and hops in the driver's seat.

"Why so serious?" Rags asks as we drive toward my house.

I give him a look like, *Is he really asking me that?*

Rags chuckles. "You'll do fine. You just have to get out of your head and do what you've trained to do. You did well at the end of the *River Runner* race. After you got back in your saddle, that is."

He grimaces, and now I'm the one smiling.

"You and Lottie seem to be getting along better," I venture.

Rags sighs. "Why do women always have to talk about relationships? Why can't they just *happen*?"

"So now you're in a relationship?"

Rags chuckles. He's being coy about Lottie, but I didn't miss the lift in his spirits, the way his eyes spark to life when she enters the room. It's a far cry from the hurt-fueled remarks they once slung back and forth. I despise it when my own mom and dad argue, but when two people fight, it's often because they still care. Because they're fighting to find a path back to how things once were.

I toy with my seat belt as Rags drives. "You never did tell me what happened between you two. You only said not to be angry with her."

I expect Rags to give me another half answer, or to ignore the question entirely. Instead, he does something out of character. He responds in full. "We dated for a couple of years. Too long, I suppose, at our age. I guess I took her for granted. Thought she'd always be there even if I never took the next step." Rags rubs his balding head.

I don't look at Rags as he speaks. Instead, I watch the road fly beneath our wheels and stay quiet, encouraging him to continue.

"She mentioned moving in, and I asked why women always had to mess up a perfectly good thing. It wasn't a week later that she brought up parting ways. I guess I was supposed to get mad, or cave on living together, or fight to make her stay. Whatever it is women want men to do. But I didn't. So she stopped coming around. Not two weeks later, I heard she started seeing Arvin Gambini, the same man who cost me my job. I was so mad at her for that. I couldn't even stand the *thought* of her anymore," Rags grumbles. "I may have called her up and said a few things one night when I wasn't thinking clearly. After that, I knew we wouldn't speak again."

My manager wipes his hand absently over the steering wheel. "It wasn't that I didn't want her to move in. I just didn't want anything different than what I had. We were good together the way we were. Lottie was . . . she was perfect. I was a happy man when we were together, and I didn't want that to change."

This time, I can't stay quiet. "What would have changed?"

Rags laughs, but there's no humor behind it. "You kidding? Can you imagine living with someone like me?" He shakes his head. "She would have spent one month living in my house before realizing she could do better. It's best we parted ways before that happened."

"Don't say that," I interject. "You're a good man."

"I'm a grouchy SOB, and you know it."

"You're eccentric."

"I'm a stubborn old bag."

"You're a man who knows what he wants."

Rags pauses. "I wanted Lottie."

"You could fix things. It's not too late. I see the way she looks at you."

Rags chances glancing at me. His tired eyes flicker with hope. "You think so?"

I nod.

He grins. "What do you know? You couldn't race a Titan to save your life."

Our laughter fills the entirety of the cabin. Only after I've gotten myself under control does Rags stop grinning. He grips the steering wheel and coughs. "You're a good kid, Astrid," he says. "A better person than I'll ever be. You deserve to win the Titan Derby. And you know what? I bet you will too."

My throat tightens. "I want to win for all of us."

"No, no." He shakes his head. "You win for *you*. Forget about anyone else. You think about the future you could have with that money. You think about college and a big house and a boy that'll realize what a nice young lady you are. You think about always making ends meet and sleeping soundly at night." He scratches his white whiskers, grown during the week's long practice sessions.

"You could open a business or something with all that money. Be a real success story in Warren County. You think about that, kid."

I don't tell him that my dreams aren't quite that big, or what I'd really do with the money. I simply say okay, and we drive the rest of the way in silence.

When we arrive at my house, my dad is sitting on the front porch. He has a drink in his hand, and he looks as if he's been waiting on me to get home for a long time.

Rags steps out of the truck, and my dad charges toward him.

CHAPTER FIFTY-ONE

I'm out of the truck in a flash, attempting to cut my dad off before he reaches Rags. My father doesn't drink often, and a nervous energy buzzes through me, anticipating what he might do.

"You the guy putting my daughter on that horse?" Dad yells at Rags.

Rags holds his hands up, trying to calm my father. Too late. Dad hits him with a closed fist.

I yell for Dad to stop—say that it was my decision to race—but it's no use. The two men wrestle in the grass, Dad trying to get in another lick, Rags trying to pin Dad's arms behind his back. My father's reaction time is slowed, so Rags is able to get the upper hand.

"Stop trying to hit me!" Rags yells, pushing a knee into Dad's chest. "You really want your daughter to see this? Let's talk inside." My manager grabs Dad by the shirt and hauls him to his feet. But as soon as Dad is upright, he shoves Rags.

"You're the worst kind of person, you know that?" Dad slurs. "Using my daughter because you're too afraid to do the racing yourself. I know she got that blasted horse from you. I know you'll keep all that money yourself even if she does win."

"Dad, that's not—"

Rags holds up his hand, shushing me. "You're right," he says to Dad. "I did give Astrid the Titan. And I am too afraid to race, because I'm an old man. So I found someone young and healthy to do it for me. But I won't be keeping the money for myself. If she wins, a portion will go to her sponsor. The rest will go to Astrid. All the rest."

Dad rocks back on his feet. He opens and closes his mouth like he can't make out what to fire back with. Eventually he decides on, "My daughter can't win this thing and you know it. All she's going to do is get herself hurt out there." He shoves Rags again, and this time Rags stumbles. "I saw that boy fall. They took him away on a stretcher!"

Until this second, I wondered why my father chose today to confront my trainer. He knew I was working with Rags. He must have seen him dropping me off a dozen times. But today Hart fell. Maybe for a moment, he imagined that jockey being me. Maybe on our tiny TV screen, after a mug of brandy, he thought it was.

I'm about to reassure my dad, to tell him I'm careful when I race. But he cuts me off, his voice lowering. "She's just a child," my dad says in a tone that implies he's stating the obvious. "A girl her age shouldn't be out on that track. A girl shouldn't be on a Titan at all."

His words are bee stings all over my body, leaving my skin swollen and itching. "Dad, are you saying that if I were a boy, I might have a chance?"

My dad's red-rimmed eyes narrow like it's the first time he realized I was there. He doesn't respond.

"I'm not the only woman racing." My voice is barely above a whisper. I hate how small I sound. I hate the way he's looking at me, like I'm a disappointing little kid that brought a bad note home from school, and what is he going to do with me?

"There shouldn't be a single female out there," my dad grunts, eyes back on Rags. "There's a reason why the only people who attend those blasted races are men. It's no place for women and children."

I remember what Lottie said about strength. How it has to come from inside me, and how, when it's important, I have to dismiss anyone else's opinion besides my own. "I've being going to those races since I was thirteen years old. And now I'm riding in them. I'm doing well, and I can do even better." I suck in a deep breath. "I can win, Daddy."

My dad does the worst thing he could—he laughs. He laughs, but his eyes brim with sadness as he glares at Rags. "She can't win. You know it, and I know it. She'll only get hurt."

Rags steps closer to my father until they're nearly chest to chest. "If you believed that," my trainer says slowly, evenly, "you'd never have allowed her to stay in the season this long."

My gaze snaps to my father's face, because what Rags said makes sense, and I want to gauge my dad's reaction. My dad glowers at Rags, his nostrils flaring. I can hardly fill my lungs awaiting his retort. If he expresses his disbelief in me again, I may break, Lottie's lesson forgotten.

But my dad doesn't reply. He only scowls at Rags until finally, finally, he drops his head and glances at me. He's still breathing hard as he studies my face, and I do my best to stand up straight, to take on the appearance of someone brave and worthy.

My dad turns away and marches inside. The deafening sound of the door slamming shut says what he does not—that he's scared, that his world is spinning out of control. But Rags gave him a perfect opening to deny his believing I could win, and he didn't. What does that mean?

Hope dances inside my heart, makes me feel stronger. Lottie said to find strength within yourself, but my dad is my blood.

He's the same man who stayed awake the whole night through, me sleeping small on his chest after I got my childhood vaccinations. He never moved, never asked for someone else to take me while he got some rest in the dead of night. He only held me, patting my back when I roused from the pain. He's always loved me. Deep inside, I know that.

I stare at the closed front door, hanging on to the belief that maybe, just maybe, Rags got my dad to admit what he never would aloud—

He thinks there's a chance I can win.

CHAPTER FIFTY-TWO

The following Saturday, I'm in my stall with Padlock at Cyclone Track. Magnolia works on my hair, and I play with the black headband she made for me while she braids. It's wide, with a painted bumblebee flying through the loop of an alpha sign.

"I made a stencil before I painted this one," she explains, taking it from my hands and sliding it over my head. "It's easier to correct a stencil than it is to repaint."

I grab her hand as she pats her newest work of art. "Magnolia, I'm scared. Before tonight, all I thought about was winning. But now that I'm so close, I'm terrified something will happen that'll prevent me from moving on to the Titan Derby." I grip her hand tighter. "I've been counting on that last race, but what if I never even make it there?"

Magnolia takes my shoulders. "Don't you dare think that way."

"There are seven Titans left. Only four move on to the last race," I continue, my voice rising. "Why has it never occurred to me that I might be in the three to fall tonight?"

"Because you won't."

"Why not? I've never once placed in the top four."

Magnolia cranes her neck to the side, smiles. "My dear, stupid friend, you've made the mistake of assuming the previous races have anything to do with tonight. You are not the same Astrid Sullivan you were a week ago."

"I'm not?"

She shakes her head adamantly. "I don't even recognize you!

Check this girl out—custom-made silks, polished horse, the look of danger in her eyes."

"I have a look of danger in my eyes?"

"It's unnerving, I'll tell ya."

Magnolia shudders, and I laugh. Padlock hears me giggling and nibbles at my hair, attempting to return my attention to him where it belongs. I rub Padlock behind the ears, tell him I have danger in my eyes and he better watch out.

He seems unimpressed.

Hart strides into the barn like he built the place with his own hands, then cranes his neck, searching for the cameramen. When he sees it's only us, he loops his good arm around Magnolia. "Don't suck out there, Sullivan."

"Gee, thanks," I mutter, frowning at his fingers squeezing Magnolia's waist. Knowing I'll snap his one remaining arm into twelve separate pieces if he breaks her heart. "Sorry you can't race today."

"No, you're not," he says.

I grin. "Yeah, I guess I'm not."

Remembering Hart's comments about this race being his only chance at a new life, my smile falters.

"Don't you dare feel sorry for me," Hart says. "Not you."

I flip him the bird, and he laughs.

Rags trots over to our stall, and instead of supplying a pep talk, he simply jabs his thumb at Mag and Hart, implying they should beat it. After Magnolia blows me a kiss and says my head-piece looks fabulous and not to wreck it on the track because she could totally sell it for millions, Rags jogs my shoulders.

"I haven't talked to you about your dad since that night," he says.

I break my gaze away. "Don't worry about it. I'm fine."

"Your dad cares about you, Astrid. He's not the best at showing it, I noticed, but he wouldn't have hit me if he didn't." Rags smiles. "Your dad loves his kid, and he knows how to throw a hook. That's a man worth admiring."

"His gambling is the reason I'm having to do this." The first time I admit this to Rags is the first time I feel real resentment toward my father.

Rags hesitates only a second before saying, "Then show him what it means to bet on yourself."

"He said girls shouldn't be on the track," I mutter.

"Well, he's an idiot. Admirable? Yes. An idiot? Also yes."

This time I'm the one who laughs. Rags slaps me on the back harder than necessary. "Get your behind into that saddle and race hard, Astrid Sullivan. I already know how strong you are—you just go show everyone else."

I can't speak, because suddenly I can't help imagining what it would be like if Rags were my father. He would have believed in me from the start. He would have helped me train, and pushed me back into the saddle if I fell. He would have been tough, and brutally honest, but he would have been proud of me every step of the way.

But then I think: Does it really matter whether or not Rags is my father?

He did those things either way.

My manager gives Padlock a quick smack the way he did me, and my Titan trots out of the stall. As the woman with the clipboard checks off my horse's parts, I think about what Rags said. I think about it as my pulse begins to throb behind my eyes. I think about it as my blood begins to burn.

Soon, we are corralled into the stalls. Soon, I'm hearing my last name shouted by the crowd and smelling sweat from the jockeys and feeling the static of rain threatening to fall. I'm turning on Padlock's racing capability, and sensing when his steel body hums with power.

Soon, the gate pulls away.

And the final circuit race begins.

CHAPTER FIFTY-THREE

The seven Titans break from Cyclone Track earlier than ever before and plunge into the forest, the fresh two-mile dirt path lit only by the subtle lights on the temporary gates. After a few seconds on the *Shooting Stars* track, a rumbling sound emanates from the ground. I don't slow Padlock. I can't. Not this time. Not for anything.

But the sound grows louder, and terror fires down my back when two enormous blades split the earth apart. Built like oversized throwing stars, the blades slide back and forth across the track, daring any Titan to race between them. The two stars growl from the outside of the gate, cross each other in the middle, pause, and roll outward once again. They aren't tall enough to reach the jockeys in their saddles, but they'll crush our Titans' legs and slice their underbellies.

The first jockey doesn't hesitate. He flies between the two grinding blades and continues on. It was a lucky break. Nothing else. The second jockey isn't granted the same favor. Her Titan is caught between the gleaming stars, and a screeching, grinding sound fills the air. The crowd cheers and rattles the gates, threatening to bring them down in their excitement.

As I race Padlock faster, I notice the stars only hesitate when they cross each other in the center of the track. The jam makes it seem as though you have to wait until the stars open again and rush through before they snap back together. But what about that pause? It must be there for a reason. And then I see what I hadn't before—the narrow open spaces on either side of the blades when they cross each other. The key isn't to rush through the middle, it's to sneak past on the outside.

Padlock picks up his pace as I navigate him nimbly past the far right side, almost sideswiping the gate as we race. The jockeys behind me take my lead, and the next time the stars cross, they take the outside as well. They may have mimicked my strategy, but that jam bought me fourth place out of seven, and as with all races, every second counts.

Using the controls, I push Padlock through twists and turns in the track, and come upon the second jam. The jockeys ahead of me—Skeet, Penelope, and Batter—have stopped cold. Tiny, razor-sharp stars fall from the sky, landing shy of the gates on either side. The entire mass of stars moves in a circle much like a tornado. There are narrow crevices on the outside of the falling stars, but those crevices move in a circle too, and there's no way to tell when you could—

Unless.

I watch the stars, and run through every circle I've ever studied. I can't be sure by eyeballing the swirling mass, but it appears to follow a Fibonacci sequence. These sequences are mathematical circles that wrap around tiles, so if I counted correctly, Padlock and I could walk with the rotation until we reached the other side like entering a revolving door.

I look for the pattern, try to estimate the exact Fibonacci sequence. There! I rush Padlock forward and we squeeze into a safe place unreached by the falling stars. No sooner than Padlock's hooves reach safety do we blast forward.

We've only run a few steps when a thought occurs to me.

We're in first.

I passed the other three Titans when I figured out that jam, and now we have a shot at winning. If it takes the other jockeys too long to pass the falling star cloud, then we could make it across the finish line. I sweep my eyes across the track and into the distance, and I see it.

The end is near.

The crowd screams my name, and Padlock's hooves thunder against the ground. I allow myself to believe I'm going to win. I envision Rags giving me an honest-to-goodness hug and Magnolia dancing in place. I imagine telling my father I won the last circuit race, and that means I can win the Titan Derby too. I imagine reporters asking for an interview, not because I'm a poor girl from Warren County with an old, first-gen horse, but because I know how to race.

I imagine all of this.

And then I see Batter coming up my side.

His horse catches up with mine, and a quick glance back tells me Skeet is gaining on us. For now, I concentrate on beating Batter in a head-to-head race. I saddle down and push Padlock's gas bar. Padlock responds with fierce eagerness, driven to action by the Titan running at his side.

There's little distance between us and the finish line, and though Padlock has never been best at straight runs, he's holding his own. He's really doing it! My hands sweat and my thighs burn and my world rocks as we charge faster and faster.

When I spot a turn before the line drawn in the dirt, my heart leaps.

I've got him.

Batter realizes he's going to lose, and he jerks his Titan to the left to slam into me. But no bother, I jerk harder. Padlock and I pull all the way to the left and hug the gate until we come to the curb.

We lean.

We *lean*.

I scream with triumph and watch as Batter eases back.

And then we fall.

I slam into the ground and Padlock rolls over my right leg. I hear a pop from my body as Padlock skids along the dirt. He comes to a stop as Batter charges past, and seconds later, Skeet does too.

When I raise my head, I see many things: Batter racing over the finish line, the crowd throwing their bet cards into the air, Padlock on his side, hoofing the open air. But above everything, what I notice the most is Arvin Gambini's face.

He wears the same smile he does in the papers.

He's standing right outside the gate, right where a steel, star-headed spear tripped my Titan. Arvin nods as if acknowledging his own handiwork. Then he shoves his hands into his pockets and whistles as he walks away. I can see the way his lips form a small circle, the way his throat moves merrily.

That's when I realize something horrifying. If I don't get back on Padlock, I'll finish in the bottom three and won't continue on to the Titan Derby. I push myself up, screaming against the pain of my sprained ankle, and hobble toward Padlock, who's now on his feet.

Jumping off my bad foot to get back in the saddle causes my vision to blur with pain. I push Padlock's turbo button, slam on the gas bar, and we're back in the race.

But something is wrong.

Padlock oozes black smoke from his mouth and nostrils, and though we're yards from the finish line, I'm terrified he'll break down. His insides clank and his steps begin to falter. The rush of approaching Titans reaches me, and Penelope tears past me to secure third place. Two more Titans are close behind her, threatening to overtake me.

Pain sears through my foot and ankle, and my hands shake from trying to keep Padlock straight as he runs. I worry we won't make it before we're passed yet again. But mostly, I worry for my Titan. Machine or not, he's my friend.

But as we near the end, and the other horses gain on us, Padlock seems to quicken beneath me of his own accord. I follow his lead and give him a touch more gas.

We fly past the finish line, and a breath later, the final three Titans do as well.

For a moment, we were in first. We were so close to winning that I could feel the victory draped across my chest. But in the end, we finished in the last possible place to proceed to the Titan Derby. In the end, my Titan stumbles to the side and leans against the fence, smoke pouring from his mouth and nose and eyes.

Cameramen leap over the fence, making a beeline for my horse. The crowd roars, making my ears ring, though the snapping of the camera lenses still reaches me. The flashes are blinding, and the smoke enveloping us is a raging river of black. Rags and Magnolia make it to my side—my manager asking if I'm okay, Magnolia yelling for me to lean on her.

I'm here, Astrid. I'm here!

But I can barely understand her. Because I'm limping toward my horse, calling his name. And because my brain is machine-gunning this question without pause—

What has happened to Padlock?

What has happened to Padlock with one race remaining?

CHAPTER FIFTY-FOUR

It's been six days since Padlock and I fell. Six days, and the derby is so close it's breathing down our necks.

The problem lies with the engine. The high-compression race starter is shot. The part works inside the engine, engaging the system and allowing it to operate at its fullest, and fastest, potential. Rags theorizes that when the spear slammed into Padlock's side and the horse fell, that the impact caused the part to crack and malfunction.

The problem is twofold. The part itself is no longer available through aftermarket companies because the Titan 1.0 was never introduced commercially. Also, even if Barney could create another part from memory and raw materials, he doesn't have the equipment to do so.

So we panic, and make phone calls, and panic some more.

Lottie comes through on her end as my sponsor and procures machinery with which Barney's familiar. She purchases some of the materials he needs as well. But it isn't enough.

"The problem is this piece right here." Barney holds up the starter and points to a hole that looks like it shouldn't be there. "We need this in order for Padlock's engine to turn over."

"Lottie ordered it, though, right?" I ask, rubbing my wrapped ankle.

"She did, but that doesn't mean it'll get here in time," Rags responds.

The August sun blazes, and soon Barney is working in only a grease-stained T-shirt.

Magnolia plops down on a hay bale inside the barn and asks,

"When does it need to get here in order for Astrid to be able to race?"

Rags and Barney exchange a glance. Because I've been here every day while they've worked on Padlock, I already know the answer.

"If it was going to arrive, it'd be by this evening," I say. "The company is closed on Saturday."

"So what happens when it gets here?" she continues. "You guys just pop it in or something?"

Barney turns the starter over in his hands. "It's not quite that simple. But, yeah, with some adjustments I should be able to make it work."

I run my hands over Padlock's neck for the umpteenth time. His unseeing eyes pain me, and though he's only been turned off for six days, I feel as though it's been years since I've watched him prance or felt the nip of his steel lips. I miss his attentiveness, his neighs and sweet nuzzles. I miss his head-butts and the swish of his tail. And I miss riding.

I'm not the only one who misses the horse either. Barney and Rags stare at Padlock, wearing the same helpless, sorrowful looks on their faces.

"How much longer until they get here, you think?" Magnolia asks, her voice small.

No one answers her. We just turn from Padlock and instead gaze at the driveway leading to Barney's house.

And we wait.

....

At eight o'clock that evening, Rags throws the handkerchief he's been wringing to the ground. "You can't trust anyone to do their job anymore!"

"Didn't they promise it by this evening?" Magnolia asks.

Barney pats her on the back. "They said they'd do their best."

"I bet you Arvin Gambini got ahold of every parts maker in Michigan," my manager snarls. "He probably bribed them to deliver every piece we needed except one."

"There's got to be something else we can do," Magnolia says.

Barney shakes his head. "The horse won't run without that part. It might not have run *with* it."

Rags kicks over an oil canister, and I kneel as best I can with my injury and lay my body over Padlock's still, cold one.

"I'm sorry," I whisper.

Rags yanks me upright and pulls me against him. He hugs me tight and holds my head to his chest. "Don't you cry, kid. Don't you dare cry."

But I can hear the quaking in his voice, and it causes tears to spring to my eyes.

Magnolia joins our hug, and Barney lays his hand on my head.

It's much later, maybe an eternity of holding each other in that barn, when Barney says quietly, "We started this with a discontinued Titan, two old men, two clueless teens, and a woman we thought we'd never speak of again. In the end, we made it to the Titan Derby. No one's laughing now."

We're quiet for several minutes before Magnolia mumbles, "I was *not* clueless."

....

The whole way home, I quiz my manager on what we could still try. We could scour junkyards. We could call other ex-engineers who've left Hanover Steel. We could drive all the way to Sandusky, where the part is sold, and pound on the door in hopes of finding an after-hours employee.

But Rags has an objection for every idea I offer. What infuriates me is that his rebuttals make sense. I know it's over. I just can't accept it. One week ago, I rode Padlock better than I ever have. Now my horse is a pile of lifeless metal in the back of Rags's truck.

When we come to a stop outside my house, I feel splintered. I feel helpless.

"You raced a Titan on Cyclone Track, Astrid," Rags says softly, staring ahead. "You remember that the rest of your life, okay?"

A choking sound leaves my throat and I fight back tears.

Rags reaches over and squeezes my shoulder, but still he won't look at me.

When I manage to get myself out of the truck, I glance at the man I've learned to love like I did my own grandfather, flaws and all. "Thank you for caring about me," I say. "Now go get Lottie. Don't let all this end without something good happening."

The pain in Rags's eyes is a knife through the rib cage. I shut the door and reach into the truck bed, rub the flat of my hand over Padlock's cheek.

"You were a good horse," I whisper. "You will be again when that part arrives."

Padlock will have decades of running through open fields, and if Rags allows it, it'll be me on his back. But we won't have another run like we did six days ago. We won't have another race, another starting gate, another finish line so thrillingly close. But we'll have each other. And I'll have Rags and Barney and Magnolia. At least for as long as we can stay in Warren County.

Stories don't always end the way you want them to.

Life isn't always a fairy tale.

Life is *rarely* a fairy tale.

Sometimes, the real point is pursuing a worthwhile goal, even if you fall short in the end.

My dad is awake when I step inside our house. He rises to his feet when he sees me, and I'm careful not to favor my bad ankle, to cover up my injury.

"Astrid," he says, simply. His voice is so devastatingly heavy with regret that I sink through the carpet, plunge into the center of the earth. "When I'm wrong, I say I'm wrong." He clears his throat, has a hard time making eye contact. "I was out of sorts before your last race. You shouldn't have seen me that way. It's just I didn't want you to get hurt, and I—"

I stop him, because I can't do this now. "It doesn't matter anymore," I mutter. "My Titan got damaged, and we can't fix it. It's over. I won't be racing tomorrow night."

Now my dad does look at me. There's confusion and surprise spread across his face. If he'd watched the local news channel, he would have seen my name announced with the other three jockeys going to the Titan Derby. Lottie's been careful with the media, explaining that Padlock was damaged in the final circuit race, but was quickly repaired and ready to race. So my dad wouldn't have known.

Nobody will know until tomorrow at midnight, when Padlock and I aren't there to step onto the track.

I head toward my room, but stop short of the hallway. "You need to talk to Dani about Jason. Make her tell you."

"Astrid . . ." my dad tries again.

But I'm already gone. Already slipping into bed. Already feeling the steady beat of my throbbing ankle beneath the blankets. Already imagining who will take home the Derby Cup tomorrow night.

Dani's bed is empty when I fall asleep.

CHAPTER FIFTY-FIVE

I'm not sure what to do with myself the following morning. After more than two months, it's strange to wake with no training to complete. No weekly sessions with Lottie to attend. No race to prepare for. I'm simply me again.

I walk to Rags's house, because I can't stand the idea of losing contact with him. He stands in his garage, tinkering with the same machine I saw him working on at the start of summer when I told him he was off by three degrees. Maybe more. He turns the machine on, and then off. Then he holds a silver object up to the light in his garage and stares at it cockeyed.

"What's going on?" Magnolia asks.

I jump at the sound of her voice, then hold a finger to my lips and point at Rags.

Magnolia rubs the sleep from her eyes, and I love her time and again for always appearing when I need her, which, I'll admit, is almost always.

Rags pulls down his welding mask and goes to work on whatever it is he was holding. Sparks fly as a rare August breeze sweeps past Magnolia and me on the street. My heart leaps in my chest watching Rags work with such intensity. Has he found a solution to our problem? I take in his disheveled clothing, tousled white hair, and manic movements, and wonder if he's been up all night. Then again, he doesn't look much different than usual.

He labors in silence before pausing to scrutinize his work. He holds the gadget up a second time and scratches his jaw.

Then he hurls it across the garage.

My stomach drops to my feet, and I shuffle toward him. "I thought we were moving past this and being thankful for the opportunity and all that?" I say.

Rags removes the welding mask and drops it on a workbench. "I can't stop thinking I can figure it out. But I've been at it for hours, and nothing works. See this lever?" He shows me a piece that's shaped like a question mark. "I need something to make it catch. Should be easy enough, but it's not, because once the engine turns over, this piece of junk unlatches and then the engine overheats."

I lay my hand on his arm and attempt to comfort him the same way he did for me last night. "You and Barney did your best, Rags. It's okay. We'll be okay. Let's go do something fun today, and tonight we'll watch the race and criticize every move the jockeys make."

Rags chances a smile. "I'd do well at that."

Magnolia punches his shoulder. "You win at standing still and providing useless information, my man."

Rags glances at her. "Why are you here?"

"Sustenance, remember?"

Rags sighs. "I'm sorry, Astrid. There's got to be a way to rig this blasted thing. I just don't know how to do it."

"Mind if I take a look?" a familiar voice asks.

I spin around and find my father standing in Rags's driveway. A few feet behind him is Magnolia's dad, holding a cup of coffee and a rusted toolbox.

"Daddy?" I say.

My dad shoves his hands in his pockets and his face reddens. I walk over to him slowly, smiling because I can't help myself. He's the one man who can fix anything, and him being here means everything. I stand before my father, letting the moment sink in.

Recognizing that he may have gotten me into this mess with a habit his own father taught him, but he's also the man I let down the day Grandpa died. I wrap my arms around his waist. He hugs me back immediately, and it's strange and awkward and perfect.

When I let go, he jabs a thumb over his shoulder. "I brought Frank. He's mostly useless, but he has a decent set of tools."

"At least I've got a set of something," Frank jokes.

While Magnolia hugs her dad—and steals his coffee—Rags strides down the driveway and approaches my father.

"I, uh . . . I'm sorry about the other night," my dad says to Rags. "I haven't been myself lately."

Rags touches the bruise beneath his eye. "I told your girl you've got a nice swing."

"I played baseball at Canyon High," Dad responds. Then he offers Rags his hand.

Rags shakes it. "Just so you know, I'd hit a man for putting my daughter on a Titan too."

My dad smiles. "Didn't say I was sorry for *hitting* you. Just said I was sorry."

"I see you found my house without my telling you where it was."

Dad's grin grows wider. "Remember that."

Rags laughs, and then eyeballs Frank's tools. "You really think you can fix this pile of metal?"

"We can fix anything," Frank replies, before spitting on the pavement.

Rags pats his truck and grins, excitement making him stand taller. "Well, we better get on over to Barney's place then. He's got better equipment."

....

The sun is setting when my father and Frank appear from Barney's work area. They've eaten nothing but the sour cherry danishes Magnolia made, and have sweat so much that I smell my dad before I see him.

I jump off the back of Rags's truck gate, anxiety rolling off me in waves.

Magnolia is at my side.

Neither one of us breathes.

I watch my father's face for signs of triumph, or discouragement, but as always, I can't read him. It isn't until a shadowy figure appears in the doorway of the barn that I get my answer.

Padlock trudges toward me, head held high, black steel glistening in the dying light.

I cover my mouth to stop the emotion from pouring forth. "He's fixed?"

Rags wipes his hands on his jeans. "Not entirely. Your father and Frank fastened a part to the compressor, but we have no idea if it'll hold." Rags glances at my dad before adding, "I'm not sure it's safe to ride, Astrid. If the part malfunctions during the derby, you could get seriously hurt. Even if it does hold, it'll be much harder to work the control panel than you're used to."

I look at my dad too, awaiting his response. If he says the part will hold, I trust him. But he doesn't mention his work, he only stares at me, a small smile pulling at the corner of his lips.

"Astrid can make it work," he says. "My little girl can do anything."

CHAPTER FIFTY-SIX

We make it to Cyclone Track a half hour before the race begins. I throw on my silks, breeches, and riding boots, and hug my best friend. Magnolia doesn't give me a long speech to inspire confidence. She simply smiles and says, "Remember: You're here. You made it. Love you madly." Lottie nudges Magnolia, and after giving me a small wave, she guides my best friend to watch from the crowd. I like to think she'll stand by my father instead of Hart, but he went home after repairing Padlock's part, saying that I didn't need him.

I was too proud to admit that I did.

Barney slaps me on the back, grins, and follows Lottie and Magnolia outside. I guess the time for talking is over. There's only one thing left to do tonight.

I run my hands over Padlock's side, and the horse bends his head in greeting. "I don't know what I'll do if I don't win tonight," I say to him. "My family stills needs money to keep the house. And Magnolia's family does too. My father . . . he's better, sort of. But what happens when Monday rolls around and he goes on another bad interview? What happens when that final notice on our house arrives? My parents will fight. Dani will run. And Zara will look to me because I failed to fix things like I promised." I hug my horse close. "I need this, Padlock. And you deserve it."

My horse jerks back and looks at me intently. My brow furrows watching him study me that way. It's like he's peering into my soul. Like he's trying to tell me something important, but can't say it aloud. His determined stance soothes me, tells me he'll catch me if I fall. And his eyes seem to say only: *Trust me.*

I open my mouth to tell my horse how much he means to me, but Rags chooses that moment to make an appearance. My trainer fidgets, shifting his weight back and forth, and I know it's not the race he's worried about.

"I don't have the words for this kind of thing," he says, patting Padlock on the haunches. "But you should know it's been my honor to be your manager."

My tongue is thick in my mouth as I try to respond. Unsure of what to say, I come back with, "I hope at the end of this race you still think I was the right person to race your Titan." I pause. "I hope I make you proud."

Rags meets my gaze. "You've already made me proud, Astrid. Sometimes I'm so proud I could burst."

I turn away to collect myself, because I have to concentrate.

Because I have to win.

Rags spots me as I swing into my saddle. "Remember what I said about his engine. You'll have to race smart, not fast. If you push Padlock too hard, the part could disconnect. If that happens, he'll turn off and you probably won't be able to get him started again quick enough to get back in the race."

"I understand," I say.

Rags nods, and then opens the stall gate. I guide Padlock to the parts check line, flutters tickling my insides. What if she doesn't let me compete? The part we have isn't standard issue, and isn't that what she's monitoring?

When it's my turn, Rags nervously licks his lips. The woman pops open Padlock's engine flap and starts checking off boxes on her sheet. She stops and frowns at us, and my stomach drops to my feet.

Tapping her pencil eraser on Padlock's belly, she says, "This isn't standard issue. What is this?"

"It won't give her an advantage in the race, I assure you," Rags says firmly.

"Doesn't matter," the woman retorts with a yawn in her voice. "No foreign parts."

My blood surges and my hands curl into fists. This can't be happening. Rags tells me we can hardly get Padlock to stay running, and now we can't even race with a handicap?

A man steps into the barn, someone who's been spying on our check-in. "Let them go ahead, Devon," Arvin Gambini says, casting his million-dollar smile my way. "We don't want to hold anyone back."

"No, you wouldn't want to do that, would you?" I snap.

Arvin continues to grin as the woman looks from him to me, and shrugs. She closes Padlock's hatch and waves us forward.

Rags walks beside me as we leave the barn. "I'm not going to question his intentions back there, and neither should you. Mind on the track, okay?"

"Okay," I reply, but I glance back anyway and catch sight of the tall, dark man watching Arvin Gambini. He narrows his eyes and jots something down on a notepad. Standing next to him is Theo. He doesn't appear pleased.

I return my attention to the final race. The Titan Derby—a race entitled *Darkness Falls*. I notice the starting gate is empty, and that the crowd is thin for such an important night. I'm about to ask Rags what's going on when a handler approaches.

"I'll lead you to the starting point," a young boy says.

"Where will that be?" Rags demands.

"Can't say." The boy reins Padlock and leads the horse behind him. Before we get too far away, he shoots Rags a backward glance. "Special track tonight."

My gut twists into knots. A special track? The derby track is always special—longer, or packed with harder jams—but never has the media not known some detail beforehand, and as a result, the jockeys and attendees as well.

Rags stands tall as we're guided away. Right before we're out of earshot, my trainer yells, "You can do this, Astrid. I can already see the cup in your hands."

I laugh to myself, touched by his unbreakable confidence. But as I'm led farther and farther from my manager—down, down into the blackness—my laughter falls away.

CHAPTER FIFTY-SEVEN

We're beneath the ground in some sort of mine shaft. I don't believe the engineers created the shaft itself, but they must have created the downward slope we took to arrive here. I remember my history teacher once referring to Detroit as the City of Salt because of its elaborate mining system beneath our buildings and streets and rumbling, spit-and-vinegar vehicles.

There's no crowd to be seen. No cameramen or photographers. There are only four Titans prancing next to one another, and a few minutes later, there is Arvin Gambini. The man is followed by the reporter and his brother, who don't seem to enjoy being underground.

I sidle up next to the other Titans and take my place behind a yellow line. Batter, Skeet, and Penelope look at me and scowl. They are competitors tonight, but where Padlock and I are concerned, they are united. I dismiss their looks of disapproval and instead study my surroundings, the chalk line drawn crudely along the ground and the lightbulbs hanging five feet apart and stretching into the cavern.

"Welcome to the Titan Derby, my friends," Arvin booms. "This year, we will not be announcing the exact race length. Rest assured your fans will see the race from the use of small cameras mounted throughout the track. I wish you the best of luck. Please wait for the starting flag to fall before beginning." Arvin picks up a flag from the ground, and the hairs on the back of my neck rise. This doesn't feel right. It's too dangerous down here. How would the medics get to us if something tragic happened? And what about the mine itself? How long has it lain dormant? Could the ceiling cave in?

The Titans push closer, and one by one their eyes blaze to life. I touch Padlock's small black button and, thank goodness, his racing engine kicks on, his ruby irises burning along the walls and ceiling and floor. With all four Titans' eyes glowing red, it looks as though we'll charge through the gates of hell when that flag drops.

"Arvin," Theo says, his voice holding a note of hesitation.

But it doesn't matter.

Arvin only smiles.

And lets the flag fall.

There's no time to think. No time to strategize. We're off, the sound of Arvin's mad laughter filling the space behind us as Titan hooves beat the ground. I notice almost immediately white dashes chalked into the ground, much like the marks on a road. We follow the marks instinctually, Batter taking the lead, and Penelope falling into place behind him.

Our first jam comes after only a few seconds. A swinging lightbulb overhead casts an eerie glow onto our obstacle— rolling balls sliding back and forth along the ground. They span from one side of the wall to the other, and go on for twenty feet. I don't know what's inside them, and I don't have time to care.

I drive Padlock down the middle, only a fraction behind my competitors. As always, I search for a pattern to the dark metal balls. There must be a way to predict the time it takes them to roll between the two panels placed low on the ground. But as my mind spins through the possibilities, and Padlock grows closer, the light shuts off.

Penelope releases a scream as we're thrown into total darkness. In the distance is another light, but it's evident we'll have to pass this jam blindly. I clench my jaw and push onward, but slow Padlock when something explodes, throwing flames into the air.

"What the—?" Batter yells.

Another fireball detonates, and Skeet hollers.

I understand at once what's happening. The balls detonate when they hit the Titans' legs. This time, I don't try to find a solution, because quite frankly, I don't believe there is one. While other jockeys stand still, attempting to solve the problem, I rush forward.

The first ball hits Padlock's hooves and fire burns up his leg, almost searing my injured ankle. I jerk my legs up and cross them in Padlock's saddle. My Titan is made of steel, and so there's no danger of him burning unless the heat is over a thousand degrees Fahrenheit, in which case the heat would be too great to survive at all. That means these fireballs are here only to slow us down, but I won't let that happen. Not when there's this much at stake.

Four more balls explode beneath Padlock's belly, and it isn't until we've passed the jam that I wonder about my horse's engine. His steel body is intact, but what about the fragile part connected to his engine? Has that overheated?

I don't have time to ponder more over this, because before I know it, we're closing in on the second jam.

In the light's reappearance, I'm able to see that I'm in third place. Batter is gaining on me, while Penelope and Skeet race a few yards ahead. I try not to dwell on this, for the track could go on for miles, and any jam could put me in a different position.

Scanning the walls, I notice orange nozzles hung at sporadic intervals. A silver box sits to one side—no telling what it holds. Penelope and Skeet race toward the jam, but right as they reach the perimeter, the lights switch off once again.

The sound of hooves moving reaches my ears, and a moment later a gust of fire shoots from the walls. Skeet screams, and in the fire's glow I see her pull her horse to the right and out of harm's way. But as soon as she reaches the other side, another flame shooter kicks on. As she navigates through, I notice the fire forms a zigzag pattern. So with sweat forming at my temples, I close my eyes and punch him through the labyrinth of fire.

Without my eyesight, I can't properly predict where the next gas spout lies, only that my best bet is to keep weaving left and then right. When we reach the other side, I notice I'm side by side with Penelope, Skeet still in the lead. Batter has fallen back again, but I know he's close behind.

The lightbulbs reappear as we shoot onward, following the uneven terrain up and down and around corners. When the ground takes on a strange appearance, I know we've reached the third jam.

I do my best to make out what it is. But then the lights snuff out.

And Padlock and I fall forward.

CHAPTER FIFTY-EIGHT

We plunge downward and stick in place. What should make a splash instead makes a spongy, goopy sound. Unsure of what to do, I attempt to navigate Padlock forward with the gas bar and joysticks, but something about the substance he's swimming in confuses his system. When the sound of three other Titans wading through the tacky liquid reaches me, my pulse picks up its pace.

I push Padlock's gas bar farther and hear an unmistakable grinding noise. Remembering Padlock's delicate engine, I ease off the bar and think. Pushing him harder is no use. In fact, I think we're wading in circles. I don't know how to get him to swim straight, but I have to figure it out.

I rack my brain until finally, I have it. The answer isn't in the control panel. It's not even in the saddle at all.

Quietly, I dismount. My heart sledgehammers in my chest when I slide into the muddy mass. My arms and legs feel as though they weigh a thousand pounds, and I can hardly keep my head above the surface no matter how hard I kick. But when I grab on to Padlock's neck, I'm able to calm myself enough to strategize.

Putting my hands on either side of Padlock's muzzle, I move backward, in the direction of where I believe the wall lies. With the gas bar still engaged, my Titan follows. I release a sigh of relief, because I wasn't sure whether the Titan would swim along with me without my palms on the joysticks.

When I reach the wall, I feel my way along and guide my horse. He's strong enough to power through the substance, and with me showing the way, we're quickly making it to what I hope is the other side. Eventually, my feet touch the bottom and excitement rushes through me in waves.

I limp backward out of the substance, putting most of my weight on my good ankle, until Padlock is far enough out that I can remount him. I push his gas bar back into a racing speed, and we're off. When the lights flip on, I glance around. Not a single Titan races ahead of us. Somehow, someway—we've taken first.

I revel in this realization for all of sixty seconds—Padlock and me flying through the shadowy tunnel—until we're slammed from behind. My Titan stumbles to the right as Batter pulls to my left, a sneer spread across his ruby-cheeked face.

"You're going to fall again, trash," he yells.

His words echo through the tunnel, and when I listen hard enough, I also hear the sounds of Penelope and Skeet closing our lead. I don't respond to Batter's taunts, only navigate Padlock toward a tight turn and prepare to take it. Batter cuts me off, though, his Titan slamming into mine a second time. Sparks fly as their steel bodies grind against each other.

Padlock slams his head into Batter's Titan and the two of them collide into the opposite wall from the impact. Despite my nerves, I release a laugh, because I certainly didn't make Padlock do that. More and more, my Titan is working on his own. I'm not sure if it's the EvoBox that makes him do such things, but I don't chastise him for it one bit.

Soon, our four horses are growling toward the fourth jam.

Water shoots down from ceiling sprinklers. The temporary lights illuminate a wall of water so dense I can't see through to the other side. It pounds the earth with such force that bits of rock dance at its feet. Batter bangs into me once again and takes the lead. But the moment he hits the water, he screams in pain. The intensity of the stream must be like getting hit with a fireman's hose.

I ease off Padlock's gas bar, and instead lean on his brake. Then, without slowing to a complete stop or hesitating, I swing my legs over the side and leap off, leaving the gas bar engaged. My ankle screams when I come down on it, but I bite down and tell myself the injury doesn't exist. Then I curl myself under Padlock's stomach, his steel body protecting me, and the two of us head straight through the destructive water jets. When we appear on the other side, the lights flicking back on, I see that Padlock's steel has tiny pockmarks in it from the jets—and that Skeet is in the lead. What's more, there's a good fifty feet between her and us. So I pull myself back into my saddle and bear down.

I don't manage to catch up to Skeet, but I do get close. Already, purple bruises blossom on the back of her neck. She must have ridden straight through the engineered waterfall without stopping. My focus turns from beating out Batter, to beating Skeet, the girl who's deaf to pain.

Skeet pummels forward, turning around each bend with her uncle's legacy for speed, but I stay with her, hoof for hoof. The two of us sail through the tunnel like two characters in a video game, the cling-clang of our steel horses the rat-tat of an arcade parlor.

Skeet begins to slow at last, and I wonder if her Titan has malfunctioned. But no, I see what's stopped her now. It's the fifth jam, lying straight ahead.

Just looking at it sends a chill down my spine.

CHAPTER FIFTY-NINE

Metal sheets cover the walls, ceiling, and floor of the tunnel. Bouncing around in their own cage are more throwing stars than anyone could safely pass through. Every few seconds there's a pause—the stars sticking to the metal sheets, tempting the jockeys forward—before being released again to spin about the area.

I watch for a pattern, but just as before, the lights flip off. Now there is only the metal clang of the stars. I could listen for a pattern, but math is always something I've studied in my mind's eye, and if I can't see it, I can't figure it out. I do my best to listen, but all I hear is the sound of Skeet screeching as she chances rushing through. From what little I saw, the distance to cross didn't seem that great. So maybe the answer is simply to dash straight through.

But what if one of those stars strikes my throat, or my head? Couldn't the small blades be enough to kill me if they hit the right spot?

I can just make out Batter's shape to my left, and Penelope's to my right. Penelope releases a grunt of determination, and then takes action. Soon it's only Batter and me remaining behind. I can feel him watching. Waiting to see what I'll do.

Like my trainer suggested, I focus my attention on what it is I need to do. Instead of listening to the sound of the stars clashing, I scrutinize my surroundings. Besides the faint glitter of the stars, and Batter's pacing, I see only one other thing. At first, I'm certain it's my imagination. But as I move closer, and run my hand along the wall, I find I'm right.

There's an opening here.

It's hardly two Titans wide, but when I squint my eyes, I see a glow in the distance. The oxygen solidifies in my lungs and my hands begin to shake.

The tunnel splits.

The question is whether to take the split. If I'm wrong, I'll never make it back in time to regain the ground that I lost. But if I'm right . . .

Bringing my heels into Padlock's sides and jamming his gas bar upward, we take off through the narrow space.

What am I doing? What am I doing? What am I doing?

Just when I'm sure I've made the wrong choice, I make out even more light. My scalp starts tingling. A slow smile grows upon my face. The light blooms brighter, and I race Padlock faster toward it. Soon, I'm certain I am right—the end of the mine shaft is near. I can see it sloping upward, a line of dangling bulbs lighting the way.

As the tunnel is illuminated, I can't help but roar with excitement. I may really make it. I may really win!

I can barely contain my exhilaration, until two things happen—

One—I hear Batter racing toward me with a vengeance.

Two—I see smoke swirling out of Padlock's nostrils.

I ease off Padlock's gas bar immediately, my head fuzzy with fear, but then Batter is able to eat up the stretch between us too quickly. I reapply gas and Padlock takes off again, but now more smoke pours out and up. Screaming with frustration, I navigate Padlock faster toward the incline that will take us out of the shaft. I need to get him across that finish line. Then Rags and Barney can repair him for real.

I only hope he can make it that far.

Whispering a silent prayer, I take liberties with Padlock's

engine, forcing him well into the caution area on the performance gauge. When I glance back, I see that Batter is still firmly in second place, assuming Skeet and Penelope are still behind us in the other tunnel.

Padlock and I hit the incline and race uphill, me leaning my body forward to take stress off his flight, and him grunting from the exertion. The smoke streams out steadily, but it still isn't nearly as bad as it was the day we fell, so I push onward, cringing when one of Padlock's red eyes flickers in and out against the last of the mine shaft.

As we exit the underground track, I spot a camera mounted on the roof. A green light flicks on, telling me the camera picked up our appearance. At the exact same time that the green light turns on, I hear the unmistakable sound of a crowd roaring with approval.

I hadn't heard them before this very moment. It sounds like they aren't too far away. It sounds like they just saw me appear and have waited a very long time to make any noise at all.

Which means I am most likely the first to appear from that mine shaft.

Which means I am first.

I release a wild cry of triumph as I shoot out onto the last stretch of the track that will wind through the forest and end at the final finish line of the Titan season. Behind that line is a two-million-dollar check.

Behind that line is a different life than one I've ever known.

I grip the joysticks firmly and curl my shoulders toward my Titan. I set my gaze ahead toward the end. I set my gaze so that I don't see when Batter blasts out of the mine shaft. I don't see when the final jam is detonated and a blade descends from above and comes crashing down on my Titan, barely missing my head.

The blade, sensing impact, pulls back up. But it's too late. The damage is done. Padlock skids along the ground, and I fly from my place in the saddle, small rocks digging into my palms. My Titan lies motionless on the ground as I clutch my injured ankle and scream. Batter races past, his own Titan clanking and clattering from the jams.

All my life, people told me I was good at math. *Gifted with numbers*, they said. *A mathlete*, they said. But why, then, did I miss the obvious?

Three circuit races.

One of fire, one of water, one of blades.

One Titan Derby.

Two jams with fire, two with water, two with blades.

I didn't notice the pattern.

And now I've lost the race.

CHAPTER SIXTY

I am broken heart and broken spirit and broken mind. Don't want to watch as I'm left in Batter's dust. Don't want to see the disappointment on my father's face after he worked so hard to put me in this derby.

A noise reaches me. Screeching, rattling, grinding.

The sound of a machine in need of oiled parts.

I raise my head.

Padlock is pulling himself upright. He staggers and falls. Pulls himself up a second time and remains standing. His head whips in the direction of Batter's fleeing Titan, and then he rushes over, nudges me—*hard*—with his muzzle. His one red eye blazes with such intensity that goose bumps rise along my skin.

Padlock stomps his front foot.

He stomps it again, his hoof dangerously close to my hand.

Then he does something that steals the breath from my lungs. He rises up on his back legs, his front hooves swiping the air as he releases a bone-rattling neigh and puffs black soot into the night.

When he comes down on all fours, I'm driven to action. Padlock is right. We're not out of this race yet.

I swing myself into the saddle as Padlock prances, anxious to be released.

My hands flutter to the control panel, ready to kick Padlock's racing gear back into action and work the joysticks. But I freeze. Look at the smoke rising from my Titan. Watch him throw his head and snort and stomp.

Who's to say I can finish this race better than he can?

This is the last race. The last stretch. The last shot.

And Padlock needs this as much as I do.

I don't hesitate.

Autopilot: ON

Padlock rises into the air again and I fumble for the handlebars and hang on, my knuckles whitening as he tears a hole through the sky and the moon. When he comes down, he swings his head around to look at me. His one good eye ignites with passion. But there's something else there too. Love, maybe. Affection, for sure.

His red eye glitters. He's fury and rage and retribution. He's fire and wrath. And I've just released those things onto the track.

Heaven help the Titans who stand in his way.

He's off!

Padlock runs and the world trembles. He runs and the entire universe tilts to get a better look. Smoke puffs from his nostrils and his eye cuts a crimson path and his body parts clash, steel on steel.

In seconds, we're on Batter's tail. A moment later, we're catching up. When Batter hears the sound of our approach, he looks over his shoulder. The shock on his face is worth all the prize money in the world.

He grabs the gas bar and shoves it halfway to the top.

No matter.

Padlock is on him.

Trees whip by and soon a crowd of race-goers appear on either side of us. Padlock blasts by all of it, eating up the ground, blazing past turns. He puts himself beside Batter's horse, and I see fear in Batter's eyes.

I see it.

No matter how far Batter pushes his horse, Padlock matches his speed. He's never been good at straight dashes, but tonight he's untouchable.

I used to race Padlock like I wanted to place well.

But Padlock races like he's already won.

In the distance, my eyes make out something that causes my entire body to turn inside out—the finish line. Padlock and I see it at the same time, and energy fires across both our backs.

I dare to hope we still have a chance, until I notice that the smoke pouring from Padlock's nose is now *billowing*—great, heaping clouds of the stuff shooting out his nose and eyes and ears. I cry out and start to reach for the autopilot button.

But Padlock won't be stopped.

Not tonight.

The button is jammed. I pull on the brake bar, turn the key in the ignition, but nothing moves. I try everything to stop him, to keep him from blowing his engine. But nothing works. As my mind buzzes, I recall the way my Titan looked at me in the stable an hour earlier. As if he wouldn't allow me to lose. And that if it came down to it, he'd sacrifice himself to protect my future.

Padlock's one good eye flickers, and now smoke whiffs out of that too.

"I don't want this!" I scream. "Stop, Padlock. *Stop!*"

Tears streak my face as his insides begin to rattle and crash. A bolt tears apart from his body and nearly hits me as it flies into the forest. My Titan is a machine, born to compete and that's all. But he's become so much more than that. He's made me stronger, braver. He's given me confidence I never could have found elsewhere. He's given me a friend.

And he's made me trust again.

Remembering this last part, I tighten my hold on the saddle horn and lean over.

Okay, Padlock, I think. *Let's do this, then.*

"Go, Padlock!" I scream, barely able to hear my own voice. "Go, go, go!"

Batter's horse stays with us around every turn, up every straightaway, past every flash of the cameras. Our horses are nostril-to-nostril, body-to-body, tail-to-tail. My competitor doesn't chance slamming into me. It's too risky. Not at this speed. Not this close to the end.

The finish line closes in so quickly it's as if it's racing toward us instead of the other way around. I cry out from pride and joy and madness. My blood pumps and my heart pounds and my pulse screams.

The finish line is upon us.

It's right there.

And so is Batter.

And so is a crevice.

An enormous break in the ground like the one I stopped at during our race against Hart. But this time, there's no stopping.

Batter stops short.

Padlock does not.

He soars over the crevice, and for an instant we are suspended, looking down at the crowd of screaming faces. Looking down at the world from our place in the sky. There is no sound here in the stars. There is only peace and happiness and a sublime moment I'll hold inside me until the day I die.

Then we are crashing down. We are rolling over the finish line. Noise slams into me like a tidal wave. Cheering and booing and my last name shouted over and over.

Sull-i-van!

Sull-i-van!

Sull-i-van!

But what about my horse's name? What about my Titan? Theo races out onto the track wearing a smile much warmer than his brother's, holding a trophy, golden and glistening. But I don't care about that. I care about my Padlock.

I was thrown from his back when we came down, and now I hobble toward him. I'm bruised and in pain, but I'm okay. Padlock, however, is barely moving. He lies on his side and kicks at the ground with his front hooves. I throw myself over his body as more smoke blasts out. Someone is there, trying to pull me off my Titan, but I won't let go of my horse. Padlock turns his head back to look at me, and I move my mouth to his ear.

"You are a good horse," I whisper to him, emotion making my words thick. "You are the very best horse. I love you, Padlock."

His eye flickers and I swear it, I'll forever swear it, I see amusement in that eye. And triumph. And love.

I embrace him tightly, crying into his steel-threaded mane, my tears sizzling against his neck. The camera flashes snap, and tickets fly, and a tall man with a notepad in his hand looks down upon it all, a grimace on his face.

When I'm lifted into the air, I fight against the person who holds me. I don't want to leave my Titan. But when I look down at my horse's face, I see it's him who has left me. I moan with sorrow and cling to Rags's chest, cry into his warmth for what feels like an eternity. Finally, finally, I am able to lift my head, and when I do, I find it's not Rags who carries me far from the crowd and the cameras.

It is my father.

CHAPTER SIXTY-ONE

Three weeks later, Magnolia and I lie on my bed, kicking our feet behind us as we pore through my glossy fashion magazines, Magnolia looking at a model's hair, me admiring a lifestyle I could now have, but don't need.

Two million dollars. Enough to do anything, really.

Except bring Padlock back to me.

I repaid Lottie's investment money and provided her the agreed-upon portion of the winnings—a total deduction of two hundred and seventy thousand dollars. I could tell Lottie didn't want it, but I insisted. I couldn't have done any of this without her, after all. Rags and Barney were just as stubborn, saying they got what they wanted. They saw their Titan race, and they saw their Titan win.

Last weekend, because he wouldn't accept his "blood money" winnings, I snuck behind Rags's back and had his work shed and garage remodeled. Magnolia and I oversaw the project, and even asked the contractors to make some updates to the front of his home while he was out. Rags acted offended when he returned. *I had perfectly good tools to begin with*, he growled.

But he stopped once he saw the new truck and trailer parked in his driveway. He stopped when he weighed the new tools in his hand, and I could see the desire to build things taking hold.

Things between Magnolia and me didn't change after I anonymously paid off the mortgage on her family's home. I'm not sure I got away with the *anonymous* part. The day after I did it, Magnolia showed up at my house grinning. *That was pretty cool of you, my friend*, she said. *Pret-ty cool.* Then, in true Magnolia fashion, she made me pastries every day for a week as a thank-you.

"You realize you're going to have to beat the boys back with a stick when we get to UM, right?" Magnolia asks.

"Doubt it," I say. But then I point to a hot guy on horseback in a cologne ad. "I wouldn't mind someone who looks like this, though." Even though I'm showing Magnolia the shirtless dude, my eyes still catch on the horse. My heart lurches thinking, once again, of the steel horse I will only ever see in my dreams. Lottie tells me the best way to give glory to Padlock now is to live life with intention and gratefulness. And joy. So I attempt to follow her advice and return my attention to this sunny, lazy afternoon.

Magnolia and I are officially seniors now, which means we'll be college bound next year. We have to start applying soon, but the University of Michigan has reached out to us, as fascinated with our involvement in the races as the media has been. And not just local media. The Titan Derby has received national attention since Bruce Edwards, the journalist from Chicago, broke the news about a man named Arvin Gambini putting people's lives in peril in order to franchise the track. The public didn't like this one bit, and Arvin's grandmother didn't either. She pulled the money she'd invested straight out of Arvin's pocket and gave it to Theo instead.

With a spotlight on the track, the local authorities have been forced to put their gambling tickets away and open an investigation into Arvin's actions at Cyclone Track and whether the stock he bought in Hanover Steel five years ago is considered insider trading.

The papers say Theo Gambini kept his hands clean, and has plans to continue the races. He'll discontinue the jams to make the races safer, and require all riders be over the age of twenty-one. The races will now take place during the day, with one family-friendly race at the start of the season.

Other than that, bets will still be placed.

Jockeys will still compete for glory.

Titans will still run.

Magnolia sees the look on my face and jumps off the bed, a copy of the UM brochure in her hand. "I almost can't wait to get our lives started, you know." She glances back at me. "You still going to major in engineering?"

I nod. "Barney says math nerds will be welcome there."

Zara comes in—intruding on my sisterly space—and flops down onto the floor dramatically. "I'm so booooored," she moans.

"Hang out with Mom and Dad," I suggest.

"Um, no," she says, turning up her nose. "They're outside working in the garden."

"Dad too?" I ask. Though I'm not sure I'm surprised. A few nights ago, Dad followed Mom outside when she went to work on our neighbors' yards. And a couple of nights after that, she followed after him when he left with a deck of cards in his pocket. The twosome came back shortly after, Mom giggling and Dad whispering Things I Do Not Want to Hear into her ear. She stopped him from gambling. I don't know if that'll hold, but it's a step in the right direction. Finding out Dani was involved in an unhealthy relationship really did a number on Dad and his involvement in our family. It also helped that an aftermarket Titan parts company in Dearborn got wind of Dad rigging Padlock for the derby, and said they wanted that man on their team.

"Think we can be roommates at college?" Magnolia asks.

"If I get put with anyone but you, I'll act loony until they move me." I make crazy eyes at Magnolia to show her I'm serious.

Magnolia stretches her arms above her head. "It's wild, isn't it? Soon we'll be, like, adults. Going to class and parties and meeting boys."

"Boys?" Zara's eyebrows rise.

"What about Hart?" I ask.

She grins. "Yeah, yeah. He'll be visiting too. The jerk."

I purse my lips. "Ugh. I can't believe you two are serious."

"I'm serious that he's hot." She wags her eyebrows. "You know he's going to sign a deal with Hanes? The first campaign will be him in his skivvies on a billboard with the tagline *He falls hard*. It's a double entendre, but he only has eyes for me. I made him pinkie it."

"Well, a pinkie swear *is* binding."

Magnolia hits me with my own pillow. "Zara's right. This is boring." She puffs out her lips, then holds up her finger like she has an idea. "Hey, let's go find cloud animals like we used to!"

"Only kids do that," Zara says.

"No, let's do it," I say, smiling. "I can totally find the best one."

"Yeah, right," Zara responds, already on her feet.

The three of us pull on our shoes, breezing past Mom and Dad, and race into the sunshine. I drop down onto the grass, scouring the puffy clouds for manes and equine noses, until a man's face appears over my head.

"What the heck are you doing, kid?" Rags asks.

I hop to my feet and give Rags a half hug. He brushes me off and tells me to stop acting like a girl.

"Nice vest," Magnolia tells Rags from the ground. "And I'm here because I'm her BFF, so bite me."

"You know, I was about to say you look nice today," Rags tells Magnolia.

Magnolia sits up. "You were?"

"No."

Magnolia sticks her tongue out at him. Then she returns to her hunt.

"Aren't you guys a little old to be lying on the ground like this?" Rags asks, but it seems to me he's stalling on asking me, or telling me, something more important.

"Aren't you always calling me *kid*?" I reply.

Rags smiles and digs his hands into his pockets. "Can we take a quick walk?"

"Sure." I dust myself off and tell Magnolia and Zara, "Hey, I'll be back in a sec."

"Take your time," Magnolia says.

"Take *forever*," Zara replies, giggling.

Rags and I walk across the street to Candlewick Park, so close to where I met my future trainer—him red and sweating, me insisting he sit down and remove that ridiculous vest. What a bitter old man I thought he was then.

Rags scratches his head like he's nervous to speak, so I elbow him and say, "Man up already, will ya? What is it?"

"All right," he says brutishly, but I know he's glad I prompted him. "I've been thinking about something."

"That's scary."

"What if I had an idea?"

"Even scarier."

Rags frowns, and I laugh.

"Tell me this idea," I say, because I want to know.

"What if I proposed to Lottie?"

I squeal with happiness.

Rags grabs his head like I'm killing him. "So you'll help me plan the darn thing? I'm sure she'll want it to be romantic and crap."

I throw my arms around Rags and hug him, hardly able to contain my excitement for the soon-to-be fiancé.

"One more thing," Rags says, pulling a small black box from his pocket. "An early Christmas present."

"Oh, wow, really?" I say.

"Stop staring at it, already," Rags replies. "Just open it."

When I do, I see a square-shaped necklace charm with a latch. Inside the latch is an intricate patchwork of parts and gears. "It's beautiful," I say. "But what is it?"

"It's Padlock's EvoBox," Rags answers. "It's what made him, *him*."

My breath catches in my lungs and I swallow down the lump in my throat. Since the derby, I've thought of little else besides the friend I lost. So having this . . . it means everything. I lean into Rags and hug him again. This time, though, Rags doesn't just give me an awkward pat. He hugs me back, and lets me hang on for as long as I need. Then he watches as I fumble with my newfound treasure. I slip the chain around my neck, and the last piece of Padlock I'll ever have falls into place next to my heart.

ACKNOWLEDGMENTS

The following people deserve steel, robotic horses for their help in turning this story into a book. I'll pop one in the post for each of you!

First, to my editor, Erin Black, for taking a chance on this idea after I sent her a link to a commercial and three sample pages. Where would my books be without your love and care for the story and characters? Nowhere good, that's for sure. Padlock goes to you!

To my agent, Sara Crowe, thank you for making this deal happen, and for not freaking out when I said, "Pull the other proposal. Let's do this one instead!" Here's your Titan.

Mad respect for the marketing team behind the Acura horse commercial. Your brilliance sparked the idea behind this book. Because I come from the world of advertising, I know how hard it is to create a memorable spot. And you nailed it. Bravo! I'd give you a Titan, but you already have your own.

Big, gushy hugs for my family. And this time, a special shout-out to my aunts and uncles—Peggy, Hassan, Nancy, and Tommy—for their support, and because they demanded a mention in the next book. I've got your Titans en route.

Love for my assistant, Regina, who helped me immensely as I worked on this book. And for all my readers and mega-fans—you guys are why I wake up and do this day after day. *Fires Titan cannon*

Ten Titans for everyone who worked on my book at Scholastic. For my publicist, Saraciea Fennell, my production editor, Beka Wallin, my designer, Nina Goffi, and for Lizette

Serrano, Emily Heddleson, and the entire sales and marketing team who ensure my books make it into readers' hands.

To author pals who keep things fun, and tell me when my title ideas are horrendous, thank you. For Julie Kagawa (magic tricks), April Genevieve Tucholke (*pretty please*), Lindsay Cummings (FUBS tour), Wendy Higgins (drive-by emails), Adi Alsaid (1PB), Sophie Jordan (triangle signing chairs), Kendare Blake (inspiration), Michelle Krys (witchery), and Paula Stokes (because obviously)—you guys win. How about instead of Titans, I send you galleys?

And finally, always, to my husband, Ryan. We made a pretty cute baby, huh? How about another one? Just kidding! You are intelligent, and funny, and handsome—and you have the darkest mind of anyone I know. I love that wicked little brain of yours to the stars and back. You are my person, and I am yours. Always and forever. Amen.

ABOUT THE AUTHOR

Victoria Scott is the author of *Fire & Flood, Salt & Stone*, and the Dante Walker series. She lives in Dallas with her family and is currently working on her next novel. Victoria adores getting to know her readers. Visit her online at VictoriaScottYA.com.

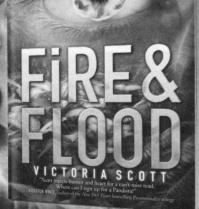
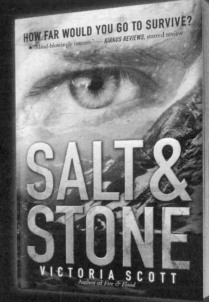